Linda —
accept yourself

SEARCHING FOR FINLEY

Eagle Point Search & Rescue, Book 5

SUSAN STOKER

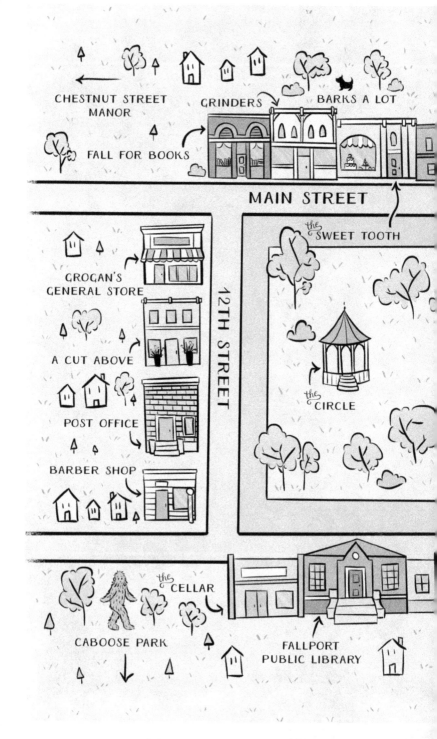

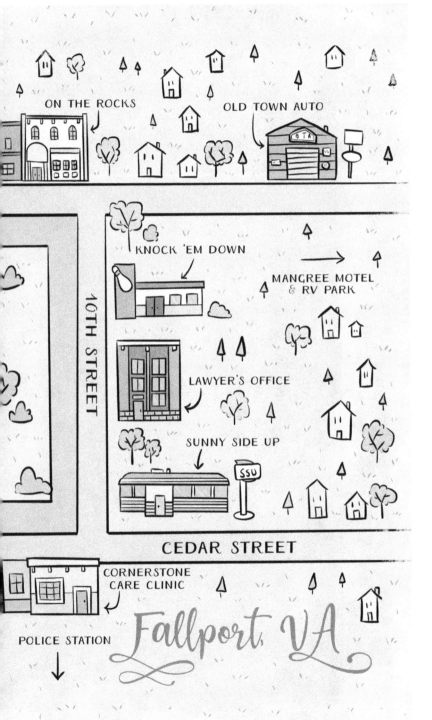

CHAPTER ONE

Finley Norris sighed in frustration as she stared down at her wrist. She'd fallen last evening. It was stupid really, she was in her own house and had tripped over nothing. It was a good thing no one was there to witness her klutzy self, sprawled out on the floor. Her wrist hurt, bad. But luckily, living in a small town had its benefits. She'd called Doc Snow and he'd agreed to see her even though it was technically after office hours.

Her wrist wasn't broken, merely sprained. But even so, it was an unpleasant surprise to find that it was virtually impossible to do what she needed to get done sooner rather than later.

Every morning, she headed into her bakery, The Sweet Tooth, located on the square downtown. Baking was Finley's passion, the one place she felt most comfortable in the world. Her culinary creations didn't judge her for being too shy, too fat, too uncool. And she took great joy in seeing the pleasure her muffins, cookies, cinnamon rolls, and other pastries gave to locals and tourists alike.

1

But this morning, there would *be* no treats because of her stupid wrist.

Tears threatened to spill down Finley's cheeks, but she held them back by sheer force of will. After twenty more minutes of struggling to measure ingredients with her left hand and failing to be able to knead a ball of dough, Finley knew there was no way she'd be able to open today if she didn't have help.

It wasn't that she was opposed to asking for help, but it was five-thirty in the morning and most people weren't early risers like she was. Except maybe Caryn.

Sucking it up, Finley reached for her phone. Taking a deep breath and hoping she wasn't waking Caryn or Drew, she clicked on her friend's name.

"What's wrong?" Caryn asked in lieu of a greeting.

Finley couldn't help but smile at that. "Why does something have to be wrong?" she asked.

"Because it's zero-dark-thirty in the morning and you're calling me. I know you get up early every morning to make those cinnamon rolls I literally can't resist, but you've never called *me* this early. So, what's up?"

"I fell yesterday. I'm fine," she hurried to reassure her friend. "But I sprained my wrist. I've been meaning to hire someone to help me in the mornings, but I haven't gotten around to it yet, and I'm finding it almost impossible to do anything. I was wondering if maybe you could help me this morning? I promise to find someone to hire soon, so this won't become an everyday thing. I'm sure my wrist will be better in a few days."

Finley was babbling, but she couldn't stop herself. She wasn't good at asking for help and felt bad that it was so early and last-minute.

"Oh, hon, I wish I could," Caryn said, regret clear in her tone. "But Drew and I are meeting with a group of ten boys and girls from the high school for their first workout as junior firefighters. Otherwise I totally would."

Finley's heart sank. "It's okay," she said, doing her best not to let any of her disappointment leak through in her voice.

"Do you trust me?" Caryn asked.

"Of course." Finley didn't even hesitate in her response. She hadn't known Caryn all that long, but she was already one of her best friends. Along with Lilly, Elsie, and Bristol. Somehow the five of them—six, if you included Khloe, the librarian who occasionally hung out with them—had clicked even though they were all so different.

"Cool. I'll get someone there to help you in fifteen minutes or so. Will that be all right? Will you be able to get your goodies out by the time you open?"

Finley closed her eyes in relief. "Yes. I mean, I won't have as many choices for people as I usually do, but if I can get a batch of cinnamon rolls in the oven, and I'll do banana nut muffins instead of bread because they'll be done faster. Oh, and I can make some pumpkin spice cookies with cream cheese frosting since it's now officially fall."

"Good Lord, woman, making me hungry this early, and before I work out, *and* when I have to deal with teenagers, is just cruel," Caryn bitched.

Finley chuckled, then said, "I appreciate your help so much."

"That's what friends are for. I'll make a call right after we hang up and get you some assistance."

"Thanks."

3

"You should've called when you fell," Caryn scolded.

"I was all right," Finley insisted.

"Your wrist is sprained. And I'm guessing you had to go see Doc. You should've called," Caryn repeated.

Finley realized her friend was probably right. But she was used to doing things on her own. It honestly hadn't occurred to her to contact any of her friends. When bad things happened in her life, she did what she had to in order to keep moving forward. "I'm sorry," she said, and she was.

"It's okay. We've got your back. I need to go and make that call. I'll talk to you later."

Finley opened her mouth to ask who Caryn was calling to help her out, but she didn't get the chance before she hung up.

Mentally shrugging, Finley clicked off her own phone and turned to the disaster that was her kitchen. Having only one good hand made for a very messy workstation. There was flour spilled everywhere, even on the floor. But since she'd had to use her non-dominant hand to measure and attempt to stir, it was extremely difficult to not make a mess.

Fifteen minutes later, there was a tap on the front door of the bakery. It was still too early for any customers, so Finley knew it had to be whoever Caryn had called to come to her rescue. Smiling, she walked out of the kitchen toward the front.

When she saw who was standing on the other side of the glass door, she almost turned around.

Brock Mabrey was waiting patiently for her to open the door.

Darn Caryn anyway! Finley definitely should've asked who she was calling for help.

Brock was the last person in the world she wanted to see. Caryn knew, or at least had an inkling, how much she admired and liked the man...and how shy she always was around him. She probably thought she was doing Finley a favor by forcing the two of them together.

In reality, having him around would be torture. She was utterly tongue tied around Brock, always feeling as if she was so out of his league. He'd been a Customs and Border Protection agent, for goodness sake, and now he owned Old Town Auto, the car shop everyone took their vehicles to when they needed servicing.

And he was so damn beautiful, it was difficult to look at the man.

He had short dark hair, huge muscular arms she just knew would feel amazing wrapped around her, a square jaw, and plump lips that she couldn't stop staring at every time she saw him. Basically, he could have any woman he wanted, and as nice as he always was to her when all their friends got together, Finley couldn't fathom Brock ever wanting someone like her for anything beyond friendship.

Sighing, and knowing there was no way she could pretend she didn't see him, Finley walked toward the front door as if she was on her way to the gallows. She unlocked the door and opened it.

"Hi," she said shyly, keeping her gaze locked on the center of his chest instead of his eyes.

"Hey. Caryn called and said you could use some help?" Brock asked.

This was her chance to tell him that no, actually, she figured things out and she was good, but since she really did need help if she was going to be able to open in less than an hour, she nodded. "I do. Thanks."

Brock walked into her shop and just like that, the normally roomy space seemed to shrink. That happened every time he was around. After he'd entered, Finley locked the door behind him, then stood there staring at him a little awkwardly.

"May I?" he asked gently, gesturing to her wrapped wrist.

When she didn't protest, he reached out. The second his fingers touched her hand, shivers shot up her spine.

He had very manly hands. They were large, calloused, and she could see the oil stains under his fingernails. Which had never turned her off. She'd witnessed him scrubbing his hands in the past, but since he spent so much time working on vehicles, his fingers were basically stained. Seeing his large hand holding hers so carefully and gently made her long once more for something she knew she'd never have.

"What happened?" he asked softly.

Finley shrugged and stared at her wrist. She liked seeing his hands on her. Probably too much. "I tripped over my own feet. Caught myself with my hand."

Brock winced. "Ouch."

"Yeah," she agreed. "Doc Snow says it's not broken, just sprained, but I'm right handed, so..."

"I bet that makes stirring difficult. And rotating sheet pans in and out of the oven."

"It does."

"Well, I'm at your disposal. Your wish is my command," he said with a grin.

For just a moment, Finley wondered what he'd do if she

6

pushed him against the counter and kissed the hell out of him. But as soon as the thought formed, she dismissed it. He'd probably be mortified.

She thought back to the day he'd come in and told her what had happened to Caryn. Finley had been so stressed and worried about her friend that she'd forgotten to be timid around him. She'd manhandled the guy, dragging him out the door of her shop and insisting he take her to Caryn right that instant, so she could see for herself that her friend was all right.

Thinking back on it now, Brock didn't seem to mind her being so demanding.

"It's a little swollen," Brock said, fingering her wrist. Finley had wrapped it that morning as the doctor had suggested, but even she could tell that it was bigger than the left wrist.

"Yeah."

"Have you taken anything for the pain?"

His concern made her blush with pleasure. Finley nodded. "Just some over-the-counter stuff."

"Good. So, where do you want me?"

For a second, Finley thought he'd been able to read her mind about shoving him against the counter and kissing him. Her gaze whipped up to his, and as she stared into his chocolate-brown eyes, she swore she could see desire there...for *her*.

He grinned. "You're cute in the morning," he blurted.

Blinking, Finley forced herself to concentrate. She was being ridiculous. Brock was just here to help. Because Caryn called him. He wasn't flirting.

Was he?

He was still holding her hand, one of his fingers

caressing her wrist, and even with the compression bandage, she could feel his touch. He was leaning into her, and the smile on his face was tender. It was...confusing.

So Finley did what she always did—dropped her gaze and did her best to distance herself from her feelings. "I need to get the cinnamon roll dough mixed. And get the muffins started." She tried to pull her hand from his, but he wouldn't let go.

Instead, he simply nodded, wrapped his fingers around hers, and turned to head to the kitchen at the back of the store.

Dazed, Finley let herself be led. She kept her gaze on their connected hands, and the sight of his rough fingers intertwined with hers sent butterflies to her belly. When was the last time she'd touched someone so nonchalantly like this? Especially a man? It had been ages.

When Brock got a look at the disaster that was her work space in the kitchen, he let out a deep chuckle. "Right...where do you want to start?"

Finley was very aware that he hadn't let go of her hand yet. She wasn't sure if he'd forgotten he was holding it or what. But she didn't want to embarrass him by pointing it out, and frankly, she was enjoying how it felt. She wanted to prolong the sensation.

"I managed to get everything added to the bowl," she said, gesturing to the large stainless-steel bowl sitting on the counter. "But I wasn't able to stir it properly."

"Right, then that's what we'll do first." He headed for the bowl, and Finley followed docilely behind him.

"I'm awful in the kitchen, but if you tell me what to do, I can probably muddle through. If anyone complains about something tasting off, just blame it on me."

"Thank you for coming to help," she blurted, feeling overwhelmed. There would've been no way she could've opened today if he hadn't.

Brock stopped in his tracks and turned to her. He lifted his free hand and brushed his fingers against her cheek. "No place I'd rather be," he said. Then he gently squeezed the hand he was still holding before finally letting go to reach for the large spoon sitting inside the bowl. The one she'd attempted to use to stir before giving up after flour and the other ingredients ended up all over the counter and floor.

Brock's muscles flexed in his arm as he began to easily mix the ingredients together. It was literally the sexiest thing Finley had ever seen in her life. She wished she could get her phone out and film him right now, but that would be super creepy.

"You want to get the ingredients ready for what we need to do next while I stir?" Brock asked.

Taking a deep breath, trying to get herself together, Finley nodded. They had a lot of work to do if she was going to be ready to open at her usual time. She turned to grab another bowl, and did her best to get her head back into baking mode.

CHAPTER TWO

Brock smiled as he stirred yet another batch of dough. His day had been made when Caryn called him. Getting a phone call so early in the morning usually meant they were about to head out on a search, but this was so much better. He hadn't hesitated to reassure Caryn that he'd go and help Finley. He wasn't thrilled to hear that she'd been hurt, but was more than willing to come to her shop and assist.

There was just something about the woman that turned him inside out. He was a rugged man. Always had been. There was nothing he loved more than getting his hands dirty. He loved camping, fishing, hiking, watching sports on TV, and tinkering with engines. But spending the morning measuring flour, kneading dough, and smelling cinnamon and sugar was literally a dream come true. Simply because he was doing it with Finley.

She was an enigma. Desperately shy one moment, then ordering him around the next.

He liked it. A lot.

One of the things he liked best about her, though, was

that she wasn't judgmental. She treated everyone as if they were a long-lost friend. He'd seen more than one person enter her store grumpy as hell, then leave with a smile on their face.

He also appreciated that she didn't give his oil-stained fingers a second glance. Didn't question whether or not they were clean. He'd scrubbed them over and over but he couldn't hide the fact that he worked on vehicles for a living. He enjoyed what he'd done for the US Customs and Border Protection, but nothing made him feel as content as when he had the guts of a car spread out in front of him, putting it all back together again.

Clearly, Finley had also found her calling. And she was a supportive friend to boot. He'd seen ample evidence of that when she was with his friends' women. She got up early every single morning to bake decadent treats for her shop, making her customers happy, then more often than not spent her afternoons with the ladies.

She'd spent hours with Bristol, helping in her stained-glass workshop. She went with Lilly to assist her with a wedding the other woman had photographed just a couple weekends ago, despite being on her feet since the wee hours already at her bakery. Brock didn't think she'd missed one of Tony's soccer games yet. When Caryn had been hurt, she'd given her enough sweet treats to ensure the next time she went to the dentist, she'd probably have several cavities.

And she'd even won over the reticent Khloe. He'd heard them chatting like old friends about the stray kittens Khloe was feeding behind the library.

For months, Brock had been somewhat obsessed with the woman. He couldn't stop thinking about her. Wanted her to look at him with affection in her eyes—instead of actively avoiding his gaze—and feel as relaxed around him as she was with his friends.

Lilly had told him more than once the only reason she got tense when he came around was because she was attracted to him. But he wasn't sure he believed it. He'd never seen any sign that she was interested in him romantically.

Until this morning.

When he'd taken her hand in his, he'd felt her pulse speed up under his fingers. For just a moment, he'd had the feeling she wanted to do more than simply stand shyly in front of him, but she'd quickly dropped her eyes and went back to being bashful.

Still, that small glimpse of the need in her eyes...it hit Brock hard.

He was making headway with her, even if it *was* baby steps. He'd take it.

As he placed a tray of muffins in the oven, and removed the dozen that had just finished baking, she sighed in obvious pleasure.

"Those look awesome," she said with a smile.

When he'd first arrived, things had been awkward between them as she'd instructed him on what to put in which bowl, how to properly stir the ingredients together —he had no idea there was a right and wrong way to mix flour, sugar, and spices, but apparently there was—but now she was much more relaxed.

"And they smell awesome too," Brock said. "I wasn't much of a pumpkin spice guy, but I think you've changed my mind."

"Just wait until they're iced. I guarantee they'll blow your mind."

Brock could only grin. She was so freaking adorable. "I'm sure they will," he reassured her.

Together, they managed to put together enough goodies for the regulars who showed up early, and Finley opened her doors just fifteen minutes later than normal.

"I really appreciate your help, but I've got it now," she said.

Brock ignored her. He stood behind her at the counter, packaging the treats people ordered as she took care of the money and making small talk. Every now and then, he'd wander into the kitchen and take out another tray of muffins or cookies. He iced cookies at Finley's direction, and between the two of them, they were able to get through the morning rush. There was practically nothing left in the display case by the time nine o'clock rolled around, but Finley looked pleased, so Brock figured things had gone as well as they could've with her only having the use of one hand and a newbie assistant.

Looking down at her watch, Finley blinked in surprise. "Oh! I didn't realize how late it was. Don't you have to get to work?"

Brock shrugged. "I called Jesus and let him know I was going to be late today."

"He's your assistant, right?" she asked.

"Co-owner of the shop," Brock corrected. "And he's used to my sometimes wonky hours. When we get called out for a search, he's on his own. But he and the rest of our employees can more than handle things without me. Speaking of which...have you ever thought about hiring someone to help you out around here?"

"Why, are you thinking about applying?" she asked with a smile.

Fuck, Brock loved seeing that grin on her face. Especially aimed at *him*. Before this morning, she'd been too shy to talk to him on a good day; forget about teasing him.

"Don't tempt me, sweetheart," he drawled.

A blush spread across her cheeks, and it was all Brock could do not to yank her close and kiss her the way he'd fantasized for months. He stuffed his hands into his pockets to try to control himself.

Finley was so damn gorgeous, and it was completely obvious she had no clue. He'd had a long talk with Bristol one day about that very topic, and she'd told him that Finley was convinced because of her size, no one would ever take a second look at her.

She was so wrong. Brock had not only taken a second look, he'd taken a third, fourth, and fifth. She was curvy in all the right places.

His mom had been a large woman, and he'd witnessed the deep love his dad had for her all his life. He constantly told Brock it didn't matter what was on the outside, but what was *inside* a person that mattered. And his old man wasn't wrong.

He'd lost both his parents four years ago. His mom had a heart attack, and Brock would always believe his dad just couldn't go on without her. Despite being pretty healthy, he'd died just a few months later. They both would've loved Finley at first sight. And he had no doubt she would've won them over just as quickly.

Brock could see the beauty Finley clearly didn't. She had thick, wavy brown hair that seemed to have a mind of its own. She kept it pulled back when she was at the shop, and he hadn't realized how long it was until recently, when she'd been hanging out with the other women. It came down to the middle of her back—and it was all he could do not to touch it that night. To run his fingers through the shiny strands...or clutch them in his fist.

Her hazel eyes were bright and curious, and he loved the laugh lines around them. She was about half a foot shorter than his six feet, but he knew without a doubt she'd fit perfectly against him.

But it was her body that kept him up at night. Brock wasn't ashamed to admit that he'd gotten himself off more than once while thinking about what she hid under her clothes. Her tits were full and lush. Her thighs thick. A waist he could sink his hands into as he took her.

Brock was a large man, muscular, and rough around the edges. He wanted a woman he wouldn't be afraid to break when they were making love. Someone who could take what he had to give, and make her own demands in bed.

He also wanted a woman who was interested in the same things he was. He didn't need her to love hiking miles and miles and miles by his side, but someone who wouldn't mind going camping with him now and then, or sitting with him while he fished, or even got as excited as he did when his favorite sports team was playing.

Brock knew he was looking for a unicorn, and until he'd met Finley, he wasn't sure such a woman existed. But after being around her, getting to know her, listening to her friends talk about her—he was well aware they were always talking her up to pique his interest—he had a feeling she was exactly who he'd been looking for all these years.

No, her size didn't turn him off in the least. It made

her more attractive in his eyes. He loved her shape, her scent—cinnamon and vanilla—and her personality. He liked her shyness just as much as he enjoyed the glimpses of sass she normally kept hidden around him.

The silence between them had grown while he daydreamed, and Brock could see it was making Finley uncomfortable, so he did his best to rein in his wayward thoughts. "But seriously, you need help, hon."

"I know," she said with a shrug. "This store was my dream for so long. And when I first opened, I was barely scraping by. Everything I earned went right back into inventory. For a while, I didn't think I was going to make it. Some people were upset that I didn't sell coffee, but that would be silly since Grinders is right next door. Eventually, people got over their irritation that they had to wait in two lines to get their coffee and sweets in the mornings, and business has stayed steady ever since. But getting hurt has made me realize that I really *do* need to hire someone to help."

"You have anyone in mind?" Brock asked.

Finley shook her head. "No. I can't hire a teenager because I'm only open when they're in school."

"I can ask around, see if I can come up with someone," he offered.

"I mean, I could probably step outside and just ask Silas, Otto, and Art," Finley said with a smile.

Brock laughed. The three older men who sat outside the post office every day, playing chess and gossiping, were a staple in Fallport. "That's true."

"But I'd appreciate knowing if you hear of anyone who needs a job. I'd love to hire someone like Elsie. She doesn't need the help now, obviously, but when she was living in the motel with her son...that's who I'd love to find. Someone who could really use the job."

Brock wasn't surprised. His Finley had a huge heart.

He wasn't concerned in the least, thinking about her as "his" even when she wasn't. He'd had his eye on her for a while now, and as he got to know her better, he was *more* attracted to her, not less. So as far as Brock was concerned, she just wasn't his *yet*. "I'll ask around, see what I can find out."

"Thanks."

"You're more than welcome. I'm gonna go and ice some more cookies before I head out. Is there anything else I can do?"

"You've already done too much," Finley told him.

"What else do you need, Fin?" The nickname just popped out.

"Maybe you can whip up another batch of batter for muffins? I don't think I need to make more cinnamon rolls, but I do need to stock the case a bit."

"You got it. But I'm guessing you probably need to supervise," he said. And he wasn't trying to wrangle more time with her. He wanted that, yes, but he didn't want to risk screwing up any of her delicious treats.

To his relief, Finley nodded. "I can help customers and supervise you at the same time."

Of course she could. Brock had a feeling she could do anything she set her mind to. If he hadn't come in to help this morning, she would've figured out a way to get her baked goods made, he had no doubt.

By the time Brock left, it was ten-thirty, he was covered in flour, smelled like cinnamon—just like Finley usually did—and he had a huge smile on his face.

17

It had been a good morning, and he already couldn't wait until tomorrow. Finley might not reach out and ask for his help again, but she'd get it anyway. Her wrist wouldn't heal overnight, and he'd make sure he was there as long as she needed him.

* * *

The next morning when Brock showed up at The Sweet Tooth, he was surprised to see Davis Woolford already waiting at the door.

"Good morning," Brock said as he approached.

"Morning," Davis replied.

"You all right?" Brock asked.

Davis nodded, but didn't explain why he was there. Brock didn't have a chance to question him further before Finley was unlocking the door.

This morning, she had on a flowery dress that came down to her knees. It was fitted around her chest and flowed out at the hips to swirl around her thighs. Brock felt himself getting hard, and it was all he could do to rein himself in. He didn't want Finley to feel uncomfortable, and if she saw his erection, she might second-guess having him around.

"Hi!" she said with a smile.

Brock was thrilled that she seemed more at ease with him this morning than the day before. "Good morning," he said.

"Davis, hi. I don't have anything ready yet this morning, but if you want to wait inside until I open, you can," she told him.

"I'm not here for food," he said. "I heard you're

looking for help. I'm not sure I can be here all the time, because sometimes I don't sleep so good, and I have trouble controlling my anger, but..." He paused, then took a deep breath. "I was a cook in the Army."

Brock turned to stare at the man. He was homeless... well, not quite as homeless as he used to be. The citizens of Fallport had built him a tiny home, basically a small shed, and placed it behind Sunny Side Up. Sandra, the owner of the diner, was doing more than her fair share of looking after him. Making sure he had food to eat, a place to wash his clothes and clean up. He was in his late thirties, way too young to be as disillusioned as he was. But PTSD would do that to anyone.

"You were?" Finley asked.

"Yeah. I could...you know...help out...if you needed it. In the kitchen. Not with people."

Finley reached out and took his hand in hers. Brock couldn't help but notice that she didn't hesitate, even though the man's hands were filthy.

"I'd love that."

"I don't have a lot of baking experience," he told her honestly.

"Neither does Brock, and he did okay yesterday," Finley said. "I'm willing to try if you are."

Davis nodded.

"There's a bathroom in the back if you want to wash up. I think I have an extra hair tie you can use as well."

Davis didn't take offense at her words, simply nodded and headed for the kitchen.

The second he disappeared into the back, Brock reached for Finley. Without thought, he pulled her close, giving her a huge hug. It wasn't until she was plastered against him that he realized he shouldn't have touched her without permission.

But she didn't seem to mind. Instead, she snuggled in and hugged him back, and Brock hadn't felt as good as he did right this moment in a very long time. "You're pretty amazing," he said softly as he took in her scent, wanting it to rub off on him so he could smell her all day.

Finley merely shrugged.

He felt her pulling away, and he reluctantly loosened his arms. She had a blush on her face once again, and Brock definitely liked how he affected her. Because she affected him in the exact same way.

She tucked a stray piece of hair behind her ear as she glanced up at him, then looked down at his chest once again. She did that all the time, looked at him without actually meeting his eyes. Reaching out, Brock put a finger under her chin and encouraged her to meet his gaze.

The second her eyes met his, he said, "Seriously, a lot of people wouldn't even give him a chance."

"Then they're stupid. Davis is awesome. If it wasn't for him, Bristol might not've been found in time."

"From what I heard, you had a lot to do with that yourself," Brock said.

"Maybe. But seriously, Davis is a good person. Yes, he's got some demons, but I've seen the kind of man he is deep down, and you said so yourself yesterday, I need help around here."

"You don't have to convince me," Brock said, lowering his hand reluctantly. But as he did, he couldn't resist running his finger down her throat.

They stood there, in the middle of her shop, staring at

each other for a long moment, before they heard Davis return.

"I'm ready," he said.

Turning, Brock saw Davis standing in the doorway of the kitchen. He'd pulled his long black hair back into a bun, washed his hands, and he'd also put on an apron he'd obviously found in the kitchen.

"So you are," Finley said with a smile. "Gosh, with two helpers, I'm gonna fill the case without any trouble today."

She wasn't wrong.

Davis turned out to be an excellent helper. Finley didn't have to tell him twice what to do. He didn't speak as he worked, but it was obvious he had experience in a kitchen. After a while, Brock turned to the sink and began to wash the bakeware they'd used, so as not to be in their way.

"I might have found someone who would be perfect to help you out in the front of the store," Brock told her.

Finley turned to him. "Really?"

"Yeah. Jesus has a neighbor who's down on his luck and is trying to raise money to send to his sister, to help with her fight against colon cancer. She's in Brazil. The guy's having a hard time finding a job around here."

"Why?"

"Why, what?"

"Why can't he find a job?"

"I haven't exactly talked to the people he's interviewed with, but I'm guessing it's because he's a big guy. Around six-four and plus-size. I think people are intimidated by him. And he's from Brazil...the people of Fallport have gotten better about being inclusive, but there are still plenty who discriminate against anyone who hasn't grown up around here. But Jesus says he's a good man. Hard-working, considerate, and despite his appearance, he's actually soft-spoken."

Finley nodded. "Good enough for me. If he comes by around three, when I'm closing, I'll have time to meet with him," she said without hesitation.

There it was again. Her huge heart made Brock want to be a better person himself. "I'll let Jesus know, and I'm sure he'll be here."

"What's his name?"

"Oh, guess that's important, huh?" Brock said with a chuckle. "Liam. I don't know his last name, sorry."

"It's okay. Having his first name is fine for now. I'd hate for someone to come in and for me to think it's the guy here about the job, only to find out it's a customer who simply wants a muffin."

Brock smiled at her. "I'm guessing with my description, you'd know it was him even if you didn't have a name. Besides, you probably *could* talk a random customer into working for you."

She shook her head as if amused.

"I'm serious. You make friends with everyone who steps foot in this shop."

"You remind me of a woman I met in Afghanistan," Davis said, speaking for the first time in an hour. "She didn't speak English, but every time I went in to buy a loaf of bread, she treated me as if I was her long-lost son or something. Pulling me behind the counter, showing off the fresh bread she'd just pulled out of the oven, and insisting on giving me twice what my money should've bought."

"That's sweet," Finley said.

"Yeah. Until the day the rebels burnt the place down,

adamant that women shouldn't be able to own a business. That it wasn't their place."

Finley inhaled sharply. "Oh no."

"Yeah. I never saw her again. I have no idea what happened to her. I'd like to hope that she's happy and healthy today, but I just don't know."

"I'm so sorry," Finley said. She took a step toward Davis, but before Brock could warn her not to touch him, she stopped, as if she instinctively knew she needed to give her new helper some space.

"Yeah. Me too. Are we good here?" he asked abruptly.

Finley nodded. "I think so. You've been a huge help. You're welcome to help me out anytime, Davis. I'm usually here by four-thirty."

The veteran nodded.

"Let me get some money to pay you for this morning."

"Don't need it. I'm gonna get going."

Brock watched as Davis took off the apron, hung it on the wall, then he nodded at him and Finley and headed for the door.

The second they heard the front door shut, Finley turned to Brock. "I hate that he's struggling."

"You're good for him."

She laughed, but it wasn't a humorous sound. "Yeah, I remind him of a woman who had her business burned to the ground. That's so good for him."

Brock couldn't keep himself from going to her. He reached out and put a hand on her upper arm and squeezed lightly. "No, you remind him of a woman who was a bright spot in what I'm guessing was a very tough deployment," he countered.

"Maybe."

She didn't sound convinced. But Brock understood where Davis was coming from. Yes, the man wasn't happy that woman had lost her shop, but when struggling with traumatic memories, it actually helped to remember the good times. And even though the outcome wasn't great, Davis obviously loved going to that woman's shop as much as she enjoyed having him there.

"How's your wrist feeling this morning?" he asked, wanting to change the subject and cheer Finley up.

She immediately rotated her right hand. "It's okay. Still sore, but better than yesterday."

"Good."

"With Davis here, you probably don't need to come tomorrow. I'm sure I'll be back to normal by then."

Brock tried not to let his disappointment show. "You *mind* me being here?" he asked.

She shook her head. "Of course not."

"Good. Because I prefer starting my day with you, rather than sitting on my duff in my house." It was a bold thing to say, but Brock was done tiptoeing around this woman.

She just stared at him with big eyes.

"Although, taste-testing all your pastries probably isn't good for my waistline." He patted his stomach as he smiled. Then he asked what he'd been thinking about all morning. "I know you close at three. You want to get together around four-thirty or so to hike the Barker Mill Trail? You said you like to hike, and the temperature should be pretty good around then, not too hot or cold."

The more she stood there, just staring at him, the more uncertain Brock became. He didn't want to give her a chance to shoot him down, so he kept babbling.

"The SAR team has been taking turns walking the paths, making sure the tourists are all right and letting them know we're there if something happens. So far it's been working out, we've found a few people who had blisters and needed a bit of first aid, and we've answered a lot of questions about the various trails in the area. Old man Grogan even gave us some of those Bigfoot squishy things he had made, to give out to kids we meet while we're hiking. It's been a good public relations kind of thing. Today's my day, and I just thought that maybe you'd want to get some fresh air. After you meet with Liam, of course. But you might have something else planned already."

He forced himself to shut the hell up, and he practically held his breath as he waited for her response.

"I...well...Why me?" she finally asked.

"Because I think you're pretty awesome. And I like spending time with you. You're funny, and kind, and being around you makes me feel good."

Her eyes widened in surprise.

"I don't want to make you uncomfortable, so if you don't think it's a good idea to go on a first date with a man who takes you deep into the forest, that's okay too. In fact, it was probably a stupid idea—"

"No!" she blurted, then blushed. "I mean, I trust you, Brock. How could I not? I just...a date?"

Brock cringed. He shouldn't have said that. But he didn't want her to think for a second that he just wanted to be friends. He valued her friendship, of course, but he wanted more.

"Yeah. We could go to dinner instead, if you wanted. Or bowling. There isn't a ton of stuff to do in Fallport, but I'm sure we could think of something. Maybe I could talk to Sandra and see if she'd pack a picnic for us or something and we could go to Caboose Park. No, on second thought, there'll be too many people there after school."

"A hike sounds nice," she said, stopping him from making more of a fool of himself than he already had.

"Yeah?" He couldn't help but ask.

"Yeah," she agreed shyly. She was back to looking at his chin instead of his eyes. "I was going to get together with Lilly to talk about the cake she wants me to make for her wedding, but that can wait. Or I can call her if I get a break today. Since she and Ethan are tying the knot on Halloween, I thought it might be fun to have a themed cake. Not with black icing though, because I can just see all the pictures of everyone smiling with black teeth. But maybe a three-tiered, white-iced cake, with silhouettes of black trees with crows on the bare branches, and the topper could be something similar."

Brock smiled as she spoke. It was obvious she was anxious about being responsible for Lilly's cake, but he knew whatever she decided to make would not only look amazing, it would taste just as good.

"Sorry, I'm babbling," she said, blushing once more.

"I don't mind," he said honestly.

"It's been a while since I've hiked. You aren't worried that I won't..."

"What?"

"That I won't be able to keep up with you? You're obviously in way better shape than me. I mean, look at you. Then look at *me*."

Brock hated the self-deprecation he heard in her tone. "I'm looking, believe me, and there's not a damn thing wrong with you," he said fervently.

They stared at each other for a long moment. He could see the hope and wariness in her gaze and was more determined than ever to make sure she never doubted how he felt about her.

He *wanted* to tell her how beautiful she was to him. How he couldn't stop thinking about her curves, and how he wanted to feel them under his hands. How he fantasized about having her in his bed. But that would be a little too much, even for someone as rough around the edges as Brock.

"This isn't a forced march, Fin. Just a casual walk in the woods. Besides, you're in shape. I've heard you talking to the other girls about how you take online yoga and Zumba classes in the evenings."

Finley swallowed hard before taking a deep breath in through her nose. "I'm not sure this is the best idea...but yes, I'd like to go on a hike with you."

"It *is* a good idea," Brock insisted, more relieved than he could say that she'd agreed. All he needed was for her to let him in, even a little bit, and he'd show her how good they could be together.

He wasn't an idiot, he was well aware that even though people appreciated what he did with the search and rescue team, he wasn't the best catch. He swore too much, worked long hours, didn't have a college education, was as blue collar as they came, and didn't care much about the right and wrong things to say in social situations. But he was loyal. And good with his hands...both on the job and in the bedroom. He'd never hurt a woman, ever, and thought anyone who did deserved to be locked away for good.

He realized Finley was staring at him, waiting for him

to finish his thoughts, and he mentally smacked his own head. "It's a good idea," he repeated firmly. "I'll be here around four-thirty to pick you up, if that's okay."

"That'll work. Thank you."

"Of course. Thank *you* for saying yes," he countered.

She blushed again, and Brock could only smile at the sight.

"I need to get the door unlocked, otherwise I might have a riot on my hands," she said after a moment.

Brock nodded and turned toward the door that led into her shop. He gestured for her to precede him, and he couldn't help but watch her ass as she walked. It was large and round...and his mouth watered just thinking about what she'd look like on her hands and knees in front of him, as he prepared to take her from behind.

She turned and caught him staring—and instead of calling him on it, she gave him a shy smile.

It was hard to believe she was finally giving him a chance, and Brock mentally vowed not to do anything to fuck it up. Of course, that was easier said than done, but now that he'd finally met a woman who seemed to tick off all the imaginary boxes he had for a partner, he wasn't about to do something that would make him lose his chance.

He was very thankful Caryn had called him yesterday morning. Without spending the last two mornings with him, she wouldn't have loosened up enough to say yes to a date. He owed Caryn, huge.

"Thanks again for coming to help me. I really appreciate it," Finley said. "I can pay you if—"

"No fucking way," Brock said with a scowl. "I'm not here for money."

"Why *are* you here?" Finley asked.

He could sense that she was embarrassed she'd asked the question, but she straightened her shoulders and managed to stare into his eyes as she waited for his response.

"Because I've been waiting for months for the most beautiful woman in Fallport to realize she's got me wrapped around her little finger. To give me a chance. And, just sayin', Fin...now that you have? I'm gonna do everything in my power to make sure you don't regret it. See you this afternoon."

Then he leaned in and kissed her cheek. Even that slight brush of his lips on her skin made him yearn for more. The scent of cinnamon and vanilla wafted into his nostrils and Brock had a feeling he'd be smelling her all day...which wasn't exactly a hardship.

He smiled down at her, then reached out and unlocked the front door and left. There was a couple waiting outside on the sidewalk for the store to open, and Brock nodded at them as he headed for his pickup truck. It was over ten years old, and his baby. He'd brought her back to life, tinkering with the engine and changing out just about all her internal parts. She purred like a kitten now, and had enough horsepower under the engine that if he wanted to, he could outrun even the fastest cop car.

As he drove toward Old Town Auto, Brock frowned thinking about Finley being alone in her shop every morning. It was something he hadn't thought about until now, and he realized it wasn't safe for her to go to work in the dark, before anyone was really up and about in Fallport. Anyone could sneak up behind her and force her into her shop when she opened.

The thought of someone hurting Finley made Brock's blood run cold. She might not need him to assist her in the mornings, but he wasn't sure he'd be able to stay away now.

Yes, Davis might be there some mornings, but that wasn't good enough for Brock. He already felt extremely protective of her, especially now that she'd said yes to a date. As far as he was concerned, she was now his to watch over. His to protect.

He knew without a doubt that she wouldn't exactly be pleased with his line of thinking. But what she didn't know wouldn't hurt her.

Nothing and no one would hurt her—ever.

CHAPTER THREE

Finley was nervous. She couldn't believe Brock Mabrey had asked *her* out. It was almost surreal. She'd felt a little less nervous around him this morning. Yesterday, it was all she could do to string two coherent words together. But the more time she spent with him, the more comfortable she became in his presence.

He'd taken her by surprise when he'd asked if she wanted to go hiking. There hadn't been a time when *any* of the men she'd dated asked if she wanted to do something physical for a date. It was always movies, dinners...sedentary things. As if they didn't expect her to be physically able to ride a bike, go roller blading, or even just walk much. She couldn't really blame them. Her size definitely screamed "give me a doughnut" instead of "let's go jogging together."

Finley had the feeling Brock was different in a lot of ways from the men she'd dated. She hadn't missed him ogling her ass as she'd walked in front of him. And the appreciation and lust she'd seen in his eyes had sunk deep down into her bones. It felt good. Damn good. Though she still wasn't sure it was the best idea to go out with him, because she knew herself, knew that it wouldn't take much for her to fall hard and fast. Hell, she was already halfway there.

She'd spent enough time around him to know he was an honorable guy. He wasn't an asshole. Didn't overcharge his customers. Was polite, but never sucked up to people. And the fact that he went out of his way to recommend his co-owner's friend because the guy wanted to help his sister back in Brazil simply tipped the scales when it came to Finley trusting him.

The meeting with Liam Silva had gone extremely well. The man was indeed soft-spoken and eager to work, as promised. He was a little intimidating at first, simply because of his appearance, but it was obvious he'd tried hard to appear harmless. Finley had talked with him for half an hour and hired him on the spot. He seemed surprised to get the job, which made her kind of sad. It was clear he'd had a difficult time finding employment, and was extremely grateful.

There was paperwork that had to be done, and she needed to check with Drew—who she'd hired to be her accountant a couple months ago—about legal crap, but it looked as if The Sweet Tooth finally had another employee.

The townspeople would be happy, as Finley always had to close the shop whenever she'd had to step out in the past. Like when she'd heard about what happened to Caryn. And when the search for Bristol was underway. While Finley had no problem closing her store when her friends needed her, it would be nice not to have to anymore. It would also free her up to take more catering jobs—like making Lilly and Ethan's wedding cake—since she could soon turn over the day-to-day operations to Liam.

The interview had ended early enough that Finley was able to go home and change before coming back to the square to meet Brock. She stopped to chat with Art, Silas, and Otto, who were at their normal spot outside the post office. It was nice to see Art, Caryn's grandfather, back to his normal self. After being stabbed in his home, everyone had been worried he might not bounce back. At ninety-one, it hadn't been guaranteed.

"There've been a lot of people coming and going from The Sweet Tooth recently," Otto said, clearly fishing for information about what was going on with Davis and Liam and Brock.

"What, you don't think I should have customers?" Finley teased.

Art chuckled.

"You hurt your wrist?" Silas asked.

Finley shrugged. "Yeah, tripped over a large piece of air someone left in front of me. It's just sprained though."

"Caryn called Brock to help her out yesterday," Art informed his friends.

They both immediately turned on him.

"You knew that and didn't say anything?" Otto demanded.

"Yeah, since when do you keep any good gossip from us?" Silas complained.

Art smirked. "It's nice to have one up on you guys. I spent too much time missing out while I was on bed rest. I'm making up for it now."

"That's just wrong," Silas grumbled. "We shared everything we could with you and this is how you repay us?"

Finley was amused by the three friends bitching at each other, even if she *did* feel a little bad that they were arguing about *her*.

Otto turned his attention back to her. "So...that's what Brock was doing there so early? Helping you bake?"

"Uh-huh."

"He didn't leave until after ten yesterday. And around nine today. That's a lot of *baking*," Silas mused.

Finley felt herself blushing, but nodded. "It was."

"And...Liam Silva? He was there after you closed..." Art said. It was a question not phrased as a question.

"I'm hiring him to help out in the front," she informed the men.

"Good choice!"

"About time."

"Nice!"

Finley smiled at the three of them.

"So what are you doing back here then? You only went home not too long ago," Otto said.

"Brock and I are going to hike part of the Barker Mill Trail."

All three men smiled huge at her, and she could practically see the wheels turning in their heads. "It's nothing serious," she quickly added, doing what she could to prevent the men from spreading a rumor that she and Brock were getting married or something equally ridiculous.

"Uh-huh."

"I'm sure."

"Finley, a man like Brock Mabrey doesn't voluntarily

show up to help a woman bake cookies and cupcakes if he's not interested in having said woman bake those same goodies in his *own* kitchen after a long night in his bed," Silas informed her.

Finley stared at him with wide eyes.

"Exactly," Art agreed with a firm nod.

"And you couldn't do better than Brock," Otto added. "The man knows his way around cars, and I'm guessing that attention to detail extends to other things as well." He winked at Finley as he said it.

"You guys, we're just going for a hike. That's it," Finley insisted. "I mean, we're as different as night and day."

"Opposites attract," Silas told her.

"Wait, what does that mean, exactly?" Art asked Finley with a frown, holding up a hand to stop Otto from commenting.

Finley shrugged as nonchalantly as she could. "Could you really see the two of us together?" she asked with a humorless laugh. "The frumpy baker and the hot former Border Patrol guy? Right."

Art shook his head and shook his index finger at her. "There's nothing wrong with you, missy. And to answer your question, yes, I could."

"He's had his eye on you for a while now," Otto added with a nod.

Silas patted his protruding belly, leaning back in his chair. "Nothing wrong with having some meat on your bones. My wife, God rest her soul, had curves for days and I'll tell you one thing, our love life was combustible. A great relationship has nothing to do with whatever the scale says when you step on it, but how you support your partner, how you're there for them in the bad or boring times. Anyone can have a good relationship during the fun times, like vacations, birthdays and the like. But it's when you're hot and tired, or cranky and upset that matters."

He wasn't wrong. Finley nodded. "I know."

"Do you?" Art challenged.

Finley straightened. "Yes. I am who I am. *This* is who I am, and people can take it or leave it. I'm never going to be a size two, and I wouldn't want to be. I like food too much. I'm a good friend, I try to be a good person, to help others when I can. And while I haven't had a long-term relationship in quite a while, I'd like to think that my friends know I'm there for them in the bad times as well as the good."

"They do," a deep voice said from behind her.

Finley froze. "Please tell me that isn't Brock," she whispered to the three men in front of her, who all had huge grins on their faces yet again.

"It's not Brock," Otto said obediently.

Finley closed her eyes and did her best to tamp down her embarrassment. It wasn't so much what she said, because she realized that Silas was right. She needed to stop denigrating herself. While she was still a little uncomfortable around Brock because he was *so* good-looking and she'd never really seen herself as particularly pretty, she really *did* like who she was. She'd come to terms with her weight a long time ago, and she'd done a fairly good job at ignoring the fat jokes and hurtful comments she sometimes heard aimed in her direction.

It had taken a long time to get to where she was today. Her mom was a freaking model, for God's sake...and she'd always been disappointed in Finley's weight. Always had snide things to say about the ever-increasing size of her clothes and the food she ate. Dinners as a child were excruciating, since she always served Finley a tiny amount of food, leaving her perpetually hungry.

She didn't know her dad; he'd apparently left as soon as he'd learned her mom was pregnant. Finley liked to think that maybe if he'd been around, he would've reined in her mother when it came to harping on her about her weight.

A large hand wrapped around her waist, then Brock pulled her snuggly into his side as he leaned down and kissed her temple. "Hey," he said by way of greeting.

Finley looked up at him and for a moment, it felt as if they were the only two people in the world. It was exciting to be held so close. And, as usual, he looked amazing. He had on a pair of cargo pants and a navy blue T-shirt with the Old Town Auto logo on the front. He smelled like soap, which let her know he'd showered not too long ago. His hair was sticking up, as if he'd run a hand through it while it was wet and it simply dried that way.

She unconsciously licked her lips as she stared at him, wondering how it would feel to have him *really* kiss her, instead of just pecking her on the cheek or temple.

A throat clearing and a chuckle brought her back to earth and made her realize where she was. Hating how easily she blushed, she turned to the three older men. They were all still smiling at her.

"Right, so...Brock is here and we're leaving. It was good chatting with you guys. Stay out of trouble, all right?" she told the trio.

"No guarantees."

"Whatever."

"Not a chance."

Their responses made her shake her head at them in

exasperation and affection. She looked at Brock again. His gaze was still glued to her, as if he hadn't looked away for a second. "Ready," he said.

Finley turned, and Brock kept his hand on her, shifting until it was resting on the small of her back. He steered her toward his truck sitting at the curb in front of The Sweet Tooth.

"I forgot about you needing to change," he said as they walked. "I'm sorry."

"Don't be. I had plenty of time after talking with Liam to run home and put on something more appropriate to hike."

"Run home?" he asked.

Finley chuckled. "Figure of speech. I didn't actually run. I drove."

"Right. That wasn't me making a judgement call on you not being *able* to run home. I was just curious. I don't run myself, always hated it. I'd rather lift weights or hike. And for the record, Finley...I like who you are. I wouldn't want you to be a size two either. Never understood the desire of women to be skin and bones. To be healthy, yes. But that doesn't equate to a particular size. Some people are at their healthiest when they're a size two, and for others it's a size eighteen."

He studied her then, with heat in his eyes. "But for me, personally...I've always been attracted to women who have curves. And you *are* a damn good friend, and person, and we all know you're here for us no matter what. So...things with Liam went well?"

Goose bumps rose on Finley's arms. She was embarrassed Brock overheard what she'd said to Art, Otto, and Silas, but his words soothed a worry she'd harbored from the moment she realized she was attracted to the man. Brock saying straight up that he not only didn't mind the shape of her body, but was attracted to her *because* of her curves, felt amazing.

She smiled shyly at him, feeling lighter than she had in a very long time. She still felt timid, but with every minute she spent with him, that shyness was morphing into something more...intimate.

"Liam was great. He's extremely enthusiastic. He's never worked in customer service, so he'll have to learn how to be tough but fair when it comes to people's demands, but I think he's going to work out. At least I hope so."

"Me too."

"He said he didn't mind working full eight-hour days, which is awesome for me. He'll come in at six, take a lunch mid-morning, and we'll both be done at three. I think with him there, I can actually get some of the next day's baking done ahead of time, or at least prep the dough. It'll save me a lot of time, since I won't be dividing my time between the front counter and the kitchen."

She knew she was babbling, but she couldn't help it.

"Thank you so much for recommending him. He told me a little bit about his sister, and I really hope any money he's able to send back home will help her get the treatment she needs sooner."

"I'm sure it will," Brock said as he steered her toward the driver's side of his truck. He opened the door and gestured. "Hop on in."

"Wouldn't it be easier for me to get in on the other side?" she asked with a curious tilt of her head.

"Probably. But this way, no one can sneak up on you while you're getting in."

That was kind of paranoid...but sweet at the same time. Shrugging and deciding it really didn't matter which side of the truck she got in on, Finley climbed inside and scooted across the bench seat. There was no middle console, and she smiled as she looked around at the nostalgic interior of the truck.

"You've done a great job restoring this," she told him.

"Thanks. You should've seen her when I first got her. Bought her for a hundred and fifty bucks from a scrapyard. Worked on her in my free time, as a way to decompress from my former day job."

"Was it that tough?" Finley asked as he pulled away from the curb. She winced. "That didn't come out right. I'm just not sure exactly what your job entailed."

"It's fine. You can ask me anything you want and I won't get offended," Brock told her easily. "I did what you probably think of when you hear about customs...stood at the border crossings and checked documentation of anyone coming into the country. I didn't ever work in airports, which I'm thankful for. I preferred to be at the actual borders. I inspected vehicles for illegal drugs, agriculture, and weapons...even people. You know, like semis full of people being smuggled into the US. I also patrolled the borders by foot, trying to catch people entering and, believe it or not, *leaving* the country illegally."

"Like along the Mexican border, the wall?"

"Yes. But also on the Canadian border. There are plenty of people who cross into the US in the forests that line our northern states."

"Yeah, I don't really think about that when I think about customs."

"There are also criminals who try to get out of the US without the authorities knowing. They usually have warrants out for their arrest. Murderers, drug dealers, child molesters...those kinds of people."

"Wow, so yeah, I'm guessing that was pretty hairy sometimes," Finley said, completely enthralled.

"That's one word for it. Desperate people will do dangerous things when they're cornered. Let's just say I much prefer looking for people who want to be found, rather than those who are trying to stay hidden," Brock said with a shrug. Then he took a deep breath and patted the dashboard of the truck. "So yeah, fixing this baby up was a good stress reliever."

"I can imagine."

They pulled into the parking area at the trailhead for the three-mile Barker Mill Trail and Brock shut off the engine. "You ready?"

"Yup."

When she reached for the door handle, Brock shook his head. "This way," he said, gesturing to his door with his head.

Finley rolled her eyes, but again did as he asked. He reached out a hand and helped her scoot across the seat. The feel of his fingers made her sigh. He was warm, and her hands were usually always cold.

"It doesn't bother you," Brock said as she hopped down from the seat. He hadn't let go of her hand, and Finley wasn't exactly disappointed.

"What doesn't?" she asked.

"My hands."

Finley looked up at him with a frown. "What do you mean?"

"They're stained. No matter how much I scrub them, I can't get the black off. I suppose if I stopped working on cars, they'd eventually go back to their normal shade, but I promise they're clean."

"My fingers are always freezing," Finley blurted. "I mean, *always*. I guess it's a circulation thing, but I've gotten used to it. I think your hands are awesome. They're really warm, and your fingers are so much longer than mine, so they wrap all the way around mine as if giving my hand a hug. Okay, that sounded stupid, sorry."

"It didn't," Brock reassured her.

"As for the stains, who cares? You've got working-man's hands, Brock. There's nothing wrong with that. Let me guess...some woman at some point in your life gave you a hard time about them."

His lips twitched. "Yeah."

"Well, she's stupid."

This time, Brock chuckled. "Can't argue with that. It's just...you didn't even ask if I'd scrubbed them before helping you in the kitchen."

"I saw you wash them at the sink before we started. Why would I question you? Oh, wait, because *she* did that too." Finley didn't know who the mysterious woman was who'd given Brock shit about his hands, but she definitely didn't like her.

"I'd taken her out to a nice restaurant, and she was embarrassed by the shape of my hands. I'd just helped a buddy replace the engine in his car and it was an especially messy job. He'd forgotten to empty the oil pan and that shit got everywhere. She asked me to go wash my hands, so I just did as she asked, instead of telling her that I'd showered before picking her up. When I got back to the table, she couldn't take her eyes off my fingers, and eventually I asked if she'd be more comfortable going somewhere else." He shrugged. "She said yes."

"I hope you dumped her ass," Finley muttered. They were still standing by his truck, her hand still in his.

Brock shook his head. "Actually, she dumped me."

"Told you she was stupid," Finley repeated. "I'm not sure I would trust a mechanic who *didn't* have stains on his hands," she said honestly. "Besides, just as you reassured me earlier that it's not how much I weigh that matters, it's not stains on your skin that matter to me."

"What does?" he asked.

Finley blushed, realizing she'd walked right into this conversation. She found the courage somewhere deep within her to answer him honestly. "The way you look *at* me instead of *through* me. How you listen to what I say. How you're always willing to drop everything for your friends. The fact that you'll spend an hour with Elsie's son, answering the same questions about something car related over and over without getting irritated. How patient you are, and how you're willing to go outside your comfort zone to help me in the kitchen when it's obvious baking isn't something you actually enjoy."

Then, because she couldn't stop herself if she tried, she brought their clasped hands up to her lips and kissed his knuckles, making sure to plant her lips right over a large stain to make her point.

The effect her words and action had on him was immediate. His pupils dilated, and she could see his chest rising and falling rapidly. She felt a little giddy herself.

"So fierce when you're defending others," he said gruffly.

Finley shrugged. She'd always been that way. It was much easier to get worked up when others were mistreated than it had ever been when she was the one maligned.

Just as Brock began to lean toward her, and Finley was sure he meant to kiss her, they were interrupted by four college-aged men leaving the trail. Brock pulled back, but she could read the promise in his eyes. It made Finley shiver in anticipation.

Brock squeezed her hand and pulled her toward the trailhead. He nodded at the kids.

"You guys goin' out to look for Bigfoot?" one of them asked.

"Depends...see any sign of him yourself?" Brock asked.

"No, but we did find a big-ass footprint. There's no way an animal made it. It has to be from Bigfoot himself!"

"Then yes, we're going to look for him too," Brock told them.

"Good luck, man!"

"Take pictures if you find him!"

"Your cell phone's not gonna work out there, found that out the hard way. So don't get lost," another said.

When they'd put the foursome behind them and entered the forest, Brock glanced at Finley. "Don't worry, I've got my satellite phone."

"I'm not worried," she told him. And she wasn't. If there was anyone she was comfortable going into the forest with, it was Brock. "You think they really did find a footprint?" she asked.

"If they did, I'm guessing it's left over from the paranormal investigations show," Brock drawled. "From what Lilly said, they were tromping all over the forest with those fake feet."

"I'd forgotten about that," Finley said with a chuckle. "You're probably right."

"Of course I am," Brock teased.

She rolled her eyes.

They walked along the well-marked trail, nodding at other hikers they passed. Being with Brock was comfortable. Finley didn't feel the need to fill the silence between them. And she couldn't deny that she loved holding his hand.

Almost as soon as she had the thought, he let go of her, and Finley figured that was the end of that.

But then he held out his other hand and wiggled his fingers at her.

"What?"

"Give me your other hand."

She switched to his opposite side and gave him her hand. They continued walking down the trail. "What was that about?" she asked after a while, not able to stem her curiosity.

"You said your hands are always cold, so I figured I'd warm this one up for a while."

Finley almost melted into a pile of goo right there on the trail. She didn't need huge bouquets of flowers from a man. Or extravagant gestures or gifts. She needed what Brock was giving her—kindness and consideration. And it scared the shit out of her. This was their first date. How was he so in tune with her already?

Was all this a ploy to get her into bed?

But as soon as she had the thought, she dismissed it.

Brock didn't have to work hard to get a woman to sleep with him. As far as she knew, however—and her friends were quick to reassure her—Brock hadn't had a girlfriend in a very long time. That didn't mean he wasn't sleeping with someone casually, but Finley didn't think that was his style.

No, like she'd told him already, he listened to people. And it was obvious Brock also had an innate sense of how to treat others. To discover what they needed and give it to them. Just as he'd done with her. He'd given her his time and assistance when she'd needed it the most. And he'd paid attention to what she'd said about her hands.

They'd walked about a mile and a half when they turned a corner on the trail and came upon a woman sitting off to the side, crying. Brock immediately went to the woman to find out what was wrong.

They learned her name was Rebecca, and that her boyfriend thought he'd seen something in the trees and had told her to stay put, that he'd be back. That had been thirty minutes ago, and she was now totally freaked out that he might have gotten lost.

Brock turned to Finley, and she immediately said, "I'll stay here with her. Go."

The relief she saw in his eyes made her feel good that she was able to help him and not be a burden.

"Take this," he said, holding out his satellite phone. "Call Ethan and tell him what's going on."

"No," Finley said firmly. "I'm not taking your only means of communication while you're out wandering around in the woods. *You* call Ethan, I'll stay here. On the extremely well-marked trail, where there will be plenty of people passing by that can help us if we need it."

Brock's lips twitched. "Right."

"We'll be fine," she told him softly. "Go. Do your thing. Wait—is it safe for *you* to go off the trail by yourself?"

"Yes. Because I've got a compass, and even if I didn't, I could find my way back to the trail with my eyes closed."

"Right. Then I'll see you when you get back."

He hesitated for just a moment, then reached for her. He wrapped one of his large, warm hands around her nape and pulled her close. His lips landed on hers—and Finley gasped as she got her first taste of the man she'd spent the last several months thinking about.

The feel of his tongue licking along her lips made Finley sigh, and she grabbed one of his huge biceps and dug her fingernails into his flesh through the cotton of his shirt, as she shyly reached out with her own tongue to meet his.

The sparks that shot through her when he caressed her tongue with his own were surprising, but by no means unwelcome.

Brock pulled back way too soon for her liking, but he had to get going. Find the woman's boyfriend before it got dark. The same heat coursing through her veins was shining out of Brock's eyes as he stared at her for another moment. Then he licked his lips sensually, as if trying to taste every last morsel of her on his skin. As he slid his hand off her nape, his thumb brushed against the underside of her jaw. It was all Finley could do to stay standing. This man was lethal...and she wasn't sure she could handle it if all he wanted was a short-term fling.

"I've dreamed about that for way too fucking long," he said quietly.

His words reassured Finley that whatever they were doing, it wasn't going to be brief. "Same," she whispered.

"Sorry our first date got interrupted," he told her.

"If you'd hurry up and get going and find this guy, we could continue," she sassed.

He chuckled. "Right. I'll be back as soon as I can. Do *not* leave the trail. No matter what. And don't let her leave it either. Got it?"

"Yes."

"It doesn't sit right with me to leave you here," he admitted.

Finley shook her head. "I'm fine. Go, Brock. Seriously."

"All right. I'm going," he said, taking a step back. Then he looked at the still crying woman. "Stay with Finley. I'll be back with your boyfriend as soon as I can."

Finley watched until Brock was out of sight in the trees, then turned to the woman.

"Do you really think he'll find him?" she asked tearfully.

"Yes. This is your lucky day...Brock's a member of the local search and rescue team. There's literally no one more qualified to find your boyfriend than him."

Her words seemed to reassure the woman, and Finley urged her a little ways down from where they were standing to a large tree that had fallen over. They sat, and Finley did what she could to keep Rebecca's mind occupied until Brock returned.

Almost an hour later, Finley looked up at the sound of footsteps approaching to find Talon coming down the trail. Standing, she frowned at him. "What's wrong?"

"Nothing," he reassured her quickly. Then he turned to the woman. "You're Rebecca?"

She nodded.

"Right, I'm Tal. My mate's the one who went off to look for your boyfriend. Turns out he found himself in a right bad predicament, stepped into a hole and sprained his ankle. But he's fine, so don't get worked up. Brock called us in, and the others are helping Mike to the trailhead as we speak. I'm here to escort you and Fin back to the cars. We'll meet them there."

"Oh! Are you sure he's all right?" Rebecca asked.

"Positive. Now, are *you* all right?" Tal asked as he gestured to the trail, indicating that the women head out in front of him. He turned and winked at Finley in the process.

She'd never been so glad to see someone in her life. Rebecca had vacillated between being hysterical about the fate of her boyfriend and downright mad when Finley wouldn't let her go off into the woods herself to look for him. She was relieved the missing man was all right, and that she was off the hook, so to speak, when it came to babysitting Rebecca.

As they walked, she learned that Brock had called Ethan, Tal, and Drew when he'd found the injured Mike. Ethan and Drew immediately went to help Brock, while Tal was sent to retrieve her and Rebecca. She was doubly glad she'd refused to take Brock's phone.

By the time the three of them reached the parking lot, there was a chill in the air and the sun was beginning to set. With the arrival of autumn came shorter days and longer nights. While Finley had never liked summer, she wasn't a huge fan of the freezing temperatures of winter either.

Mike was sitting in the passenger seat of a Ford Excursion, talking to the three search and rescue guys. When Rebecca saw him, she ran toward the car, crying hysterically.

"She's a little dramatic, huh?" Tal asked.

Finley did her best to choke back a laugh. He wasn't wrong.

"Looks like Brock's just as eager to see you as Rebecca was to see her boyfriend," Tal observed, as Brock hurried in their direction. "It was good to see you," Tal told her with another wink. He gave Brock a chin lift as he passed, but he didn't even seem to notice as all his attention was on Finley.

"You all right?" he asked when he got close.

Finley frowned. "Why wouldn't I be?" she asked.

Brock took a deep breath as he stopped in front of her. "I don't know. I just hated leaving you alone back there."

"I wasn't alone. And I'm not helpless. I was on the trail the whole time. I was fine."

"I know, I just...*shit*." He ran a hand through his hair, and Finley couldn't help thinking he was kind of cute when he was frustrated.

She reached out a hand and placed it on his chest. "I'm *good*, Brock. But thank you for worrying."

"You don't have to thank me for that," he said, grabbing her hand with his. Then he frowned. "Crap, you're freezing."

Finley chuckled. "I'm not really. I told you my hands run cold."

Without a word, Brock turned and towed her toward his truck.

"Don't you have to, I don't know...do something official

since you were the one to find him?" Finley asked as she followed.

"Ethan will take care of the report."

He opened his door and gestured for her to get in. Without a word, Finley climbed in and scooted over to the passenger side. Brock climbed in behind her, then took a deep breath before turning to face her.

"Thank you for making me take the phone."

"What happened?" she asked.

"Found him about twenty minutes after I left you. He'd stepped right into a large hole covered with debris and hurt his ankle bad. He wouldn't let me touch it, and he was screaming in pain. Also, you saw him, he's not a small man. I probably could've swung him over my shoulder and carried him, but he would've bitched and moaned the entire time. I figured it would be better to call for backup. I hated not being able to let you know what was happening."

Finley shrugged. "It's okay. I wasn't worried."

He tilted his head and stared at her. "You really weren't? I was gone for an hour."

"No, why would I be? Brock, you're more at home in the woods than you are in town. I knew whatever was going on, you had it under control."

"Fuck," Brock said under his breath. "How'd I get so lucky?" Then he shook his head and said, "This isn't how I saw our first date going."

Finley chuckled. "Well, you can make it up to me with the next one." Then she blushed. Darn, what if he didn't want to go out again? She was being awfully presumptuous.

"Damn straight I will," he muttered. Then he reached over and picked up her hand. Instead of holding it, he lifted his thigh slightly and stuffed her fingers under it. "To warm you up," he said gruffly, then reached for the ignition.

Finley's belly did somersaults. It wasn't the most conventional or romantic thing, but to her, it meant the world. She inched closer to him on the seat, as far as her seat belt would allow, and sighed in contentment as he drove them back toward Fallport.

When he turned onto the road where her small house was located, Finley frowned. "I need to get my car," she reminded him. "It's behind The Sweet Tooth."

"I'll come pick you up in the morning, take you to work."

"You don't have to—"

"I know I don't. But I'm going to."

Finley could only smile at the determination in his tone. "Okay. Thank you."

His shoulders relaxed a fraction, as if he'd been afraid she would argue with him. "You're welcome."

He pulled into her driveway and climbed out. Finley didn't even try to get out on her side, knowing he preferred for her to get out on his. She quickly scooted across the seat and he took her hand again as he helped her out. Then he walked her to her door. After she'd unlocked the dead bolt, she turned to him. "Thanks for the hike."

"Sorry it didn't go as planned."

"I don't know...We got out and stretched our legs. We got to talk a bit. You rescued a dude in distress. I think it went all right."

Brock smiled. "Promise our next one will go better. Speaking of which...wanna go bowling with me?"

"When?"

"Tomorrow?"

Finley chuckled. "I need to meet with Lilly."

"Right. You've got stuff to do. All right, you let me know when you're ready. You've got my number, right?"

"Uh-huh. Lilly made sure we all had everyone's numbers."

"Good." Then he stepped closer and said, "May I?"

Finley knew exactly what he was asking, and she nodded shyly. She'd wanted his lips back on hers ever since that first kiss on the trail.

He palmed the side of her head, brushing his thumb across her cheek. Finley's eyes closed and she sighed as their lips met. At first the kiss was slow and gentle, but then Brock groaned deeply and his hand slipped into her hair. He held her still as he slanted his head and opened his mouth.

They devoured each other as if the world was in imminent danger of exploding and this was their last moment alive.

By the time Brock lifted his head, they were both breathing hard. Finley's nipples were rubbing uncomfortably against her bra and it was all she could do not to clench her thighs together to try to control the need between her legs. This man was *lethal*.

"*Damn*," Brock whispered.

It was nice to know she wasn't the only one affected by their kiss.

"Go in and lock the door," he said after taking a deep breath. But he hadn't let go of the back of her head. His fingers caressed her scalp, sending tingles down her spine.

"I will...but you have to let go first," she told him, smirking a bit.

"Yeah, I know. Trying," he mumbled.

It was exhilarating to know he was just as attracted as she was. Finley's hands were on his chest, stroking absently, and she couldn't help but feel his own hard nipples under his shirt. He finally took a deep breath and stepped away from her.

"See you in the morning. Four twenty-five all right for me to pick you up?"

"Are you sure you really want to get up that early?" she asked.

"Positive."

"All right, then yes, four twenty-five is great. Thank you."

Brock nodded and backed off her small porch. He didn't turn around as he walked toward his truck. "Inside, Fin. Lock the door."

She kept her eyes on him as she pushed the door open and stepped into her house. She smiled at him one more time before shutting herself inside. She turned the dead bolt, then took a deep breath and leaned against the door. One hand went up to her lips, and she smiled.

Today had been...surprising. She'd gained two new employees, had her first date in forever, and was kissed as if she was the most important person in the world.

Yeah, she could take more days like this one.

CHAPTER FOUR

It had been almost a week since Finley hurt her wrist, and since Brock had started showing up in the mornings to help with her baking. Her wrist was completely healed, but Brock hadn't stopped coming by. Davis had also shown up every other day since he'd first knocked on her door. Both men had been a huge help.

But it was Liam who'd already changed her life as far as her bakery was concerned. The man was seriously perfect. He was charming and friendly, and he'd immediately mastered the art of the upsell. If someone bought a cinnamon roll, he could usually could talk them into getting a muffin or a cookie for later. Not only had Finley's sales increased in just the few days he'd been working for her, but it felt as if the general vibe of the store had lightened as well.

Usually she had to split her time between working the front counter and baking in the kitchen. But with her being able to concentrate solely on mixing, icing, and getting trays in and out of the oven the past couple days, she'd been way more productive, and her regulars didn't feel like they had to rush when they were deciding what they wanted.

Finley had even been able to try out a few new recipes and keep the front racks better stocked. She should've hired someone a long time ago.

If Liam continued to work out, Finley hoped to expand her business. She hadn't had any time to offer special-order cakes and other baked goods, but she'd always hoped to provide that service one day. She was super excited to make Lilly and Ethan's wedding cake, and she knew her friend wouldn't have any problem recommending her to others...particularly clients who hired her to photograph their own weddings.

All in all, things were going extremely well, both professionally and personally. She saw Brock every morning and, more often than not, he stopped by after The Sweet Tooth closed to chat some more. They hadn't gone out on their second date yet, but they planned to do it soon.

Bowling wasn't really Finley's thing, but she didn't really care *what* they did, as long as she got to spend time with Brock. It seemed silly that she'd been so reluctant to get to know him, and she regretted the lost time her insecurities had cost them. He was down to earth, friendly, and amazingly, he seemed to really be into her.

She heard the bell over the front door ring as another customer entered the store. She heard Liam greeting whoever it was, then he was at the door leading into the kitchen.

"There's a Khloe here, asking to speak to you," he informed her.

"Really? Send her back. And for the record, she's always welcome in the kitchen when she comes in. Just like my other friends."

Liam nodded. "No problem. I'll send her back."

A few seconds later, Khloe appeared in the doorway. While Finley had hung out with the woman a time or two, she didn't know her nearly as well as she did Lilly, Elsie, Bristol, and Caryn.

This morning, Khloe looked...stressed. That was the only word Finley could come up with. The quiet librarian had always been pretty reserved. None of Finley's inner circle knew much about her. She'd shown up in town around a year ago and had snagged the librarian job. Sometimes she and Raiden—another member of Brock's SAR team—seemed to get along so well, Finley wondered if there wasn't more going on between them than boss and employee. But other times, they seemed to barely tolerate one another.

No matter what was going on between them, Raiden's dog *always* adored Khloe, much to everyone's surprise. The bloodhound was completely devoted to Raid, and didn't seem to even notice anyone else...except his employee.

Khloe came into the shop frequently to get a breakfast cinnamon roll, but never to talk to Finley, specifically, so she was very curious as to what prompted the visit. "Hi," she said brightly.

"Hi," Khloe returned. "I don't mean to interrupt."

"You aren't," Finley reassured her. "Is something wrong?"

"No," she said without hesitation. "But I need your help."

"Of course. What's up?"

"I have to go out of town for a while...and you know about the kittens I've been taking care of behind the library. I'm worried about leaving them. I was wondering if you could keep an eye on them for me?"

"Of course I will!"

"I've been feeding them in the mornings and checking on them throughout the day. I made a cat house for them, to keep them out of the sun and dry when it rains. It's just a wooden box with a hole in one end, but they seem to really like it. It's next to the dumpster out back, and people who park back there have left them alone so far, but I'm still worried."

"Aw, of course you are. I would be too. I'll be happy to keep my eye on them. How long will you be gone?"

Khloe's eyes dropped, and she suddenly found the floor extremely interesting. "I'm not sure."

Finley's brows furrowed. She didn't like that the other woman was suddenly looking anxious. "You know you can tell me anything and I won't say a word to anyone, right?" she felt compelled to say.

Khloe looked back at her. "Of course. It's not a big deal, just something I have to do back home."

Finley wasn't fooled by her attempt at acting nonchalant. Whatever she was doing, wherever she was going—she didn't even know where "home" was for Khloe—it was important...and clearly stressing out the librarian.

The last thing Finley wanted to do was add to the woman's stress level, so she said, "All right. Do I need to get some cat food?"

Khloe shook her head and her shoulders dropped a little from their defensive hunched position. "No, I've got it. You want to come over and let me show you what I've been doing?"

"Yep. Good timing. I just took these cupcakes out of the oven and they can cool while I'm over there," Finley said with a smile. "Is the mama cat there too?"

"Sadly, no. I haven't seen her around, which is why I've been taking care of her kittens. I don't know if she got run over or some other animal got her..."

"Oh, that *is* sad."

Khloe nodded.

"Are they healthy? Have you brought them to the vet?"

Surprisingly, Khloe's lip curled in derision as she said, "I wouldn't bring *any* animal I loved to see that jackass."

Finley blinked at her harsh assessment of the only veterinarian in town. Dr. Ziegler was in his fifties and had been Fallport's vet for years. "Um...okay," she said tentatively.

"He's so old school he might as well have gotten his license in the eighteen hundreds," Khloe griped. "He has no clue about the new procedures that have been approved for the simplest of ailments. Not only that, but he won't let owners be with their pets when they need to be euthanized. Who *does* that? He claims it's less traumatic for people, but that's bullshit. What about the animal? While I have no proof, I *know* they're aware that they're dying. Would you want to be dying and surrounded by strangers? No, having your loved ones around would bring you comfort when you're scared and confused. It's barbaric —and I don't trust him as far as I can throw him."

Finley frowned. "Yeah, that's not cool. I don't have any pets, but I can't imagine not being with them if I needed to put them down."

"Exactly. He's too set in his ways. Not willing to even consider alternative treatments like acupuncture or homeopathic remedies. So to answer your question—no, I haven't brought the kittens to him. He'd probably want to put them down because they're strays," Khloe said.

Finley had never seen Khloe so worked up before. She seemed like a completely different woman at the moment than the one Finley had gotten to know a bit. Normally she was very succinct with her words, as if she didn't really want to talk at all, didn't want to be noticed. Except when she was arguing with Raiden, of course. But right now, she was standing with her hands fisted, practically shooting daggers from her eyes. If Dr. Ziegler had been there right that second, Finley had no doubt he'd been quaking in his boots.

"All right then, the vet is out. Do the kittens look okay? Should I be on the lookout for anything? And if something does happen, should I take them to Christiansburg?" That was the closest town to Fallport. It was forty minutes down I-480.

Khloe took a deep breath, as if to calm herself down. "They're fine. Healthy. Nothing's going to happen. I just need you to make sure they're fed. They do tend to wander away from their home these days, they're old enough now, but they always come back at night. If a storm or anything is forecasted, you can bring them and the box inside the back of the library. They always come back if bad weather's approaching."

"Inside? Does Raiden know about them? Wait—why don't you ask *him* to look after them?"

"Of course he knows." Khloe grinned, and Finley

thought when she smiled, it changed her entire countenance. Made her look more approachable. She wrinkled her nose adorably. "I *would* ask Raid, but...he's got a lot on his plate right now. He works really hard at the library, and then with the search and rescue obligations. I just don't want to bother him with one more thing. Besides, Duke doesn't think much of the kittens, and the feeling's mutual. Just make sure you shut the door that leads to the main part of the library, and let Raid know they're back there, and they'll be fine."

"Okay."

"I really appreciate this," she said.

Finley nodded and went to the sink to wash her hands. She'd had no idea that the woman was so passionate about animals. Finley had lived in Fallport for a while now, and she hadn't even met the local veterinarian. She didn't know how Khloe had gotten such a bad impression of the man, but she decided that the kittens couldn't have found a better champion.

After telling Liam she'd be back, Finley and Khloe cut through the square to get to the library. It was located directly opposite The Sweet Tooth. They waved at Art, Otto, and Silas. Two people were sitting in The Circle, the gazebo in the middle of the grassy area of the square, and Finley smiled at seeing the small The Sweet Tooth bag between them. It never got old, seeing people enjoying the things she baked.

They walked around the southeast side of the library, away from The Cellar. The library was between Doc Snow's medical clinic and the pool hall, and some people laughed at the irony of the staid building next to the notorious bar, but it's not like the respective patrons really mixed. The library closed well before the rowdiness ramped up next door.

Finley spied the box between the dumpster and the building as soon as they turned the corner. There were no kittens in sight, so she assumed they were out exploring, like Khloe mentioned.

Khloe opened the top of the box. There was a blanket inside, which she shook out before returning it to the box. She told Finley she'd bring her some clean blankets and towels to switch out with the dirty ones, as well as a bag of the food she'd been giving them.

They ooh'd and aah'd over the pictures on Khloe's phone of the kittens. There were three of them, a calico, a black kitten, and a brown and white one.

"They're pretty used to me, but don't be offended if they don't take to you right away. They tend to run when anyone other than me gets too close, which I'm not totally upset about. The last thing I want is someone from The Cellar messing with them. But since you'll be feeding them, they'll get used to you fairly quickly, I think. And I'm pretty sure everyone else thinks the box is simply trash, so they don't bother to come investigate. That, and they're too invested in getting into the bar quickly to get drinking," Khloe said dryly.

"Are you going to try to find them homes?" Finley asked. "I mean, you can't let them live out here forever, can you?"

Khloe sighed. "No. And yes, I'd love to find homes for them."

"What about Bristol or Lilly?"

"What about them?"

"They both have fairly large properties. I bet they wouldn't mind taking them."

"You think?"

"It couldn't hurt to ask."

"Maybe I will. In the meantime, I appreciate you keeping an eye on them for me while I'm gone."

"Of course," Finley told her. "And you really have no idea how long you'll be away?"

Just like that, a shutter seemed to fall over Khloe's eyes. "No. I'm hoping not more than a week, but honestly, it could be longer."

"Are you sure everything's all right?"

"It's fine," she said curtly, making it clear she didn't want to answer any more questions about where she might be going or why. "I usually feed them in the mornings. I don't live that far away, just a few streets over. I come over before any businesses open. When cars start pulling into the lot, the kittens tend to head off to do whatever it is they do during the day."

"That's not a problem. I'm at work around four-thirty every morning anyway."

"I know," Khloe said with a small smile. "It's why I asked you for help."

"Do I need to do anything with them when I leave for the day?"

"No, they should be fine. Just keep an eye on the weather app. I appreciate this so much."

"Of course. And please know...if you *do* ever want to talk, I'm a good listener."

Khloe looked almost melancholy for a moment before her features cleared once more. "Thanks. But I'm good."

"Promise?" Finley asked.

"Promise. Now you probably need to get back, and I'm sure Raiden's grumbling under his breath about me being gone so long."

"Really? He doesn't seem like the kind of guy who'd care about that sort of thing."

Khloe shrugged. "Yeah, you're right. He probably doesn't even *know* I'm gone," she said with a small chuckle.

Finley wasn't so sure about that. While trying to avoid staring at Brock when she was with their group of friends, she'd noticed Raiden eyeing Khloe the couple times the woman joined them. She wasn't sure of the dynamic between the two. They really were hot and cold, some days fairly friendly, and others doing their best to stay away from each other.

"You've got my number. If anything seems off, please text me," Khloe said.

"I will. Although I'm not sure what you'll be able to do from wherever you are."

"You'd be surprised," Khloe said mysteriously. "Anyway, while I didn't want to ask Raiden to take care of the kittens, I'm sure he'd help if you needed him to."

Finley nodded. "When are you leaving?"

"This evening."

Her eyes widened. "So soon?"

"Yeah."

"All right, well, travel safe."

Khloe smiled. "I will. Thanks again."

Finley took that as her cue to return to the bakery. She said her goodbyes to Khloe and headed back around the side of the building. She could've cut through the library, but she was enjoying the crisp fall afternoon. It was October, and Lilly and Ethan's wedding was right around the corner. From what she'd heard, the renovated barn on Bristol and Rocky's property, where the ceremony was going to be held, looked awesome.

She'd met with Lilly a couple days ago, and she'd approved the vision Finley had for the Halloween-themed wedding cake. The ceremony was going to be laid-back, and while it wasn't a costume thing, Lilly wanted everyone to be comfortable...which meant no suits and ties and no fancy gowns. And that was more than all right with Finley.

Liam gave her a chin lift as she entered, and Finley was pleased to see how much he'd sold even in the short time she'd been with Khloe. Yeah, things were definitely looking up for her, and Finley couldn't help but smile as she headed into the kitchen to ice the cupcakes she'd made earlier.

* * *

Looking at his watch, Brock saw it was three-thirty. Finley should be done at the bakery, unless she was staying late... which was more often than not. She worked damn hard to make her business a success, and Brock was extremely proud of her.

"Gonna take a break," he told Jesus.

"Got it. Time to see Finley. No problem," his partner said with a grin.

Brock didn't even care that all of his employees knew he was head over heels for the pretty baker.

"Liam told me she paid him his first paycheck early. Said she knew he wanted to send money home to his sister, and she wanted to make sure he could start doing so quickly. I swear I thought he was going to cry," Jesus told

Brock. "Not only that, but she included an extra five hundred dollars...a gift to help make sure his sister got the care she needed as soon as possible. As far as I'm concerned, I'm never getting my kids' birthday cakes and treats anywhere but from The Sweet Tooth from now on."

Brock wasn't surprised at Finley's generosity. That was just who she was. He made a mental note to give his own donation to Finley to pass on to Liam. He didn't think the man would take money from him directly, but from his boss? If it was simply included in his paycheck, that might work. "She'll appreciate that," he told Jesus.

He pulled out his phone as he walked toward the enclosed yard behind the shop. Caryn and Drew used the area for working out some mornings, and Caryn had even arranged for some of the less-damaged vehicles in their lot to be used in training for both the Fallport Fire Department and the junior firefighters program she was starting. The FFD was going through a major change in personnel and training regiment, which in Brock's eyes was a good thing.

When he was employed by the government, he'd constantly gone through additional training, not only to keep his skills up to par, but to learn the new ways smugglers were trying to get their illegal goods into the country. The fact that the FFD hadn't bothered to do any kind of training in several years was appalling and downright negligent.

Brock wandered out into the yard, enjoying the feel of the sun on his face after being cooped up in the bays most of the day working on cars. He clicked on Finley's name and realized he was smiling as he waited for her to pick up.

"Hi," she said when she answered.

"Hey back," Brock said. "How was your day?"

"Good. Busy. I finalized the last of the details for Lilly and Ethan's cake. I'm planning on baking a trial run cake next week, so I can tweak anything that doesn't work from the design, and to make sure Lilly likes it. We sold an extra three dozen cupcakes today, and I just pulled a new batch of pumpkin spice cookies out of the oven for tomorrow. I'll ice them in the morning. Oh, and Khloe brought over stuff for me to take care of the stray kittens she's been looking after, while she's out of town."

"Where's she going?" Brock asked.

"I don't know. She wouldn't say. In fact, she seemed downright mysterious about it, but I didn't want to pry. Said she's not sure when she'll be back either."

"Hmmm," Brock murmured.

He made a mental note to ask Raiden about his employee, make sure she was okay. Their relationship seemed complicated, but surely he had more info than Finley. Brock liked Khloe. She was a little standoffish, but she hadn't done or said anything to make him think she wasn't a good person. Besides, Duke liked her—hell, the bloodhound *loved* her—and Brock had always trusted an animal's instincts.

"So...do you have any plans for tonight?"

"Well, I was going to go home and try a new recipe for pumpkin sugar cookies. And I want to make sure I remember how to make my molasses cookies before I put them on sale in the shop."

"Yum," Brock said with a hum. "If you need a taste tester, I'm available."

Finley giggled, and Brock couldn't remember hearing a better sound. He loved when Finley was happy.

"I'm not sure I can trust you. You have the palate of a starving man who hasn't had sugar in years."

She wasn't wrong. He didn't have the patience to make anything sweet on his own, and when he shopped, he usually stuck to high-protein, low-sugar items. Being with Finley this past week had shown him exactly what he'd been missing. He'd loved every single thing she'd asked him to taste, including the oatmeal cherry cookies he hadn't thought he'd enjoy. "True. But I think it's more that the things you make are just that good," he told her. "Any chance you'd like some company while you bake tonight?"

"If that company's you, then yes," she told him.

Once more, Brock sighed in contentment. He loved that she didn't play games with him. She wasn't coy, didn't try to pretend she didn't want to see him as much as he wanted to see her. "And what about tomorrow evening? I thought maybe we could try that bowling date we talked about."

"I'd love it," she said immediately. "Although I have to warn you, it's been years and years since I've played."

"No problem."

"In fact, I'm guessing you'll probably be embarrassed by the way I bowl. You know, standing at the line, holding the ball in both hands, before leaning over and lobbing it down the lane...where nine times out of ten it ends up in the gutter."

Brock laughed out loud. But he was already looking forward to standing behind her, checking out her sweet ass every time she bent over to roll the ball.

"Brock? Did I lose you?"

"Sorry, no, I'm here. And I don't give a shit how you

bowl or how many gutter balls you roll. I just want to spend time with you."

"Same," she said quietly. Then asked, "How was *your* day? You put any cars back together?"

Brock chuckled. "It was good. And I didn't get to put together any engines or anything, but I did get to do about eight oil changes and rotate three sets of tires," he said wryly.

"*Wooo*. Thrilling day then, huh?"

Brock had already told Finley that he much preferred puzzling out what was wrong with a car's various systems, keeping it from running at peak performance. Oil changes weren't high on his list of favorite things to do, but money was money, and he'd change oil all day long if it meant keeping his business going. "Pretty much. You want me to grab something for dinner before I come over?" he asked.

"How about if I make something for us?" she countered.

"I don't want to put you out," he told her.

"Brock, throwing some chicken breasts into the lower oven while I use the upper for my cookies isn't going to put me out. You like broccoli?"

"Yes."

"Good. I'll bake some of that too, with lots of spices and maybe a little cheese on top. I've been lazy this week with dinner, and I need some good stuff to counter all the crap I've eaten."

"You aren't lazy," Brock countered immediately.

She chuckled. "When it comes to cooking real food, trust me, I am. Anyway, come over whenever. I'm finishing up here and should be home in thirty minutes or so."

Brock wanted to hang up and immediately head to her

house, just so he could spend as much time with her as possible, but he had another oil change to complete before he could leave. "Sounds good. I'll text when I'm on my way."

"All right. Brock?"

"Yeah, Fin?"

"This week has been great. And you're a big reason why. Thank you for recommending Liam. And helping me in the mornings. And for encouraging Davis when he's here. It...it means a lot."

"You're welcome. I've had a good week too."

"I'm glad. I'll see you later."

"Later," Brock said before clicking off the connection. He stood in the yard, daydreaming about his sweet baker for a full two or three minutes, before turning and heading back into the shop. The sooner he finished his work for the day, the sooner he could go home, shower, and get to Finley's.

CHAPTER FIVE

Finley headed out of The Sweet Tooth with the bag of cat food and a clean blanket in her arms and a smile on her face. The night before with Brock had been...wonderful. She'd been perfectly relaxed around him, so much so that she wore a pair of old, thin leggings and an oversized T-shirt with a small hole near the hem. Her go-to comfort clothes. And he didn't seem to mind a bit. In past relationships, she wouldn't even think about wearing something so casual around someone she'd just started dating. It always took at least a few weeks before she felt comfortable enough to do so.

But with Brock, everything was different. He made her feel as if she could simply be herself. And that meant wearing whatever made her happy and saying whatever was on her mind.

Last night, he'd helped with the baking and profusely praised the cookies she'd made. He'd admitted that he didn't understand the obsession with pumpkin-spice everything, but after tasting her pumpkin sugar cookies, he claimed he was a convert. He'd enjoyed the simple baked chicken and broccoli...and she was still thinking about the kiss he'd given her before leaving for the night.

The more Finley was around Brock, the more she wanted him. He made her feel beautiful, which was no easy task. While she'd learned to accept her body years ago, the way his gaze heated and his obvious erection pressing against her as they kissed...well, it gave her even more confidence when it came to her sexuality.

She could admit to nervousness at the thought of being naked with him, if their relationship progressed to that point. He was so damn muscular, and Finley had a feeling he didn't have an ounce of fat on his entire body. The last thing she wanted was for him to be disappointed when he saw what she looked like under her clothes. He'd told her time and time again, in words and with his actions, that he liked her exactly how she was, but she still had that small nagging doubt.

However, today wasn't the day she needed to worry about that. They were going on their second official date that evening, even though they'd seen each other every day for the last week. She would've been content to have him come over and chill at her house again, but Brock was determined to take her out. He said he wanted to show her off. Which was just another way he made her feel special.

He wasn't embarrassed to be seen with her in public.

She'd dated one particular guy in the past who never took her to dinner, never went shopping with her, never so much as held her hand or touched her in any way the few times they were out in public. When they broke up, he'd admitted that he was embarrassed for his friends to see him with someone like her. That particular blow had taken a while to get over.

But she didn't have to worry about that with Brock. Every chance he got, he was putting his hands on her. While walking anywhere, sitting on her couch watching a movie, standing in the kitchen at The Sweet Tooth...he was always touching her.

So if he wanted to go bowling, she'd gladly go. It didn't matter if he called it their second date, their fifth, or their sixtieth. She was just pleased he wanted to spend time with her.

But first, she needed to get through the day. Starting with looking after the stray kittens Khloe had been caring for. Davis was currently in the kitchen of The Sweet Tooth mixing the first batch of dough for cinnamon rolls. She told him she'd be back within ten minutes or so and headed out the door.

Fallport was quiet this early, and quite dark. The stars overhead twinkled as she walked across the grassy square. She turned left and went around the clinic, as she and Khloe had done the day before. She walked quickly to the box by the trash—and was thrilled to see a little brown head peeking out from inside.

Finley knelt and slowly pulled the plastic food bowl closer. She murmured quietly to the kittens, not wanting to scare them, as she filled the bowl. Then she pushed it toward the opening of the box, and within seconds, all three kittens were standing around the bowl, chowing down. They didn't exactly come up to her for pets, but at least they hadn't run when she approached. Finley supposed the food was a great incentive.

She didn't want to startle them by attempting to pet

any of them while they were eating, so she stayed on her knees next to the box and watched as they heartily ate.

A noise to her left startled Finley, and she looked up to see a black pickup pull into the parking lot behind the pool hall. It was so dark, she knew whoever was driving probably wouldn't see her kneeling next to the dumpster, so she kept her eyes on the vehicle in case it reversed back toward her. The last thing she wanted was for any of the kittens to be spooked and run off—right under the wheels of the truck.

To her surprise, a man came around the corner of the pool hall and leaned into the passenger side of the truck. Whoever was driving had rolled down the window on that side. The driver and the man had a short conversation, before the man reached into the truck, coming away with a backpack. He stepped away as the truck drove off, slinging the pack over his shoulder before disappearing around the corner.

The entire thing had taken no more than a minute and a half, and in that time, the kittens had managed to finish their meal. The calico had gotten up the nerve to come near Finley to smell her.

The black truck forgotten, Finley reached down and gently ran a finger over the kitten's head. It immediately started purring. The other two kittens, obviously feeling as if they were missing out, came up to her as well. Soon, Finley was sitting on her ass on the dirty ground with three kittens on her lap.

She stayed there in the dark, soaking up the innocence of the kittens, for way too long. "I wish I could stay here all day," she whispered. "But I've got cookies and goodies to make. I've brought you a clean blanket though."

She leaned over and pulled the soiled blanket out of the box as all three kittens slowly climbed out of her lap. She exchanged the dirty blanket for a clean one, making a mental note to bring a second bowl and a bottle of water the next morning. She watched as the kittens scampered away and disappeared into the trees bordering the back of the parking lot.

More determined now to convince Bristol and Lilly to take in the cats, Finley stood and brushed dirt off her butt. She picked up the dirty blanket and the bag of food, pushed the plastic bowl closer to the box, then headed back to her shop.

Brock arrived to help her out not long after she got back to the bakery, and with his and Davis's help, making the morning goodies was fast and easy.

The day went by fairly quickly, much to Finley's relief. She was doubly grateful for Liam's presence when there were several customers who seemed determined to take out their bad moods on someone else. Finley hated conflict and usually just ended up giving the obnoxious customers whatever they wanted. But Liam had more backbone. He was soft-spoken, which seemed to help ease tensions, but more than that, he was able to resolve the customers' issues and complaints without simply rolling over and giving anyone free food to get them out of the shop quicker, like Finley might've done.

By the time three o'clock came around and they closed up the shop, nervousness was just starting to get the better of Finley. It was silly. She'd hung out with Brock every day this week. Just because they were going out instead of staying at her house, or his, didn't mean anything.

But it did. It made things between them more official.

She could tell herself they were just friends and hanging out if they were at her house, but going out in public, letting others see them together, was very different. It opened them up to being the topic of gossip, which this small town loved. And Finley *hated*.

She knew what people would think. They'd wonder what in the world Brock was doing with someone like her. He was fit and athletic, and she was...not. They'd probably assume he was feeling sorry for her or something, going out with her on pity dates or maybe even just to get laid.

Taking a deep breath, Finley shook her head. No, she wasn't going to worry about what others thought of her. She was positive Brock didn't give two shits about the opinions of strangers, and he wouldn't waste his time dating her if he wasn't truly interested. If she'd learned anything about the man in the last week—and really, in the last few months that she'd been around him, thanks to her friends—it was that he didn't do anything he didn't want to.

She waved goodbye to Liam and headed for her car. There was still plenty of time before Brock said he was going to pick her up. She could relax a bit, get off her feet. She was used to standing all day, but couldn't deny that sitting on her butt for a while sounded like heaven.

Three hours later, Finley sighed when she realized she hadn't sat down at all. From the moment she'd gotten home, different nerves had struck. She'd spent way too much time trying to decide what to wear. She didn't want to look like she was trying too hard, but she also didn't want to look like a slob. After rifling through her entire wardrobe, she finally decided on a pair of jeans and a flowery top. It was tight across her boobs but loose and flowy around her stomach, hiding the extra weight she had there.

She'd left her hair down, which she never did. It got in the way when she baked, and the last thing she wanted was hair getting into the treats she made. It was thick, and in the summers she couldn't stand the weight of it on her neck, but because cooler weather had finally hit Fallport, she knew she wouldn't sweat to death if she kept it down.

She wasn't a high-heel kind of person, so she put on a pair of red Sketchers and examined herself in the mirror. She actually felt pretty. Her cheeks were flushed, and the little bit of makeup she'd used really brought out the changing colors of her hazel eyes.

At six o'clock on the dot, there was a knock on Finley's door. Her heart beating hard in her chest, she quickly opened it.

Brock always took her breath away, but tonight, he was even more handsome.

His hair looked damp, as if he'd recently gotten out of the shower. He smelled like some sort of spicy body wash, and her gaze greedily took him in from head to toe. He was wearing black jeans that hugged his muscular thighs, a forest-green polo shirt, and black hiking boots. His biceps strained the elastic at the sleeves, making Finley's mouth water. She loved how buff he was.

"Hi," she said belatedly.

But he didn't even seem to mind that she hadn't greeted him right away, because his own gaze had been taking her in as well. At the sound of her voice, his gaze came back up to her face. Instead of speaking, he stepped toward her.

Instinctively, Finley backed up. He kept coming until

they were inside the small foyer of her house. Using his foot, Brock shut the door behind him, then reached for her. He framed her face with his hands and leaned in.

Finley went up on her tiptoes, more than eager to meet him halfway.

He held her still as his lips touched hers. They went from zero to one hundred in seconds, and Finley's palms curled into his chest as he kissed her senseless.

Brock pulled back but didn't go far. He stared down at her for a long moment before saying, "You're so damn beautiful."

Finley let out a huff of breath. It wasn't that she didn't think she cleaned up well, but she'd never been that good at taking compliments about her looks. If someone wanted to praise her food, she had no problem basking in the pleasure the comment evoked. But she knew what she looked like, and it wasn't like anyone she saw in magazines and in movies. Over the years, Hollywood had gotten a little better at employing men and women who didn't fit the typical mold of what society deemed beautiful, but those actors and actresses were few and far between.

"Thanks," she finally replied.

"You don't believe me," Brock stated.

Finley didn't hear any irritation in his tone so she merely shrugged. "I know what I am and what I'm not."

"Obviously you don't," Brock said. "When you opened that door, I saw a woman so delectable, it was all I could do to control myself."

Finley's lips twitched. "This is you controlling yourself?" she couldn't help but ask. "Backing me against the wall and kissing the daylights out of me?"

"Yes. I *wanted* to sling you over my shoulder, throw you

78

on your bed, strip you naked, and bury my face between your legs."

Finley's heart skipped a beat and her cheeks heated. "Oh," was all she could manage to say. The image that sprang to her mind at his words was so carnal, she almost had a spontaneous orgasm right there and then.

"You didn't slap the shit out of me," he said with a grin. "I'm gonna take that as a good sign."

"Yeah, well, it's not every day a girl like me hears that kind of thing," she informed him.

"A girl like you?"

Finley took a deep breath. "I'm fat, Brock. I know you've noticed, because everyone does. I'm always going to be this way. I've dieted, and sometimes I even lost a good amount of weight. But I felt like crap. I was always tired and miserable and it was all I could do to get out of bed in the mornings. I like food too much to be on any kind of long-term diet. But I see my doctor every year, my blood pressure is good and my cholesterol is normal. I work out when I can, yoga, hiking, workout programs on the internet, things like that. But I'm probably always going to be bigger than what society deems acceptable."

She took a breath and stared up at Brock. He hadn't let go of her face and her fingers were still digging into his chest.

"You done?" he asked.

"Um...yes. I guess so."

"You're right. I haven't missed your size, Finley. And I believe I already told you this, but I'll tell you again. I don't give a shit what the scale says. In my eyes, you're fucking *perfect*. I'm a big man, all over. I work out, lift weights. A lot. It's my way of letting off steam. I can't think of anything sexier than feeling your softness against my hardness. I love every single curve on your body, and the thought of having you under me, and over me, makes me lose my damn mind. I don't *want* you to lose weight. I want you to be healthy, of course, but I wouldn't be kissing and touching you like I am if I didn't want you exactly how you are."

Finley wanted to cry. She'd had men tell her in the past that her weight didn't bother them, but they eventually proved otherwise. Now, held in Brock's possessive hold, feeling his erection against her belly and hearing the sincerity in his tone...she had no choice but to believe him.

"Thank you," she whispered, almost overcome with emotion.

"You wouldn't thank me if you could read my mind and knew what I was thinking right now," Brock said dryly as his gaze went from her face down to her chest.

Finley could feel that her nipples were hard. And the shirt she wore had a fairly low, scooped neckline. It wouldn't take much for him to push the material down and—

She cut her thoughts off. It was too soon for sex with Brock. Wasn't it? In the past, she tended to wait at least a couple months before trusting a man enough to go to bed with him. But she was finding it difficult to come up with her usual reasons to wait with Brock.

He cleared his throat and inhaled deeply before dropping his hands from her face and taking a step back. "You ready?"

Ready? She was more than ready for him.

Finley swallowed hard. That wasn't what he was talking about and she knew it. "Yeah."

"I thought we could eat at Knock 'Em Down. They've got decent burgers and their seasoned fries are awesome."

"Don't let Sandra hear you say that," Finley joked. "She'd be appalled that you find bowling alley food acceptable."

"What she doesn't know won't hurt her," Brock said with a wink. Then he leaned toward her once more. This time, the kiss he gave her was short and sweet.

"What was that for?" she asked as he reached for her hand and turned toward the door.

"Just because," he said with a shrug. "Does it bother you?"

"Does what bother me?" she asked as he took her keys after they'd exited the house, locking her front door.

"Me touching you. Kissing you. I'm finding it difficult to keep my hands and lips off you, honestly, and I need to know what your level of comfort is with PDA."

"PDA?" she said with a small giggle. "What are we, in middle school?"

Brock grinned as he walked her toward his truck with a hand on the small of her back. "Nope. But Fallport's a small town, as you're well aware. And the second I kiss you in the middle of Knock 'Em Down, word's gonna be all over that we're seein' each other. I just want to make sure you're comfortable with that."

"I am," she reassured him immediately.

"I'm just a mechanic," he reminded her.

Finley frowned at him as they stopped in front of the driver's side door of his truck. She was startled to realize in that moment that he had his own insecurities when it came to others' opinions of him. She reached up and palmed the side of his face, much as he'd done to her earlier. "A damn good one," she said softly. "The only thing I know how to do to keep my car running is put gas in it when the little line gets too close to E. And you aren't 'just' anything, Brock Mabrey."

He tilted his head into her palm and closed his eyes for a moment. When they opened again, he looked at her with such intensity, Finley found herself holding her breath as she stared back.

"I'm not going to fuck this up," he said after a moment.

"Of course you aren't," Finley said in surprise.

"I mean it. It's been a very long time since I've found something I want as badly as I want things between the two of us to work out."

"Same," Finley admitted. It was kind of scary to lay herself so bare like this, but it also felt right.

"Good. Now, you want to go knock down some pins?"

"Well, yeah, but that doesn't mean I'm going to be able to," she quipped.

Brock chuckled, and the powerful moment they'd had was over. He turned and opened the door and gestured for her to crawl over to the passenger side.

"Are you ever going to let me get in on my side?" she asked as she scooted up into the seat.

"Probably not," Brock said with a shrug. "It's safer this way."

Finley wanted to roll her eyes and remind him that this was Fallport. That the crime rate was ridiculously low. But then again, after what had happened to Lilly, Elsie, Bristol, and Caryn, she figured he might have a point, so she kept her mouth shut.

They drove to the square and Brock parked behind the bowling alley. Finley could see the tiny house the town had made for Davis on the other end of the parking lot, and she smiled. There were definite disadvantages to living in a small town, but there were pros too.

Brock held her hand as they walked into the bowling alley, and Finley was shocked to find the place so crowded. "Holy crap, have there *ever* been this many people here at one time before?"

"Maybe on half-price bowling nights," Brock said with a small frown on his face. He walked them up to the counter where bowling shoes were handed out.

Before he could tell the kid behind the counter their sizes, he said, "We're completely full at the moment, it'll be at least forty-five minutes before a lane opens. Here's a card reserving your spot. When you hear your number over the loudspeaker, you can come back and get shoes."

Brock took the laminated card and sighed.

Finley squeezed his hand. "It's okay. We can grab something to eat while we're waiting. It's hard to eat and bowl at the same time anyway."

Brock nodded and they headed for the food counter. There was a long line, and Finley heard Brock sigh again as they took their place at the end. She leaned against him and put her arm around his waist. He immediately wrapped his arm around her shoulders and held her tightly. "Sorry about this," he said.

"About what? You can't control who decides to go bowling on the same night as us," she said with a shrug. "And while I'm not always thrilled with the tourists, this is really good for business. I've definitely had an increase in sales myself."

"I know, I just...I just realized I don't like sharing you."

If Finley wasn't mistaken, Brock was pouting. Honest-to-God pouting. She couldn't help but chuckle.

"What's funny?" he asked.

"You," she said with a shrug.

"I've gotten used to having you to myself. Chatting with you in your shop in the mornings, hanging out with you in the evenings. All these people are..." His voice trailed off.

"Peopley?" Finley finished for him.

"Exactly," he said with a smile. Then he leaned down and kissed her forehead.

Luckily, the line moved fairly quickly. Brock gave the harried-looking boy behind the counter their order and they received another laminated paper with a number on it.

"Not sure we can find a seat, but shall we try?" Brock asked.

Finley nodded and, as it turned out, they had to wait just five minutes or so before a couple got up to leave. Brock moved faster than the twenty-something kid who'd spied the table at the same time, claiming the sticky tabletop first.

"My hero," Finley said with a sigh, batting her eyelashes at him playfully.

"Not sure she needs to eat anything else, she already looks like she swallowed an entire cow," the kid muttered spitefully under his breath.

Finley felt Brock's muscles tighten and she grabbed hold of his forearm before he could get up and confront the inconsiderate asshole. "Don't," she warned.

"You think I'm gonna let that shit go?" he asked with a lift of an eyebrow.

"Yes, you are. Because that's not the first insult I've heard about my size and it won't be the last. I'm used to it, Brock. It's fine."

"It's not *fine*," he insisted. "It was rude as fuck and there's no way I'm gonna let anyone talk to you like that."

"Here's the thing," she said, leaning into him. "That's unfortunately normal for people my size. Being fat means I'm fair game. I'm used to it, and while I admit comments like that used to bother me, now I pretty much see it as *his* problem, not mine. Other than feeling self-conscious now and then, I've accepted my body for what it is. Going after him will only embarrass me, and it wouldn't change the way he thinks anyway."

"It's bullshit," Brock complained, but Finley was relieved when he relaxed into his seat once more.

"It is," she agreed with a shrug.

Brock wrapped his fingers around her hand and stroked the back of it gently. "You're gorgeous," he said softly. "And I'm a lucky son-of-a-bitch to be here with you tonight. I've wanted this for a long time now."

"Really?" she asked.

He nodded. "But you would barely look at me when we were together with our friends. I had to bide my time until you were more used to being around me."

Finley shrugged. "I'm shy," she said.

"You aren't telling me anything I don't already know," Brock said with a grin. "And I like it."

"You're weird," she informed him.

"Nope. I just know that under that shyness is a passionate woman who's worth the wait."

"You think so?" she asked with a tilt of her head and a small smile.

"Definitely. I see the energy and effort you put into baking. The passion you have for your creations. The way you stand up for your friends. How concerned you are about them. You've got more passion in your little finger than a lot of people have in their entire bodies. So yeah, I knew once I got past that bashful exterior, I'd be rewarded with the real Finley."

She stared at him in disbelief. He made her sound almost mysterious. It made her feel all tingly inside that he wanted to get to know her, and that he'd been patient for so long in order to gain her trust.

She opened her mouth to say something, she wasn't sure what, but their number was called over the loud-speaker.

Brock picked up her hand, kissed the back, and said, "Save my spot?"

Finley rolled her eyes. "I'm guessing there isn't going to be a rush of men trying to take it."

"Then you aren't paying attention. Your ass in those jeans? Woman...I'm surprised some of these guys haven't come hit on you with me sitting right here. I'll be back."

Finley watched him walk over to the counter to grab their burgers and she pinched herself to make sure she wasn't dreaming. Brock was hands down the best-looking man in the building. It wasn't even so much his looks, although he definitely wasn't hard on the eyes. It was the confidence he exuded. She had no doubt he could take on an entire flotilla of men if they started a fight over her.

She had no idea what a flotilla was, but she was sure Brock could take it on.

She was still smiling when Brock returned with a plastic tray loaded with their burgers and fries.

"You look happy," he observed.

"I am. This is fun. Thank you for bringing me."

He chuckled. "So far we've found out we have to wait an hour before we can bowl, had to stand in line for food, had to fight for a table, you were insulted, and I forgot the drinks. Oh yeah, loads of fun."

Finley giggled. "I've actually learned things I didn't already know about you tonight, which makes it all worth it."

"Like?" he asked, sounding genuinely curious.

"You aren't as self-confident as you appear, which is actually a huge turn-on. You're protective, which I already knew, but probably even more so than I thought. You're touchy-feely, which is awesome, and you're really patient."

"Patient?" he asked with a chuckle.

"Yup. If you weren't, you would've turned around and left when that kid told us it would be an hour before we could bowl."

"Okay, that's probably true. I learned the power of patience sitting in the woods, waiting for someone trying to cross into the US illegally to make their move and reveal their hiding spot. And while waiting for a certain beautiful baker to give me a shot."

Finley smiled at him.

"Eat," he ordered, nodding at her burger. "Before it gets cold."

"Yes, sir," she sassed, picking up her hamburger and taking a bite.

"Good?" he asked after a moment.

Finley nodded enthusiastically, as her mouth currently full and she couldn't speak.

Halfway through their burgers, Brock got up and

bought them both a beer, and the rest of their meal passed quickly. After he'd thrown away their trash and put the plastic tray on top of the trash can, their number was finally called for bowling. They got their shoes and headed for their assigned lane.

Finley was as bad at bowling as she'd warned, but since Brock didn't seem to care, she didn't either. They were halfway through their first game, and Brock had just bowled another strike, when the machine that reset the pins stopped working.

"You have *got* to be kidding me," he muttered, running a hand through his hair in agitation.

Finley could only laugh.

Brock went to tell someone about the problem, and while he was gone, Finley couldn't help but eavesdrop on the couple in the lane next to them. They were arguing about whether or not to stay in town another night. The guy wanted to stay and go back out in the forest the next day, while his girlfriend was obviously over tromping around the woods looking for Bigfoot.

"They said it would probably be ten minutes or so before anyone's free to go see what the issue is," he said in a disgusted tone of voice.

Finley shrugged and took a sip of her beer. It had gotten a little warm, but she wasn't going to complain. Not when poor Brock was already thoroughly frustrated with their night out.

He sat down beside her and shook his head. "Second date, second time things haven't gone according to plan. I'm thinking we should just stay in from now on."

"You mean you don't ever want to take me out again?" she asked.

"Oh, I want to, but with my track record, I'm not sure it's smart."

"Brock, shit happens. It has nothing to do with you or me. And it's fine. I'm still having a good time. Aren't you?"

"Of course I am. Any time I get to spend with you is awesome."

"I feel the same. So...where do we want to go on our third date?"

"I think we should go to Sunny Side Up. That should be safe enough."

Finley wasn't going to remind him about the man Caryn had saved in the diner while he was choking. Or that it was likely to be as crowded as the bowling alley. She simply smiled at him and nodded.

The argument between the couple next to them got more heated just then. The woman accused her boyfriend of not caring about her feelings. Raged about the "backwater town" they were in and how it didn't have a decent restaurant and how she was sick of him being cheap as hell with their vacations.

Unfortunately, the man didn't have a lot of common sense, and he retorted, "Let me guess, you want to go to Chicago or New York City, which you know I hate, and shop all day. Spending hundreds of dollars on shit you'll never wear or use. That's not a vacation, that's just plain stupid."

Finley's eyes were wide as she looked at Brock, and she saw him desperately attempting to smother a chuckle.

But the smile on his face quickly faded when the girlfriend, obviously sick of her boyfriend's shit, stood up and threw her almost-full cup of beer at the man.

The guy, not being an idiot, ducked.

And the beer meant for her boyfriend ended up hitting Brock instead.

They'd been sitting on the other side of the plastic booth from the couple, and it was all Finley could do not to laugh from utter shock as Brock blinked back at her, beer dripping off his hair and onto his face and shoulders.

Turning, Finley saw the woman's eyes widen almost comically, then she burst into tears and ran toward the restroom.

"Shit, man, I'm so sorry!" her boyfriend said as Brock stood. He looked terrified as he stared up at Brock from the other side of the booth. In comparison, Brock was huge—and he could easily squash the smaller, far-less muscular boyfriend.

But Brock just shrugged and said, "Don't sweat it, man. I would recommend, though, that you apologize to your woman...and take her on a shopping spree tomorrow, instead of looking for Bigfoot."

"Yeah, good idea," the guy said before grabbing his girl-friend's purse, their shoes, and heading toward the bathroom.

Finley couldn't hold the giggle back any longer. Poor Brock looked miserable. She wasn't laughing at him, but at the entire situation.

"Come on, we're leaving," he told her, bending down to take off his shoes. Beer dripped from his hair onto the floor, and when he turned, Finley saw how drenched he actually was. The entire back of his shirt was soaked, and she could see the material of his jeans darken from his ass down to his knees even as they stood there.

After they put their street shoes back on, she followed him to the counter, where they informed the kid they weren't going to wait for someone to fix the problem with their bowling lane and were, in fact, leaving. Brock didn't ask for a refund, even though it probably would've been perfectly acceptable.

Brock grabbed her hand and towed her toward the exit. She silently let him lead her back to his truck, and she got in without a word of protest. He drove them back to her house, and after she'd climbed out of the front seat behind him, Brock moved to get back behind the wheel.

She put a hand on his arm. "Brock?"

"Yeah?" he asked, one foot inside the truck.

"Will you stay a bit? It's early."

"I stink. I'm irritated. And I'm soaking wet. I need a shower, and I'm in no mood to be good company. I'm sorry, Finley."

She didn't want their night to end. Even with everything that had happened, she'd enjoyed spending time with him. And she was pleased to see that even when things didn't go his way, he didn't go off the deep end. Too many people would've lost their shit on the woman who'd thrown the beer. Or on the boyfriend. Or even on the shoe guy. But not Brock. He'd kept his cool.

"You can shower here. One thing about being my size is that I should have a T-shirt that will fit you while we wash your clothes. I can't do anything about underwear or sweats or anything, but I do have big towels you can use until your jeans are dry."

He stared at her for an incredibly long moment. "You're okay with me sitting around your house in nothing but a towel?" he asked.

She noticed he hadn't said anything about putting on one of her T-shirts. She hadn't lied, she had a feeling that the large T-shirts she liked to lounge around in would probably fit him, but she didn't bring it up again. "Yes," she said simply. "Why? Are you going to attack me or something?"

"Fuck no!"

"Then..." She let the word trail off.

Brock took a deep breath, then turned and slammed his truck door. He grabbed her hand once more and marched toward her house.

Smiling, and feeling relieved that he was going to stay, Finley docilly followed behind him. He held his hand out for her keys and she willingly handed them over.

"Shower?" he asked.

He was obviously still upset, so Finley didn't say anything, simply pointed toward the hallway and the guest bathroom. When he headed that way, she said softly, "If you put your clothes outside the door, I'll get them in the wash."

Brock nodded and disappeared down the hall.

Whew. He was *intense*. But not in a bad way. Finley appreciated that he wasn't ranting and raving. He was upset, yes, but he didn't act in a way that would scare her or otherwise make her leery to be around him.

She heard the bathroom door open and shut and peered down the hallway, spotting his clothes sitting in a pile. Quickly gathering them up, she got them started in the washing machine, then changed into a pair of comfy pants with an elastic waist and a long-sleeve T-shirt before heading into the kitchen to put on a pot of coffee. She also got out some of the pumpkin sugar cookies she and Brock had made. She arranged them on a plate and put them on the coffee table. By the time she returned to the kitchen to grab two cups of coffee, Brock had finished with his shower.

Sensing him, Finley turned—and almost swallowed her tongue. He had one of her large bath towels around his waist and his hair was still wet. But it was the expanse of muscular chest that had her thighs tensing and her lungs sucking in a deep breath.

My God, the man was *gorgeous*. He was built like a Greek god—or at least what she imagined they'd look like. The muscles in his arm flexed as he grabbed hold of the knot of the towel at his waist. His jaw tightened as she continued to stare at him.

"If you don't stop looking at me like that, I won't be responsible for my actions."

His words didn't scare Finley because she had a feeling she was staring at him the way a little kid drooled over ice cream. She definitely wanted to lick him. She'd start at his nipples and work her way down to...

She closed her eyes and turned to fiddle with the coffee mugs. She needed a minute to get her equilibrium back. She'd known Brock was stunning, but having all that smooth skin right there in front of her was almost overwhelming.

"Is that coffee I smell?" he asked nonchalantly, as if he always hung around in women's houses naked with nothing but a towel on.

"Uh-huh," she said, still not able to get her words to work.

She felt him come up behind her, and a hand landed on her hip as he leaned down. He nuzzled the side of her neck as he said, "Have I told you how much I love your hair down?"

Finley shook her head.

"Well, I do. And I appreciate you being cool about this. I know this is...awkward."

"It's not," she said firmly, turning to face him. "I mean, if I'd been the one who had that beer poured on me, I wouldn't have taken it nearly as well as you did."

"If you'd been the one who'd had that beer poured on you, things would've ended much differently than they did," he said in a deep, dangerous tone.

Finley shivered.

"Come on, you want to watch a movie?"

Sit beside him *now*, when all she had to do was tug on that towel and he'd be naked? No, she didn't want to. But she nodded anyway. He was being cool about this, so she would be too.

She carried their coffee cups to the couch. Brock smiled at seeing the plate of cookies. "You can't help yourself, can you?"

"What?"

"The cookies?"

Finley shrugged. "I figured they'd be a good dessert."

"You figured right," he said. Then, as if it was the most normal thing in the world, he sat and pulled her down next to him. He tugged her close, until she was plastered against his side.

Finley wasn't sure where to put her hands, but he solved that for her when he grabbed one and placed it on his chest. His skin was warm, almost hot, and of course her fingers were chilly. He had a slight smattering of chest hair, and it was literally the sexiest thing Finley had ever seen.

She remained tense against him until he murmured, "Relax, Fin."

Amazingly, she did. Practically melting against him.

A few minutes went by as he searched for something to watch on the movie app. He settled on *Signs*, an oldie but one of her favorite flicks, before he said, "This is much better."

Finley smiled. "What, being practically naked on my couch while your clothes get washed after being drenched in beer?"

"Yup. I get you all to myself now."

She shook her head.

"I'm sorry I was so short with you when we got here."

"I don't blame you."

Finley hadn't forgotten that Brock didn't have any clothes on, but he didn't make things weird, which she appreciated. He also didn't make a pass at her. Didn't try to take advantage of the situation. After about thirty minutes, she got up and moved his things to the dryer, then settled back into the same spot beside him.

She was almost sorry when the dryer dinged, letting them know his clothes were done. Without a word, he got up, and when he returned, he was once more in his jeans and polo shirt. Finley was almost sorry her dryer was so effective.

The second he sat beside her, Brock pushed her shoulders gently until she was lying on her back, and he was hovering over her. Then he kissed her. Long, hard, and quite thoroughly. She could feel his erection behind his jeans pressing against her thigh.

When he pulled back to gaze down at her affectionately, she frowned.

"What's wrong?"

"I'm just trying to understand you," she said, caressing the skin of his muscular arm as she spoke.

Knowing exactly why she was confused, he explained, "I wasn't about to kiss you when I was only wearing a towel. I didn't want to make you nervous that I might want more, that I would lose control and take what wasn't being offered freely, and I knew if I *did* start kissing you, it would be extremely difficult for me to stop."

"You wouldn't lose control, and for the record...it definitely would've been offered freely," she said shyly.

Brock inhaled deeply before smiling down at her. "I think you have more faith in me than I do."

"Probably," she said with a shrug. "You're a good man, Brock. Down to your bones."

"It's gonna be a while before we go on that third date," he said.

Finley frowned in dismay. "It is?"

"Uh-huh. With our luck, I don't even want to imagine what would happen. So I'll keep helping you in the mornings, even though I know you don't need it anymore, and we'll hang out like this. But we aren't calling them dates, okay?"

She rolled her eyes. "Okay."

"And I know you're making Lilly and Ethan's cake, and that you're going to be helping with the wedding...but I was hoping you'd sit with me? Dance with me?"

"Like, be your date?" she asked.

"No!" Brock exclaimed.

Finley giggled this time.

He smiled. "No dates. Just hanging out. We are especially *not* calling it a date at our friends' wedding. There's no telling how we might ruin their big day if we did."

"Yeah, you're probably right," she said, rolling her eyes. "And yes, I'd love to *hang out* with you at the wedding then."

"Good. You need a ride?"

"Would you mind?" she asked tentatively.

"Wouldn't have offered if I did."

"I need to get there pretty early. And it's a pain to transport a cake. It won't be completely put together, because that's just asking for it to fall over or something while on the way, but I'll have a bunch of pastry boxes and supplies and stuff to bring with me, so I can get it all finished once there."

"Not a problem," he said evenly. "How do you usually get cakes to a venue?"

"Well, I've only made a few birthday cakes since opening the shop. There hasn't been time for special orders. But generally, I hold my breath and hope the boxes don't go flying across the floorboards and stuff."

"I can be your assistant," he said easily. "Whatever you need me to do."

"Thanks."

They stared at each other for a long moment before Brock sighed and climbed off her and held out his hand.

"You're going?" she asked.

He nodded. "I'm sorry the night didn't go the way we planned."

"I'm not."

They both smiled.

It was fifteen more minutes before Brock actually left, neither of them particularly eager to end their kisses at her door. When he pulled out of her driveway, Finley leaned against her door and smiled. It was safe to say she was extremely happy with how things were working out with Brock. She never would've thought they'd click as well as they did, but she was looking forward to seeing where things would take them after their next non-date.

CHAPTER SIX

Four days later, Finley was behind the library, sitting with the kittens. They recognized her now, and started meowing loudly the second they spotted her, wanting the food she brought. She'd heard from Khloe late last night, just a short text informing her that she was going to be gone at least another week.

Finley was worried about her friend, but until Khloe was ready to share what was going on, she didn't know what she could do to help her. She could at least make sure the kittens Khloe had befriended were safe and sound when she returned from whatever mysterious trip she was on.

Finley needed to get to work on the day's baking, but she was enjoying the peace and quiet of the morning. Just as she was getting ready to stand up and leave, a vehicle pulled into the lot and stopped behind the pool hall. It was the same black truck she'd seen the other day.

She hadn't given the truck much thought when she'd first seen it, but now the hair on the back of her neck was sticking up. As she watched, the same man as before came around the side of the pool hall with a familiar backpack. He handed it over through the truck window, took another pack from the driver, and disappeared around the building a minute later.

But this time, the black truck didn't immediately leave. It sat idling in the parking lot.

The longer it sat there, the more nervous Finley got. She didn't think she could be seen, sitting as she was between the dumpster and the building, with no sunrise in sight. Still...she memorized the license plate, then stood slowly and backed toward Doc Snow's clinic.

When she was halfway to the corner of the building, the brake lights on the truck came on.

They were bright in the otherwise dark lot—and Finley had no doubt that she could be seen if the driver looked in the rearview mirror.

Not wanting to know what she'd just witnessed, she turned and walked as fast as she could around the corner. As soon as she was out of sight of the truck, she broke into a run. Cutting across the square and praying whoever was inside the truck hadn't seen her.

She had her keys out and ready as she approached The Sweet Tooth. She fumbled a little with the key, but then she was inside, safe and sound. Finley was breathing hard, not because the jog across the square had winded her that much, but from the adrenaline coursing through her veins.

This was apparently one of Davis's not-so-good mornings, as he hadn't been waiting for her when she arrived. For the first time ever, Finley was nervous to be alone in her shop.

It was that thought that had her straightening her

shoulders and taking a deep breath. No, she wasn't going to be scared to be here. This was Fallport. She was safe. And there was no proof that whatever she'd seen had been anything nefarious...

Okay. While Finley wasn't sure what she'd seen, she also wasn't an idiot. No one met at o-dark thirty in the morning in an empty parking lot, behind the pool hall at that, and exchanged something through the window of a truck if they *weren't* doing something suspicious.

A knock on the door behind her scared Finley so much, she let out an undignified squeal and spun around. Relief swept over her when she saw Brock standing there. There was a back door to the bakery, just as there was for each of the businesses in the square, but Finley rarely used it for whatever reason. She'd gotten used to coming around to the front, to make sure the sidewalk and the front of the shop was clean and professional looking.

Quickly unlocking the door, Finley smiled at Brock. "Hi!" she said a little too loudly.

"What's wrong?" he asked, picking up on her weird mood immediately.

"Nothing. I'm good."

"Finley—what's up?" Brock insisted. "And don't say nothing again. I know you. Something's wrong. You haven't even turned on the light in the kitchen yet and when I walked up, I could see you just standing here, staring off into space."

For some reason, Finley didn't want to talk about what had happened that morning. Mostly because nothing *had* happened. It was likely she was blowing things out of proportion. She'd feel stupid if she got someone in trouble for nothing. "Seriously, I'm fine. I'm just running a little late this morning," she told Brock, feeling bad for even the small white lie. "I spent too much time with the kittens, and I was just standing here thinking about what I wanted to make for the day."

Brock stared at her for a long moment before nodding. "All right. But if something was wrong, you know that you can talk to me about it, right? I don't care what it is, don't be afraid to come to me."

"I do know, and thank you," Finley said. The more seconds ticked by, the more she was sure she'd overreacted.

"Good. Now...how about a good-morning kiss?" he asked, holding his arms out.

Smiling, Finley walked into his embrace and gave him a hard hug. Being held by him felt so damn good. Safe. She lifted her head after a moment without letting him go and he lowered his lips to hers. The kiss wasn't devastatingly passionate, it was just the right amount of tender and adoring for the situation.

He didn't drop his arms when he lifted his lips. He stared down at her long enough for Finley to feel a little uncomfortable. It felt as if he could read her mind. As if he could tell how badly she wanted him. How scared she was that she was going to do something to mess things up between them.

How nervous she was about what had happened in the parking lot behind the library.

But he didn't say anything other than, "What's on the menu this morning?" when he finally released her.

By the time Liam showed up, and the cinnamon rolls, muffins, and cranberry pumpkin bread were done, Finley had all but forgotten the weird incident from that morning. In the light of day, she felt silly for being scared. She put the incident out of her mind...but not before jotting down the license plate number of the black truck on a piece of paper and putting it in the box of recipes she kept on one of the kitchen counters.

* * *

That night, Finley found herself at the small house Caryn was now living in with Drew. It was a rental, but they were both perfectly all right with their living arrangement for the moment. The house was near Caryn's grandfather's, and she was still nervous about leaving Art by himself... even if he was almost one hundred percent healed from being stabbed.

She'd called to invite Finley over because Lilly was freaking out about her wedding. Not getting cold feet, per se, but wondering if it was too soon to get married. Elsie and Bristol were already there when Finley arrived.

The other women each had a glass of wine in their hands and Finley saw a bottle of moonshine sitting on the counter. Caryn was friends with Clyde Thomas, who made some of the best hooch in this part of Virginia, and she'd obviously brought out the big guns. She no longer drank herself—not after a scary night at The Cellar, where some local firefighters intentionally got her wasted—but she had no problem with her friends imbibing.

"Do not pass go without taking a shot," Elsie ordered, pointing to a shot glass and the moonshine sitting on the counter as Finley entered the house.

Grinning, she did as ordered, wincing a little at the burn of the moonshine as it went down. If someone had asked her last year if she'd ever be doing shots with her girl posse, she would've said no way in hell. But in just a few short months, these four women had become the best friends she'd ever had, and she'd walk through fire to make sure they were safe and happy...and she knew they'd do the same for her in return.

She sat, and Bristol said, "To catch up...Lilly's worried that she and Ethan moved too fast and that she's crazy for marrying him right now. We all think she's wrong, and I personally think she's just freaking out because of all the last-minute wedding stuff."

Finley curled her legs under her on the couch. She took a sip of the wine she'd poured before sitting down and looked at Lilly. The other woman did look extremely stressed. "Do you love him?" she asked.

"Yes." Lilly's answer was immediate. She didn't have to think about her response at all.

"Have you talked to him about this?" she asked.

Lilly sighed and shook her head as she looked into her wine glass.

"Right," Finley said. "I'm probably the last person whose advice you should take, since I've never been engaged or even in a long-term relationship, but I've seen you and Ethan together, and I don't think I've ever seen anyone as in love as you guys are. Ethan's eyes are always on you, even when you aren't paying attention. He watches out for you as if he's ready to leap in front of a speeding bullet for you at any moment. If I had a guy like that? If a man loved me as much as Ethan loves you? I wouldn't wait for a wedding ceremony. I'd drag his butt down to the courthouse and get his ring on my finger, pronto."

Lilly's shoulders relaxed as she contemplated Finley's words.

"What's really bothering you?" Elsie asked. "What can we do to help take some stress off your shoulders?"

"I don't know. I'm just being stupid," Lilly mumbled.

"You are the least stupid person I know," Elsie countered. "Now spill."

For the next hour, the five friends brainstormed ways to mitigate the stress the upcoming wedding ceremony was putting on Lilly. Even though it was late to make changes, less than two weeks until the wedding, the women did so anyway. Instead of doing a plated dinner for the guests, Elsie would meet with Sandra to come up with a menu that could be served buffet style. Since Lilly was the town's only videographer, and she obviously couldn't film her own wedding, Caryn volunteered to get in touch with someone she knew. The woman was a photographer back in New York, where Caryn used to live. Her studio had caught on fire, and as a firefighter on the scene, Caryn had managed to save almost all of her cameras. The woman had told her anytime she needed a favor, she only needed to ask.

Finley volunteered to come even earlier in the morning with the wedding cake and help with whatever needed doing, and Elsie had said she'd bring Tony over as well. Her son was still young, but he had a ton of energy and wouldn't mind being put to work setting up chairs and whatever.

By the end of the hour, Lilly was feeling much better. It might've been the alcohol mellowing her out, but since she'd only had one glass, Finley figured it was mostly because of her friends.

"I don't know what I'd do without you," she said sappily. "You're the bestest friends ever! And now I'm sick of talking about me. Honestly, I can't wait until this wedding is over. I just want my life to go back to the way it was...except I'll be Mrs. Lilly Watson."

"I have to say that I'm pretty happy Zeke and I agreed not to do a big ceremony," Elsie said with a small grin. "I mean, there are days where I feel kinda sad I didn't get the white dress and everything that goes along with it, but then I think about how much money and how many headaches we saved ourselves, and I'm relieved."

"Don't even get me started on the money," Lilly moaned.

Everyone chuckled.

"You know as well as we do that Ethan couldn't care less about the money," Bristol said.

"I know. And I am grateful for you, Bristol. We couldn't have found a better place to get married than on your property. I can't believe how awesome your barn turned out."

"It *did* turn out really good, didn't it?" she asked with a smile.

"How's that stained-glass piece for Sunny Side Up coming along?" Finley asked.

"It's almost done," Bristol said.

"Tell us honestly, how much would something like that usually cost if you were selling it?" Elsie asked.

Bristol grinned. "You don't want to know."

"Yes, we do!" the others all said together.

"Well, it kind of depends on what the buyer is willing to pay. But based on the size and how long it's taken me... probably mid six figures," Bristol said with a shrug.

Finley stared at her in shock. And realized the others were all looking at her the same way.

"Seriously?"

"Yeah," Bristol said with a small grin.

"That's so freaking awesome!" Elsie exclaimed.

"And to think, Fallport has a Bristol Wingham original!" Lilly added.

"And we know her!" Caryn threw in.

"Please tell me you got Bigfoot in there," Finley begged. They'd all heard the plans for the stained glass, which included the elusive creature peeking out from behind a tree, but no one had seen it yet.

"Of course it does," Bristol said with a laugh. "It's the best part of the piece. Well, that and my man's ass."

Everyone burst out laughing.

"I didn't *tell* him it was his ass, but I couldn't resist. I might be biased, but it's the best ass in Fallport," Bristol said.

A short but spirited debate ensued on whose man had the best ass, but Finley kept quiet as the others went on and on about their men's butts.

Then Caryn smirked and turned to her. "We might think our guys have the best butts, but I'm thinking Brock wins hands down when it comes to muscular arms."

Finley blushed. She wasn't sure why. They weren't talking about *her* arms.

"Oh my God, right?" Bristol said. "I swear he could bench press a bear."

"I'm guessing they feel pretty damn good wrapped around you, huh, Finley?"

She could only nod.

"And propping himself up while he makes slow, sweet love to you," Elsie teased.

It was obvious the alcohol she'd consumed was making her friend bolder than she would've been otherwise, but Finley didn't take offense. How could she when she'd fantasized about the same thing?

"Well, I don't have any firsthand knowledge of that, but I'm guessing you aren't wrong," she told her.

"Damn, I lost that bet," Elsie said with a pout.

Frowning, she asked, "What bet?" All of a sudden, no one would meet her eye. "Guys? What bet?"

"It was all in good fun," Caryn said after a moment. "We just had a slight wager on whether you and Brock had already been together or not. And if not, when it would happen."

Finley wasn't sure if she should be mad at her friends or not, but decided if the roles were reversed, she'd be just as curious and want in on that action.

Brock had certainly been spending a lot of time with her. He'd been to her shop every morning and they'd spent every evening together. Not only that, but the incident at the bowling alley had spread like wildfire, as well. Everyone knew that Brock had been drenched with a beer thrown by a tourist. Hell, the fact that he'd gone to her house afterward had also been discussed. So she wasn't surprised her friends just assumed she and Brock had slept together already.

"You aren't mad, are you?" Elsie asked, biting her lip. "We didn't actually wager money. We each put our favorite candy bar in the pot."

Finley frowned. "I can't believe you," she said softly. "I thought we were friends." She paused dramatically, then let everyone off the hook by saying, "Leaving me out of a bet that involves chocolate is just *mean*."

Everyone laughed in relief.

"Girl, you had me going. I thought you were really pissed," Lilly said.

"I'm not," Finley said. "I mean, if I were you, I'd think the same thing. And for the record...I'm ready. More than ready. We've only been hanging out a couple of weeks, but Brock is...well...he's pretty darn amazing."

The others all agreed.

"He's had his eye on you for as long as I've known you both," Caryn said. "And I'm the newcomer to this group. If I noticed, that means he's probably been watching you for a lot longer than I realized."

"You aren't wrong," Bristol said. "I remember noticing at the Fourth of July parade that he couldn't take his eyes off you."

"Every time we get together, he spends the whole night staring our way. I actually thought at first he didn't like me or something, or maybe he didn't like all the women crashing their guy time...until I realized it's Finley he's always looking at," Elsie added.

"You guys are exaggerating," she argued, but deep down, she couldn't help but feel all warm and fuzzy.

"Nope. But then again, you weren't exactly subtle in the looks you were giving *him* either," Elsie said.

"Right? Staring at him all longingly, and the second he turned her way, she'd study the ground as if it was the most interesting thing she'd ever seen," Bristol said with a laugh.

"Can we talk about something else?" Finley asked desperately.

"Nope. We already did that, now we're talking about you," Lilly told her.

"Fine. I like him. He likes me. And for whatever reason, he doesn't seem to mind the extra weight I'm carrying."

"Of course he doesn't!" Lilly exclaimed.

"There's no 'of course' about it," Finley said. "Most men aren't into big women like me."

"But Brock clearly is. He's a large guy himself. I can totally see why he'd be into you. Aside from the fact you're gorgeous, he doesn't have to worry about hurting you if he gets...overexuberant," Caryn said, wiggling her brows.

"Right? Could you see him with someone my size?" Bristol asked. "No way."

Finley wasn't offended. And her friends weren't wrong. "All right, all right. We're both sexy and perfectly suited... now there's just one problem," she whined.

"What?" they all asked at once.

"Now you've got me all hot and bothered and all I can think about are his biceps flexing when he's propping himself over me."

They all burst out laughing.

This felt good. Really damn good. Finley had never had close girlfriends she could talk about sex with. And while she and Brock weren't having sex yet...she had a feeling it wouldn't be long. And she was perfectly all right with that. She wanted Brock, and it was obvious he wanted her too. She didn't give a damn how fast things between them were moving. She'd seen her friends' relationships move just as quickly, and they were some of the most in-love people she'd ever met.

Honestly, Finley wanted that too. Whether or not she'd

have it with Brock was still to be determined, but she wasn't going to let any opportunity to have sex with him slip away.

"I needed this," Lilly said. "I feel stupid that I was freaking out now. I love Ethan so much, and of course I want to marry him. I appreciate all your help more than I can say. And if any of you ever need anything from me, all you have to do is ask. Or even hint. I'll be right there to help you out."

"Same here," Elsie said. "You've all been so great with Tony. He loves seeing you at his soccer games. You're all honorary aunts to him."

"And I can't begin to thank you all for what you've done for me," Bristol added. "I'm not the most outgoing person, and being laid up with a bum leg didn't exactly help. But you guys never hesitated to come over and keep me company when I was bored out of my mind."

"You mean to annoy you," Elsie quipped.

Everyone chuckled, but Bristol said, "You guys are never annoying."

"Never?" Caryn asked.

"Okay, maybe I should've added *usually*." Bristol grinned. "And I'm thankful that Lilly's going to work all the kinks out of the wedding thing in the barn," she went on. "By the time it's my turn, we'll know what works and what doesn't." She winked at Lilly.

"It's all going to work just fine," Finley said firmly. "And even if it doesn't," she said, addressing Lilly, "will you care? Please tell me you aren't going to turn into a bridezilla. You've been pretty even-keeled so far, and tonight doesn't count."

"No bridezilla," Lilly reassured them.

"Even if it rains?" Elsie asked.

"Nope."

"What if I drop your wedding cake?" Finley asked.

"Then someone will run to the box store and grab as many cupcakes as they can get and we'll eat those," Lilly said firmly.

Finley shuddered. "Bite your tongue. You can't give your guests that crap!"

"Then don't drop my cake," Lilly countered.

Laughing, she nodded. "Right."

"Honestly, now that I'm feeling more mellow, I've remembered that the only thing that matters is being with Ethan. I don't even care what people show up wearing, although I really would prefer this shindig to be laid-back and not stuffy or anything. And I don't care what we eat, or if the music is loud enough, or *anything*. I just want my friends and family there to see Ethan and I get married."

"And that's what you're going to get," Elsie said firmly.

"Love you guys," Lilly said with a sniff.

"No crying!" Caryn exclaimed.

"The big bad firefighter doesn't want to be seen sobbing," Finley teased.

She wasn't sure who started it, but the next thing Finley knew, she was in the middle of a huge pillow fight. Everyone was giggling and laughing and even getting beaned with a pillow to the face wasn't enough to dim Finley's good mood.

When they were suitably tired, all five women lay sprawled out around the small living room. Pillows were all over the floor and someone had knocked over a half-full glass of water, but Caryn didn't seem to care.

"Khloe should be here," Bristol said after a moment.

"Yeah, anyone hear from her?" Lilly asked.

"I got a text from her asking if I could continue to look after the kittens a little while longer. That she should be back in a week or so, if things went well," Finley said.

"If what things went well?" Elsie asked.

"I have no clue," she said with a shrug.

"Do we think she's in trouble?" Caryn asked.

"Why would she be in trouble? She barely says a word to anyone," Bristol said. "But I do think she's got some pretty deep secrets."

"Would Raiden know?" Lilly asked.

"If he doesn't, I bet he's not happy about being in the dark," Bristol observed.

"He likes her, doesn't he?" Elsie asked.

"I think so. But he's definitely not ready to admit it," Lilly told them.

"I just hope he doesn't wait until it's too late," Bristol fretted.

Everyone was quiet for a while, thinking about what in the world Khloe could be hiding...any maybe whether or not Raid could get anything out of her.

"Right, so...when she gets back...Operation Befriend Khloe will start?" Lilly asked.

"She's already our friend," Bristol protested.

"I know, but we need to step it up. If something's going on with her, something she needs help with, we need to figure out what it is before anything bad happens," Lilly said, then held up her hand as if to stop any protests. Not that anyone was about to say anything. "All I'm saying is that we need her to truly understand that we're here for her. Enough shit has gone down with all of us that we know sometimes bad things happen to the best people."

She wasn't wrong. "What about Talon?" Finley asked.

Four pairs of eyes swung in her direction.

"What about him?" Caryn asked.

"He's the only one without a girlfriend. I mean, Raiden and Khloe aren't dating, but it's obvious that's only because they're both so stubborn. We need to find Tal a girl."

"I'm thinking no one 'finds' women for our guys. Can you imagine what he'd say if we tried to set him up?" Lilly asked.

"Besides, who would we set him up *with*?" Elsie asked.

"I think he hides how sensitive and serious he can be behind that British humor," Bristol added. "He's always trying to lighten the mood, but deep down, I think he wants what his friends have."

Finley nodded. "I've noticed that too."

"He needs someone to take care of," Caryn said quietly. "And I don't mean that in a bad way."

"I understand," Bristol said. "Out of all the guys, he came to visit me the most. He was always bringing me food and things to read. He even drove to Roanoke one day to go to this bead store because he heard me talking about how I got most of my supplies from there."

"He did?" Lilly asked.

"Uh-huh. And I agree with Caryn. He wouldn't last long with someone super independent. He should be with someone who needs him," Bristol mused.

"Do we know anyone like that?" Finley asked.

The room was silent as they all racked their brains.

Elsie sighed. "I don't."

"Me either," Lilly said.

"Well, crap. We can't exactly put out an ad in the newspaper that says, "If you're down on your luck, or running from an ex, or have fourteen kids and need a sugar daddy, we've got the guy for you," Caryn complained.

Finley laughed along with the others, though she also felt a little sad. Caryn wasn't wrong. Talon needed a partner he could take care of, who'd take care of him in return. But most women these days were pretty independent. Society had taught them to be that way, which wasn't a bad thing.

"Everyone keep your eyes open," Lilly ordered. "Talon can't be the only one of our guys without a woman."

"You think someone perfect for him is just gonna drop out of the sky?" Elsie teased.

"Well, *we* all found ourselves here in Fallport kind of unexpectedly. Who's to say the perfect woman for him won't show up out of the blue?"

"True. All right. Are we all good now?" Elsie asked. "Everyone's happy? No one's thinking about backing out of any weddings?" She eyed Lilly and Bristol as she said it.

Both women shook their heads.

"Don't look at me," Caryn said with a laugh. "Drew and I aren't ready to get married. We're totally committed, but for now, we're just taking things one day at a time."

"And you're good, Finley? You'll let us know how amazing and awesome Brock is when he rocks your world?"

"Only if I can get some of the candy bars you guys were betting on me," she retorted.

"Deal!" Elsie said. "And for the record, Zeke and I are good. Great. And now I'm gonna go home and fuck my man and see if he can't put a baby in my belly."

Pandemonium broke out at that, as everyone wanted

to know how long they'd been trying, and if she could actually be pregnant already.

"Well, I don't think so, I wouldn't have been drinking tonight if I thought I was. And I'll be damned if I tell Zeke the second I *do* get pregnant," Elsie said.

"You won't? Why not?" Lilly asked in concern.

Elsie winked. "Because I'm enjoying the hell out of him doing everything in his power to knock me up. I know the second I tell him he succeeded, he's gonna treat me as if I'm a piece of glass."

"Right, that actually makes perfect sense," Lilly said.

Finley agreed.

"So...since we're all good, I'm calling Zeke. Anyone else need a ride?"

No one did. They all said they'd call their men to come and get them, since they'd been drinking. Finley didn't even think twice about calling Brock as well.

All the guys arrived around the same time, and Finley hugged each of her friends goodbye before letting Brock escort her to his truck. She climbed in, scooting over to the passenger side as usual.

"Have fun?" he asked when they were on their way.

"Uh-huh."

"Good."

"You don't want to know what we talked about?" she asked.

"Nope."

Finley grinned.

"Although...with that grin, I might be rethinking my answer," Brock said.

He stayed at her house for a while, after making sure she drank a large glass of water and took some painkillers, to try to mitigate any kind of hangover. They made out on her couch, and Finley couldn't keep her hands off his biceps. She'd encouraged him to take his shirt off, and it was all she could do not to shove her hands down his pants.

"We need to stop," he sighed, lifting his head.

"Why?" Finley whined.

Brock propped himself over her, and Finley stared up at him. She was horny, damn it—and she wanted this man.

"Because I want our first time to be special. You have to get up in about five hours. And I want you completely clear-headed when we make love."

That was sweet, but Finley felt compelled to say, "I'm not drunk."

"I know. And I'm already looking forward to fucking you when one or both of us has had too much to drink. But not tonight."

She knew enough about Brock to know once his mind was made up, he wouldn't budge. So she merely pouted at him.

In response, Brock threw his head back and laughed. Even that was sexy as hell. When he had himself under control, he traced a brow with one of his fingers as he studied her with a tender look in his eyes.

"For the record? I'm ready," she informed him. "I know it hasn't been too long since we started dating, but I've wanted you for what feels like forever. I'm kinda over waiting."

His pupils dilated as she watched. "Good," he said after a moment.

"Shoot. That didn't convince you?" she asked plaintively.

He chuckled. "For tonight? No. But did it move my timetable up? Definitely."

"Good," she echoed.

"I'm willing to wait for as long as it takes for you to be completely sure of this. Of us."

"I'm sure," Finley said. "I'm old enough to know a good man when I have him. And you, Brock, are one of the finest men I've ever known. It's icing on my specialty chocolate cherry cheesecake that you don't seem to care that I'm overweight. Or that I'm shy around people I don't know...or people I want to like me."

"I more than like you," he said without hesitation. "And you're perfect, Fin, don't let anyone tell you otherwise. Come on, see me out," he said as he prepared to get up.

Finley gripped his biceps tightly. "Brock?"

"Yeah?"

"Don't make me wait too long."

"I won't," he promised, his gaze heated.

"Good. Because the girls have a bet going about when we'll get together, as in, you know...get *together*. And it involves candy bars."

Brock laughed. "What's your favorite?"

"Candy bar?"

"Yeah."

"Anything with caramel in it."

"Done. I'll bring you a whole stack."

Finley giggled. "Cool."

He leaned down and kissed her again. And by the time he heaved himself up and off her, his erection was impossible to miss and Finley's underwear was soaked. Grabbing her hand, he hauled her off the couch and held on as he walked to her door. He kissed her once more, a long, almost desperate kiss, and it was obvious how difficult it was for him to leave.

"See you in the morning," he said as he backed down her front sidewalk, prolonging their goodbye.

Finley nodded. "You know that you don't need to keep coming in the morning, right?" she asked. "Davis has been a huge help, and I'm actually able to keep up with the baking now that Liam is there."

"I know. Do you not want me there?" he asked.

"No! It's not that. I just know how hard you work at your shop. I feel guilty that you're getting up early to help me and then going to do your own work afterward."

"It's not a hardship," he said. "I'd much rather start out my day with you than alone in my bed."

It was on the tip of her tongue to say that he could start out his day with her and *not* be alone in his bed, but she swallowed the words. He said he wanted to wait, and she wasn't going to force him into anything he wasn't ready for. "Then I'll see you in the morning."

"Yes, you will," Brock said. Then he finally turned and strode to his truck. He waved with two fingers and motioned toward her door with his chin.

Knowing he wouldn't leave until she was locked behind her door, Finley waved and turned to head back inside. She smiled as she continued toward her bedroom. There was no way she'd be able to get to sleep without releasing some of the sexual tension inside her.

"Soon," she said out loud, smiling at the thought. Soon she'd have Brock to help her relieve her tension in the best way possible. She couldn't wait.

* * *

"If you think I'm gonna let some small-town asshole of a police chief take me down, you're fucking stupid," the deep voice on the other end of the phone seethed.

"I said I'd take care of it, and I will," the person known only as "The Boss" said tersely.

"She fucking *saw* me," the man said. "I don't know where she came from or what the hell she was doing lurking in that parking lot so early, but when I looked in my rearview, she was standing there staring at my truck. I need to know what she saw."

"I know," The Boss said, already bored with the conversation. The entire operation depended on this asshole. He came to town three times a week, bringing the pills necessary to keep the narcotics business in Fallport up and running. No one suspected who the local connection might be, and they'd never find out...as long as the fucking baker kept her mouth shut.

"So, what are you going to do about it?" the supplier demanded.

The Boss didn't like being questioned, but if the money was going to continue to flow uninterrupted, the supplier needed to be appeased. "I'm gonna send some guys to question her. Find out what she saw."

"And if she saw too much? Told people? Then what?" the supplier insisted.

"Then they'll take care of her."

"Just like that?"

"Just like that."

"Fine. But the next delivery's on hold until I'm sure

things are clear. Again, I'm not being busted by some backwoods cop. No fucking way."

Irritation swam in The Boss's veins. Fuck this guy for withholding the pills. People were counting on this fucker. The business was counting on him. There were people to pay. This asshole's reluctance to return to Fallport meant customers might start looking elsewhere for their needs. And that was unacceptable. "I'll come to you then. I'll send one of my guys to Roanoke to make the exchange."

"Not one of your guys. *You.* I don't fucking trust anyone until I know what that fat bitch saw."

"Fine. When?"

A time and place was determined for the meeting, and The Boss fumed after hanging up the phone.

Fucking baker. She shouldn't have been in that goddamn parking lot. And if she told anyone what she'd seen, she'd regret it.

Clicking the disposable phone back on, The Boss tapped the number of a client. He wasn't the smartest tool in the shed, but he'd do what was asked of him without question.

"Yo, Boss, what's up?" he answered.

"I have a job for you."

"Cool," he said.

By the time The Boss hung up, things had been arranged. Pete and Cory would follow the baker and get her alone. Then they'd find out how much she saw of the drug drop and if she'd mentioned it to anyone. Whether she'd seen anything or not, they'd rough her up enough to scare her into staying silent.

If she dared tell anyone about that little chat...they'd

go back and make sure she couldn't open her big mouth ever again.

Satisfied that things were smoothed over for now, The Boss turned off the burner phone and went into the garage. Once it was smashed into a hundred pieces, it was placed inside a plastic bag, along with a week's worth of dog poop from the yard. On the way to do some errands later, it would be thrown into a random trash can in town. There were a dozen more phones where that one came from.

A trip to Roanoke was inconvenient, but not impossible. And hopefully it would be the last one for a very long while. The operation needed to continue as it had been... but with a different meeting spot for the handoff. Behind The Cellar had been ideal. One of the bartenders was a very loyal customer, and he had no problem meeting the supplier to grab the pills. Now the handoff would have to take place elsewhere. All because of that fat fuck.

Pastries and other fattening shit wasn't The Boss's thing, but it looked like a trip to The Sweet Tooth was in order to check the bitch out. Learning all there was to know about the enemy was not only smart, it was imperative if the operation was going to continue to run as smoothly as it always had.

Smiling, The Boss put the bag of shit and the destroyed phone on the driveway to be picked up when it was time to leave. Things with the baker had been taken care of as well as they could be right now, so it was time to get ready for a trip to the bank. Money from the latest transactions had to be deposited, then it would be time to pick up the kids from school.

It was just another normal day in Fallport.

CHAPTER SEVEN

Brock found himself smiling like a lunatic as he walked toward The Sweet Tooth. The bakery was certainly aptly named, as his Finley definitely had a sweet tooth. He couldn't wait to see her reaction to the gift he'd brought her this morning. It had been three days since he'd picked her up from her girls' night, and he was looking forward to this evening.

Sandra had invited them to come to Sunny Side Up for a special themed dinner menu she was trying out. It was geared especially for the tourists who were in town to hunt Bigfoot, and everything on the menu had something to do with the legendary creature.

Hotdogs were now called Big Footlongs. There was Yeti Spaghetti, Mountain Meatloaf, a Sasquatch Sandwich, Bigfoot Burrito, Sasquatch Burger, Bigfoot Steak and Eggs, Bigfoot Balls (which were sausage balls with jalapenos and cheese), and Squatched Potatoes and Sas-squash as sides. There were several more items on offer, and Brock couldn't help but be impressed by Sandra's imagination. He had a feeling the menu would be a huge hit.

Impressive or not, he still thought it was hokey as hell, but he could tell Finley was enamored with the idea. This would be their third official date, but honestly they were well past counting what number they were on. Spending every evening with her was definitely the highlight of his days. While he enjoyed spending time with her in the mornings before her shop opened, he liked having her complete attention better.

They would usually watch TV, snuggle on the couch... and of course, there were the long make-out sessions.

And tonight was the night he was going to move their physical relationship forward. It wasn't fair to either of them to keep calling things to a halt just before they'd reached the point of no return, ending their nights in frustration.

If asked a couple months ago if he thought Finley would be so enthusiastic about being physical with him, he would've said no way. Her extreme shyness had made him think he was going to have to carefully ease her into *any* kind of physical relationship. But that wasn't the case at all.

Once she'd gotten over her initial timidity, and after he'd convinced her there wasn't *anything* about her that he wasn't attracted to, it was almost as if she'd emerged from a self-imposed protective bubble. She'd blossomed right in front of his eyes—and Brock couldn't wait to experience everything she had to offer.

So tonight, after their dinner, he was taking her back to his place. He'd washed his sheets, bought flowers for her, which were sitting on his counter, and he even made sure to buy an extra toothbrush and Finley's brand of shampoo and conditioner. He figured it would be less awkward to be prepared with the personal items than to tell her to pack a bag.

It was a surprise for Brock to realize he was actually nervous. It had been a while since he'd been with a woman, and even longer since he'd had deep feelings for a sexual partner. He wanted Finley to be comfortable, to not worry about anything but relaxing enough to allow him to give her pleasure.

But that was tonight. For now, he had a surprise for her this morning, and that was the reason for the smile on his face.

After he'd knocked on the door—he'd insisted she keep it locked, even though she hated that he had to wait outside for her to let him in—Brock impatiently shifted back and forth as she emerged from the kitchen.

"Good morning," she said cheerily after she'd opened the door.

That was something that probably would've annoyed him with anyone other than Finley—she was definitely a morning person, and she was always so cheerful when he saw her.

"Morning," he said, leaning toward her.

She immediately went up on her tiptoes and eagerly met him halfway. She tasted like cinnamon, as if she'd been tasting her creations, which she probably had. Brock wanted nothing more than to pick her up, carry her into the kitchen, and bend her over one of her counters, but not for their first time.

Besides, she probably wouldn't be too excited about the prospect of him fucking her in the kitchen anyway. She was a stickler for cleanliness, which he highly approved of. The last thing he wanted to think about was someone's ass being on the surface where his food was prepared in the restaurants where he liked to eat. But that didn't mean the fantasy would leave his brain.

"What are you so smiley about this morning?" she asked, keeping one hand on his arm after their kiss ended.

"I have a present for you," he said, holding out a plastic bag she'd obviously missed.

"Oh! For me? You don't need to buy me things," she said, but her eyes were sparkling and she couldn't take her gaze from the bag.

Brock chuckled. His Fin liked gifts. He'd have to remember that. "It's not a huge deal, but something you said the other day made me think of you when I was at the store."

She took the bag eagerly and peered inside. Then she burst out laughing, and upon seeing the joy on her face, it was all Brock could do not to haul her against him and take her right then and there.

Shit, he was a goner. He'd never been this eager to sleep with anyone before.

Still chuckling, Finley began to pull the candy bars he'd bought out of the bag. Snickers, several kinds of Milky Way bars, Twix, 100 Grand, Caramello, Whatchamacallit, Rolos, and Reese's Take 5.

"Wow," she said.

"You said you liked candy bars with caramel," he said with a shrug.

"I do! Thank you so much."

"You're welcome," he said.

Then Finley's wide grin became a little more calculating. "Does this mean what I think it means?" she asked.

"It means I was at the store and was thinking about you," Brock said, not wanting to pressure her in any way.

"Which is super sweet. But I'm hoping maybe it also means that the winner of that silly bet will be determined tonight..."

Her cheeks reddened as she spoke, and Brock could feel his heart start to beat faster in his chest. He took the bag from her, making sure all the candy was safely inside for her to indulge in later. Placing the stash on a nearby table, he took her in his arms once more. One hand shifted to her nape, and the other pressed on the small of her back.

His erection was hard against her belly, but she didn't seem to mind in the least if the way she rocked against him was any indication. "I want you. That's not a surprise. Would I like to finally make you mine tonight? Yes. But there's no timetable or schedule, Fin. If it happens, it happens. If we wait, that's okay too. I want our relationship to progress naturally, not to fit into any predetermined slot or meet some stupid milestone that someone else thinks we should be meeting."

She smiled up at him and when her fingers caressed the nape of *his* neck, he shivered almost violently. He'd never realized how sensitive he was there.

Finley seemed to know how she was affecting him, because her thumb stroked his hairline lazily as she spoke. "Agreed. And I want you too. I hate having to leave at the end of the night or watching *you* leave. I want to go to sleep with you beside me, and wake up the same way."

Then she stiffened, and her fingers stopped moving.

Hell, it was almost as if she stopped breathing. "Unless you don't want to spend the night," she said uncomfortably. "I mean, I can understand that."

"There's nothing I want more than to hold you all night and wake up to your beautiful face in the morning," he said quickly, reassuring her.

She sighed in relief. "Good," Finley said quietly. "Um... should I bring an overnight bag when you pick me up for dinner?"

Fuck. His dick twitched against her. "If you want. But I picked up some toiletries for you, so you won't need to pack any. And if you wanted to wear one of my shirts in the morning, I'm completely on board with that."

Her eyes got wide. "You picked up toiletries for me?" she questioned.

"Yes," Brock said simply.

"Wow, um. Okay. And as much as I want to wear your shirt, I'm thinking that's probably not appropriate for wandering around Fallport."

"Maybe not. But I'll enjoy it," Brock said with a grin.

She laughed.

Their intimate conversation was interrupted by a small tap on the front door. Turning, Brock saw Davis on the sidewalk with a smirk on his face.

He kissed Finley chastely one more time before stepping away.

Her gaze went to his crotch, and it was her turn to smirk. "I'll get the door. That looks...uncomfortable," she told him.

Brock chuckled. "I'm used to it," he answered with a shrug. "I feel as if this is my natural state when I'm around you."

"Then we'll see what we can do about that later, huh?"

"You aren't helping," Brock said with a grimace.

She giggled again and headed for the front door.

Things felt different between them as the morning went on. More relaxed. As if now that they'd decided to actually consummate their relationship, the tension was lessened. Even Davis seemed to be in an especially light-hearted mood, probably thanks to their ease in the kitchen.

There were more customers than usual that morning, and Brock had no problem sticking around to help Liam. He'd always thought Fallport was a small town, but he was amazed to realize half of the customers who came in this morning, he didn't even know. Of course, some were tourists picking up a sweet breakfast treat before they headed out into the woods, but many more were locals.

And Finley seemed to know them all. From the principal of the high school, to housewives and local business people, to the PTA parents. When she delivered more treats to the cases, she greeted everyone by name. And when she didn't know someone, she quickly *got* to know them. Asking questions about their morning, what their plans were for the day, things like that.

It was hard for Brock to believe she'd ever been shy with him. She was a natural with people, and it made him smile every time he saw her interact with her customers. She wasn't great with people who were upset about something, but Brock and Liam had no problem handling those customers. Luckily, there weren't many people who were in shit moods. How could they be, when Finley's desserts were always perfectly made and enough to lift anyone's spirits?

He didn't get a chance to do much more than give Finley a short peck on the lips when it was time for him to get to the auto shop. He couldn't exactly kiss her the way he was dying to when there were customers in the store. Still, it thrilled him when she didn't shy away from his touch around others.

"I'll pick you up at your house around six?" he asked.

Finley nodded. "That's perfect."

"Sandra said she'd save us a table."

"That's good, because I have a feeling Sunny Side Up is going to be completely packed. Especially since she said twenty percent of the proceeds the week the Bigfoot menu is up will go to the junior firefighter club and your search and rescue budget."

"She's good people," Brock said.

"She is," Finley agreed. "Now go. Make sure Fallport citizens' cars are working properly."

Brock grinned. She was a goof. "Yes, ma'am. See you later."

She nodded, and he could see her desire for him bloom in her eyes. It was all he could do to turn and leave her there. They both had responsibilities, but by this time tomorrow, she'd be his in every way that mattered. Just as he'd be hers.

* * *

That night, precisely at six, Brock pulled into Finley's driveway. He'd been half hard for the last couple of hours, simply thinking about seeing her again...and what would most likely happen tonight.

He didn't want to go out, wanted to bring Finley back

to his house and show her exactly how much he'd been thinking about her and how badly he wanted her. But she was looking forward to eating at the diner tonight, and Brock would bend over backward to give her what she wanted.

He strode quickly up to her house and smiled as she opened the door before he could knock.

"Hi!" she said brightly enough...but she was back to not meeting his eyes. Her gaze was fixed on the hollow of his throat instead.

Brock stepped toward her and put his finger under her chin, gently lifting her head until she was looking at him. "What's wrong?" he asked.

"Nothing, why?" she said a little too quickly.

He snorted. "Talk to me."

Finley sighed. "I guess I'm just...nervous."

"About being with me?"

"No. Yes. I don't know. It's just...I was packing a bag and it hit me that it's been a long time for me, and suddenly I'm not sure about this. Seeing me naked is completely different than seeing me with my clothes on. I'm a big girl, Brock. I've got lumps and bumps and I'm not toned at all. I don't—"

Brock cut her off the easiest way he knew how. He kissed her senseless. By the time he pulled back, they were both breathing hard.

"Stop stressing," he ordered gently. "We'll play things by ear. If all we feel comfortable doing tonight is cuddling, that's what we'll do. There's no pressure to do anything more. And as far as seeing your body...trust me, the first time I see your tits, nothing else will even register. Don't you know guys are a sucker for boobs?"

She giggled, which was his goal. He wasn't being entirely honest, he couldn't wait to see every inch of her naked body, but he didn't think that would comfort her right now. He made a mental note to make sure his bedroom was dark when they finally got there later, but not so dark that he couldn't see her. There would be a time when she'd be comfortable being naked around him with every light in the room blazing, but for their first time, he'd do whatever it took to make her think about nothing except the pleasure he could provide.

"I don't understand the obsession with boobs," Finley said finally.

"I can't explain it. It's a guy thing," he said. "You ready?"

She nodded and leaned over to grab a small bag already sitting by the door. Just seeing it made Brock's cock twitch. He wouldn't have to say goodbye to her later and go home and masturbate to the thought of her. He'd get to hold her all night, whether or not they actually had sex. He'd get to have her vanilla-cinnamon scent surrounding him. He couldn't fucking wait.

He wondered if she'd mind going straight to bed when they got home from dinner.

He walked her to his truck with a hand on the small of her back, threw her bag into the back seat, then opened the front door for her. He loved how she no longer even blinked at him wanting her to scoot over the bench seat instead of getting in through the door on the passenger side. It just felt safer to have her get in on the same side as he did.

The drive to the square didn't take long. It actually

took longer to find a place to park than it did to drive there in the first place.

"Wow, it's packed," Finley said as they walked hand in hand toward the entrance.

Suddenly, Brock stopped dead in his tracks and stared at the front of Sunny Side Up.

"Holy crap," he breathed.

Finley had a huge grin on her face. "They put it in today. I didn't want to ruin the surprise."

They stared at the stained glass Bristol had made for the diner. It was around eight feet wide and two and a half feet tall. The various greens and browns in the glass made the trees look as if they were alive. A lone figure was captured mid-step from behind on a trail in the middle of the trees. The man had on an Eagle Point Search and Rescue T-shirt, and he was carrying a backpack in his hand.

And just as Bristol promised, a hairy creature was peeking around the edge of one of the trees in the corner, as if watching the man traverse the trail.

"It's..." Brock's voice faded away. He didn't have the words to express how amazing the piece of art was.

"I know," Finley said as she cuddled up to his side.

People around them were taking pictures of the stained glass, and the Sunny Side Up sign as well. This was going to be huge publicity-wise for Sandra and her diner, for Bristol, and for Fallport in general.

Brock sighed. "I'm guessing this is gonna bring even more people to our peaceful town."

Finley patted his arm. "Yup."

He smiled down at her. "You might need to hire another assistant," he told her.

"I can do that."

Of course she could. He was impressed that she didn't even seem rattled by the idea. "Come on, let's see if Sandra saved us that table she promised."

They managed to get past the people waiting inside the door and the hostess looked extremely rattled as they approached. But when she saw them, she smiled. "Hi, guys. Isn't this crazy?" she asked. Without waiting for a response, she grabbed two pieces of paper—the temporary Bigfoot menus, most likely—and asked them to follow her. She led them to a table against a wall on the far side of the room. There weren't any private eating spots in the diner, which Brock kind of regretted.

"Karen will be by to take your order as soon as she can."

"No problem. We can be patient," Finley said warmly.

The hostess gave her a thankful smile then turned to head back to the hostess stand.

"Wow," Finley said after she'd left. "I figured it would be busy, but this? It's crazy."

"Bristol's stained-glass reveal, combined with the Bigfoot menu, is obviously a good draw," Brock said.

Finley snort laughed. "Ya think?"

It was ten minutes before Karen was able to get to their table, but Brock didn't mind. He was enjoying talking to Finley about her day. They ordered not only their drinks, but their dinner as well, in case it was another ten minutes before Karen could get back to them to take their order. Finley's eyes lit up as she ordered the Bigfoot Burger with a side of Shaggy Potato Strings and the Sas-squash. He got the Bigfoot Steak and Eggs with a side of Sasquatch Stew, which was apparently minestrone soup.

"This is fun!" Finley exclaimed, when Karen left to put in their orders.

Brock reached for her hand and held it tightly as he smiled at her. They were sitting across from each other at the small table for two. He would've preferred to be in a booth, at her side, but it would've been rude to take a table for four when it was just the two of them. So he had to be content with holding her hand across the table and staring into her beautiful face.

They made small talk as they waited for their dinner to arrive. The cooks must've been working overtime in the back, because Karen returned with their meals after only twenty minutes.

Several people who knew Finley had passed their table and stopped to say hello. Brock was impressed once again by how many locals she knew.

They were just finishing up their meals when the one thing Brock had been dreading happened.

He'd tried hard not to think about their first two dates, and how something had gone wrong during both. But considering every time they were in public together, something seemed to ruin it, he'd been a little leery since they walked in the door.

Just when he'd let down his guard and was beginning to think they'd be able to get through one date without shit hitting the fan, a waitress approached from behind Finley with a tray full of food.

The customers at the table next to theirs chose that moment to get up. A man stood, pushing his chair aside— right into the path of the waitress.

Everything seemed to happen in slow motion. Brock

tried to reach a hand out to steady the waitress, or to grab the tray somehow, but he didn't have time.

The tray she was holding tilted sideways as she tried to avoid getting slammed by the man's chair. The plates and cups slid toward Finley, and gravity took over.

A plate of Yeti Spaghetti, Bigfoot Balls, and a Sasquatch Burger spilled down Finley's shoulder and into her lap. Two glasses of water and another of Coca-Cola splattered onto the table top, spraying both Finley and Brock with their contents.

For a moment, no one in the entire place moved or said a word.

Everyone just kind of stared at them with wide, shocked eyes.

Then, as the waitress began to apologize profusely, the man grabbed some napkins from his table and thrust them at Brock, and Sandra rushed to their table from across the diner...Finley began to laugh.

At first it was a small giggle, but it expanded until she was laughing so hard she couldn't even talk.

Brock was *pissed*...but at seeing Finley's mirth over the situation, he couldn't help but sigh, shake his head, and eventually smile himself.

"Oh my goodness!" Sandra exclaimed. "Oh my...this is... here, take these napkins."

For some reason, that made Finley laugh even harder. She pushed her chair back and stood, noodles falling from her shoulder even as a meatball bounced off the floor and rolled a few feet away.

Finley was covered in sauce and noodles—and Brock hadn't seen anything more beautiful in his life than she was at that moment, head thrown back and laughing over the absurd hilarity of the situation. She could've been furious, had every right to be upset or even crying, but instead, she chose to see the humor in the moment. The man hadn't meant to disrupt the waitress, just as she hadn't purposely dropped the food in Finley's lap.

That didn't mean Brock didn't wish he'd been the one to be dumped on.

"Wow, that's it," she told Brock, delicately picking stray noodles off her blouse and tossing them to the table. "You were right. No more dates."

He froze for a moment, wondering if this was *literally* it. If she'd decided they were through. But then she went on.

"When we go out together, we're just hanging. Chillin'. Having dinner or lunch. Hiking. You were right the second time—no more calling our excursions outside the house dates. Better yet, maybe we should just stay in our houses and never go out again."

Brock gently eased the waitress out of the way. She was attempting to pick up the broken plates and some of the food. He pulled Finley against him with one arm.

She screeched and, still giggling, said, "I'm gonna get you all yucky!"

"You could never get me all yucky, and I got enough soda on me to make me just as sticky as you."

"But at least you aren't wearing the Yeti Spaghetti," she said with a laugh.

Brock palmed her cheek and leaned in close. "We aren't hiding in our houses. I want to show off the woman who makes me laugh over spilled food, makes me want to beat anyone who dares to look at her cross-eyed, and who has me thanking my lucky stars I took the job here in Fallport five years ago."

Her laughter stopped as she stared up at him. "I want to show you off too," she said simply.

They shared an intimate smile before he leaned down and kissed the tip of her nose. Then her forehead.

"I'm so sorry," the waitress said miserably.

Finley turned, keeping one arm around his waist. "It's okay. It was an accident," she said magnanimously.

"I feel horrible. Your pretty shirt is probably ruined."

"Probably," Finley agreed. "But it's not the end of the world."

"I'll pay to have it replaced," Sandra told her.

Finley shook her head. "No, you won't. It's fine."

"And your dinner is on the house. Were you done? Beth, go tell the cooks to re-do their orders immediately."

"No!" Brock and Finley said at the same time. They shared a smile and quiet laugh before he turned to Sandra.

"We were practically done. We don't need more food. What we had was excellent, as always."

Sandra was practically wringing her hands in agitation. "What can I do then?" she asked.

"You can clean this up and continue on with your night," Finley said firmly. "It was an accident. No one was hurt."

"And we're still paying for our meal," Brock added.

Sandra sighed. "Fine—but I'm putting all of it toward the charities, not just a percentage."

Brock nodded, satisfied with that. He turned to Finley. "You ready to go?"

"Yeah."

Sandra hovered behind them as they made their way

through the diner toward the register. People gave them a wide berth, which wasn't exactly a surprise, since Finley was covered in spaghetti sauce.

"Wait!" Sandra ordered when they reached the door. "Don't go anywhere. Give me a second!"

They didn't have a chance to ask what she was doing before she rushed off toward the kitchen.

"If she brings back a doggy bag of Yeti Spaghetti, I'm not sure I'll be able to keep from laughing again," Finley told Brock quietly.

He loved her sense of humor. Leaning down, he put his lips near her ear and whispered, "Just think about being naked in my shower instead." He couldn't help but nip her ear playfully before he straightened.

She shivered as she stared up at him. "You aren't taking me to my house to get cleaned up?" she whispered back.

"No. I want you in *my* shower. My bed. The plan all along was to get naked together, so this will just expedite things."

Her pupils dilated right in front of his eyes, and just as Brock was taking a step to propel her out of the diner, Sandra returned.

"Here! You can't sit in your car like that. Take these towels, they'll protect the seats."

It was actually a very useful and thoughtful suggestion. Brock took the towels.

"Thank you so much," Finley said.

Sandra snorted. "It's not right, you thanking me when you got food dumped on you," she muttered.

"I'd give you a hug, but then you'd be messy too," Finley said. "So tomorrow, expect a huge hug from me."

"Deal," Sandra said, looking a little less stressed.

"Go do your thing...and enjoy the success of tonight," Finley said quietly. She patted the other woman's arm then looked up at Brock. "I'm ready."

There was so much more to those two words than the people around them shameless eavesdropping understood. Brock nodded at Sandra and pushed open the door to Sunny Side Up.

He walked Finley to his truck, both lost in their own thoughts about the upcoming night. After unlocking his door, he leaned in and spread one of the towels across the passenger seat. Then he held Finley's hand as she climbed into the truck. She scooted across to the other side, and Brock put his own towel down. He quickly started the engine and, once on the road to his house, reached for her hand.

Once again, no words passed between them on the short trip. It wasn't until the front door shut behind them that Brock took a deep breath and said, "There're two ways this can go. One, after you shower, you can put on the robe that's on the back of the bathroom door. I'll shower in the guest bathroom and after we're both clean, we can find something to watch on TV and when we're tired, we'll head to bed and sleep. That's all. Or...I can meet you in my bed after your shower."

"There's a third option," Finley said, a bit of trepidation easy to hear in her tone.

Brock had no idea what that would be, and if she said she could change into the clothes she'd brought with her and go home, he was going to shoot that option down point blank. "What's that?"

"You could shower with me, *then* we could go to bed," she said softly.

Brock's dick immediately sprang to life once more. He even felt a bit of precome leak out of the tip at the thought of having her naked, wet, and soapy in his shower.

Without a word, he grabbed her hand and stalked through the living room toward the short hallway. He heard Finley giggle behind him, but it was as if he was hearing her through a thick fog. All he could think about was being naked with her in his shower.

He pulled her into his en suite bathroom and shut the door behind them. Loving her initiative and courage in asking him to bathe with her, but knowing she was probably having a few unkind thoughts about her body, Brock turned off the overhead light at the same time he flicked on the light in the small alcove that held the toilet. It gave enough light to see by, but it wasn't as harsh as the overhead one. Shadows filled the room, and he could see the relief in Finley's entire expression.

"Strip," he ordered, as he reached for the hem of his own shirt.

CHAPTER EIGHT

Finley shivered at the tone of Brock's voice. And for the first time ever, she wasn't thinking about how many rolls her stomach had or about the size of her thighs, all she could concentrate on was Brock.

He'd already taken his shirt off over his head, and Finley swore she was practically drooling. Yes, she'd seen him bare-chested before, but it was different somehow knowing they were about to be naked together in his shower.

She managed to get her shirt up and over her head, but apparently she was moving too slow for Brock, because by the time her head emerged from the material, he was standing in front of her. *Right* in front of her. As promised, his gaze was glued to her boobs, which were overflowing the lacy bra she'd put on earlier. Generally, she lived in sports bras. They gave her more support while she was working, but she'd wanted to feel pretty for Brock tonight.

More relieved than she could admit that she'd given in to the vanity—because there was nothing sexy about getting out of a sports bra—Finley arched her back a little as Brock leaned down.

His hands went to the fastening of her jeans even as he placed open-mouth kisses all along her upper chest and cleavage. Her nipples were hard as nails and every breath pressed her skin to Brock's lips. He shoved her jeans and underwear down at the same time, and Finley toed off her shoes before stepping out of her clothes. As his hands snaked around her back to undo the clasp of her bra, Finley reached down and ripped off her socks. To her mind, nothing was less sexy than being naked, but still wearing socks.

Brock didn't stand back to take in all of her naked glory. The second her bra dropped to the floor, his lips covered one of her nipples.

Finley couldn't help but let out a long moan. God, his mouth felt so good. Her nipples had always been extremely sensitive.

Even as he sucked, Brock grabbed one of her hands and brought it to the button of his own jeans. Taking the hint, Finley fumbled with the button and zipper until it loosened. She flattened her hands against his hips and shoved the material down.

When he was as naked as she was, one of his arms wrapped around her waist, his large, calloused hand on the small of her back, as he ushered her into the shower. He turned so his back was to the nozzle, and Finley let out a small screech when he turned the water on. It was cold... and she wasn't even in the direct path of the spray. She had no idea how Brock could stand it, but she didn't have time to care when he used his free hand to plump her breast as he opened his lips wider and took even more of her into his mouth.

Finley reached around him, one hand clutching his butt cheek while the other gripped his massive biceps, and she got lost in a haze of sensation. One of her legs lifted automatically as she tried to get closer to Brock...which was practically impossible.

"So fucking gorgeous," he breathed as he lifted his head long enough to switch to her other nipple.

"Brock," she said on a groan as her pussy convulsed with every pull of his mouth on her nipple. She'd never been this turned on. Ever.

Vaguely, she realized the water had turned warm and steam began to rise around them. Then Brock moved, turning her sideways and pushing her against the wall. The juxtaposition of the cold tiles at her back and the warm water splashing against her side and front made her head spin.

Before she knew what he was doing, Brock was on his knees in front of her, turning her to lean against the adjacent wall, the water hitting his back. Finley blinked at him in surprise. His hands gripped her hips tightly and he stared at her pussy in the shadowy stall for a long, intense moment.

Finley hadn't been with a man in too many months for her to count, but she was fond of keeping herself neatly groomed. Other than a small bit of hair right above her clit, she was completely bare. She held her breath, waiting to see what Brock's reaction would be.

"Good Lord, woman!" he exclaimed. He moved one of his hands between her legs, running a single finger through her folds. Finley could feel how wet she was, and for once in her life, she wasn't embarrassed about it.

"I hadn't planned on doing this in the shower, but fuck it," Brock swore, right before diving forward. Finley's head fell back and the slight pain of hitting the tile wall behind her barely registered. All she could feel was Brock's lips and tongue between her thighs.

He lifted one of her legs and placed it over his shoulder. She was completely open to him then, at his mercy. She teetered for a moment, but his strong grip steadied her.

Looking down, Finley could see the top of Brock's head as he licked and sucked on her as if she was a sweet treat he'd been denied for too long.

Goose bumps broke out on her arms as he feasted on her pussy. Had anyone ever gone down on her this enthusiastically before in her life?

No, the answer was definitely no.

As she watched him devour her like a starving man, doing her best not to think about suffocating him between her thighs, he looked up. For once, she didn't see the pooch of her belly. Didn't think about how much harder his body was than hers. Didn't think about all her extra flesh on display. All she could think about was how good Brock was making her feel. As he stared back, she could see in the dim light that his pupils were completely dilated, and the raw lust in his expression only ramped up her own desire.

"Brock," she whispered.

He smiled against her, then closed his eyes and went back to driving her out of her mind. He seemed to know exactly what would send her soaring, as he concentrated his attention on her clit. Her inner muscles clenched, wanting something to hold onto and squeeze as Brock brought her closer and closer to a monster orgasm.

Finley grabbed hold of his hair with one hand and his shoulder with the other. She felt off-kilter. Shaky. The last thing she needed to do was fall mid-orgasm. That would ruin the mood for sure.

"I've got you," Brock breathed into her tender flesh. "Let go. Come for me, Fin. I want to taste you. I want your juices all over my face."

She shouldn't have been surprised that Brock was a dirty talker, but she still kind of was. And she couldn't deny it was hot as hell. Her fingers curled into his shoulder as he began to lick her nub over and over again. Fast and hard. She rocked her hips, and the leg she was standing on began to quiver as she neared orgasm.

Brock wrapped an arm around the thigh that was braced on his shoulder and pushed her harder against the tiles. The hand that had been clutching her hip moved between her legs, and he pushed one long finger deep inside her body as he licked her clit.

"Yes, there! Brock!" Finley cried out.

Her entire body was at the edge of the precipice. Every muscle felt taut as a bow. She wavered between holding on and letting go. Then he added another finger to the first, stretching and filling her. He thrust in and out of her body gently as he sucked on her clit, hard.

She couldn't hold back even if she wanted to. A deep-throated grunt escaped her mouth as she thrust against Brock's face and let herself go.

A satisfied moan came from Brock's throat, but it hardly registered in Finley's brain.

"That's it, fuck my fingers," he urged in a husky tone as he drew her orgasm out for as long as he could. By the time she came down from the high of the pleasure he'd just given her, Finley felt as boneless as a wet noddle. But Brock didn't let go; instead, he held her thigh on his shoulder and kept moving his fingers in and out of her body.

"I can't wait to feel this around my cock," he said, not taking his gaze away from her pussy stretched around him. "You're gonna strangle me so hard. I'm gonna blow the second I get in there, I just know it."

Finley had a feeling her face was bright red. She shouldn't be as embarrassed as she was with his dirty talk, and with sex in general. But this was more than sex. Most men she'd been with had barely gotten her wet before climbing on and getting themselves off. Brock was so different. He was...worshiping her.

And Finley knew he'd already ruined her completely for any other man.

After a moment, she tentatively said, "Brock?"

"Hmmm?"

"I think I'm getting a cramp in my calf."

That got him moving. He leaned in and sucked her clit once more, licking his lips as he lifted her thigh off his shoulder and placed her foot back on the tile floor. But he didn't stand. Simply held onto her hips as he knelt at her feet and stared up at her. The steam was thick in the shower stall now as the water continued to rain down on them.

"Thank you," Brock said after a moment.

Finley frowned. "I think that's my line."

He shook his head. "No. I lost control. I couldn't wait

to taste you. I appreciate you trusting me to make sure you didn't fall. For giving that gift to me. And for the record...I fucking *love* eating you out. I'm gonna want to do that a lot in the future."

Finley's face felt like it was burning. Did he think she was going to complain? No way in hell. "Um...okay."

He grinned, and his hands slid up her sides until he was cupping both her breasts. She looked down, and the sight of his huge stained hands on her skin was erotic as hell. Her gaze traveled over his chest, past his six-pack abs to his cock, which was bobbing up and down slightly as he balanced on the balls of his feet with his legs spread. He was long. And thick. And the desire that had waned a moment before ramped right back up again.

She wanted him. Inside her. Now.

She must've made a needy noise in the back of her throat, because Brock grinned and slowly stood. He gathered her to him, and she could feel his hardness against the softness of her belly. Never had their differences as man and woman been so evident as they were right this second.

But instead of taking her right there against the wall like she wanted him to, Brock turned her so her back was to the water. He leaned over and picked up a shower pouf and a bottle of liquid soap. He poured a dollop onto the pouf and rubbed it vigorously with his hands.

"Brock?"

"Yeah?" he said as he began running the pouf over her shoulder.

"I want you."

"I want you too. And I'm gonna have you, just as you're gonna have me."

Finley reached for his cock, which was smearing

precome against her belly with every move he made. But Brock caught her hand in his and brought it up to rest on his chest. "Patience, Fin," he said with a small smile as he began to wash her skin. The scent of vanilla wafted up to her nostrils...

The soap was the same brand she had back in her own shower.

"Look who's talking. And you expect me to be patient after the orgasm you gave me, and after seeing how hard you are for me?"

"Yup," he said, his grin never faltering. "Need to get that Yeti Spaghetti off you. And that soda. Relax. This is a marathon, not a sprint."

Good Lord. The man was seriously trying to kill her. "Just remember that I don't have the stamina you do," she muttered, even as she arched her back when his hand dipped down her ass with the shower pouf and lower to between her legs.

"You don't have to do a thing but lie there and let me pleasure you," Brock whispered into her ear as he used his other hand to lather the soap he'd wiped over her pussy. And just like that, Finley's legs went weak again.

The rest of the shower was a lesson in patience, which Finley didn't have. After he'd rinsed the soap off her, and she'd turned the tables on him, taking the pouf and making sure every inch of his skin was sparkling clean, he turned the water off and opened the shower door to grab a towel.

When he'd turned back around, Finley was the one on her knees in front of him.

"Finley, you—"

His words were cut off when she grabbed the base of

his cock and took him into her mouth. She couldn't keep her hands, or mouth, off him a second longer. She wanted to give back some of the pleasure he'd already given her.

He smelled like vanilla and sex. It was a heady combination, and Finley used her hand to jack him off as she bobbed up and down on as much of his length as she could. He was thick, and it was difficult just to get her mouth around him. There was no way she could take all of him, but she did her best.

She felt Brock pushing her hair out of the way so he could watch.

"Fuck yeah, Fin! That feels so damn good. Suck me harder. Yesssssss, just like that." His hips thrust against her as she sucked, and she reveled in having this amazing man at her mercy. One hand thrust into her hair, clenching tightly, but he didn't try to direct her movements, simply held her as she gave him the best blow job she knew how to give.

Way before she was ready, he tightened his grip in her hair and pulled her off his cock. As if she weighed nothing at all, he pulled her to her feet and gathered her close. They were both breathing hard, and Finley's nipples brushed against his chest hair. He stared at her for a heartbeat before leading her into his bedroom. They were both wet, her hair dripping down her back, but he didn't seem to care or notice.

He threw her almost roughly onto the mattress and immediately crawled toward her when she scooted to the middle of the bed.

Just as in her fantasizes, the muscles in his arms flexed as he hovered over her. The wet tip of his cock brushed against her inner thigh, making Finley immediately open her legs to him. She'd never needed a man so badly in her life.

"I'm clean," he said gruffly.

"Me too."

"Are you protected?" he asked.

Finley frowned. "Shit. No."

His eyes closed, but he didn't move from his position over her. "I should've picked up condoms today when I was at the store, but I got distracted by looking at the candy bars and trying to find all the ones with caramel."

Finley couldn't help but feel disappointed. Not about the candy he'd bought for her, but because the lack of protection meant she wouldn't get to experience all that was Brock. She wanted him. So damn bad. Wanted his monster cock inside her. Wanted to be fucked. *Hard.*

His eyes opened, and she stilled under him at the look on his face. "Fuck it. I can't wait. I'm gonna take you now, Finley. Want to be buried so deep inside you that we can't tell where I end and you begin. If there are consequences from tonight, if we make a baby, I'm gonna take care of you both. No matter if we end up together permanently or not.

"I know that's irresponsible as fuck—but I don't care. This isn't just sex, Fin. It's so much more. And this isn't just me wanting to get off; I can do that with my own hand, and recently, I've done it every damn night. There's something about you that makes me a little crazy. I literally can't resist you."

He took a deep breath. "Say something," he begged. "Tell me to get the hell off you. That you aren't willing to take the chance on getting pregnant. Or that I'm insane for not caring if I knock you up. *Something.*"

Finley was shocked by everything he'd said. But she couldn't deny a big part of her was jumping up and down, yelling at her to let him fuck her already.

To let him fill her up with his come and get her pregnant.

She'd always wanted kids, but hadn't found anyone she wanted to have them with. And she hadn't been thrilled about the idea of artificial insemination. Now, she knew instantly that a little girl with Brock's beautiful brown eyes would be a dream come true. Or a boy who'd follow him around, wanting to learn everything he could from his dad about cars and the forest.

"Finley?" Brock asked, lifting himself off her. "Shit, I fucked up. I'm so sorry."

In response, Finley reached down and wrapped her fingers around his still-hard cock. She wiggled until he was right where she wanted him, opened her legs even wider, and notched the tip of his cock between her pussy lips.

"Take me, Brock. I'm yours." And she was. From this moment on, she belonged to this man. He had her heart, body, and soul, and she couldn't imagine ever being with anyone else.

This might be a mistake...but so be it. She was living for the moment, and she knew this moment with Brock was going to be one of the most beautiful in her entire life.

With a groan, Brock shifted and sank into her in one long, slow thrust.

* * *

Brock literally thought he was going to orgasm right then and there. Without any other stimulation beyond being buried in Finley's delectable body.

She hadn't even protested his caveman talk about knocking her up.

He'd never been so reckless in his life. Always wore a condom, *always*. But with Finley, he needed to be inside her raw, skin on skin. He couldn't stand being with her any other way. Maybe some animal part of his brain knew that already, when he forgot to buy condoms.

He hadn't lied, if they made a baby tonight, so be it. He'd always make sure both Finley and their child had everything they ever needed.

"Brock?" she whispered under him. "Move. *Please!*"

Her nails dug into the skin of his biceps, and he hadn't missed her slight flinch as he'd plunged all the way inside her. She was tight. Almost too tight, despite still being wet from earlier. He could feel her hot juices soaking the skin of his cock.

"I'm afraid to," he blurted.

She frowned. "I'm okay. You aren't hurting me."

"Yes, I'm scared about doing anything that might cause you pain, but I also think if I move, I'm gonna come. And I don't want this to end. I want to stay here as long as I possibly can. You feel so goddamn amazing, Fin...you have no idea."

He savagely enjoyed seeing the blush on her face. She was passionate and eager, and yet he could still bring out that blush in her. He fucking loved that.

Her inner muscles squeezed him then, and almost involuntarily, Brock's hips rocked forward and back.

They both moaned.

"Do that again," he ordered.

She did. She squeezed his cock harder than before, and Brock clenched his teeth to keep from exploding.

She giggled, and he felt her shifting against him even as he was buried deep inside her. Looking down at Finley, Brock couldn't believe she was finally here. That she trusted him with her body—and what a fucking body it was. Full in all the right places. Soft as silk and so damn lush.

And with that thought, he pumped into her once again. Her tits shook as he bottomed out, and he wanted to see that again. So he thrust his hips once more and smiled at seeing her generous breasts shimmy.

The vision of him taking her from behind and watching them in a mirror strategically placed so he could watch her tits swing back and forth as he took her almost had him coming right that second. As it was, a long burst of precome escaped his cock as he closed his eyes and did his best to regain control.

"Fuck me, Brock," she ordered. "Stop torturing yourself. Get the first one over with, then we can take our time on the second."

She was right. He had no plans on letting her out of his bed or his arms anytime soon tonight. Now that he'd gotten her here, under him, naked, he wasn't going to let her go.

He began to fuck her. *Hard.* The sound of their skin slapping together was as much a turn-on as seeing her tits bounce on her chest. Finley bit her lip as he took her, arching her back, doing her best to thrust, her fingernails digging into his skin. He had the thought that he hoped she left marks. He wanted a reminder of tonight. Of the first time he took the woman he wanted to spend the rest of his life with.

The thought didn't freak him out. No way. Jesus, he was already hoping he *did* knock her up; thinking about moving her in and having her delicious body all to himself for the next forty years or more didn't stress him out in the least.

She was slick and hot and so tight, and the friction of his cock tunneling in and out of her tight pussy was more than his overwhelmed brain could handle. He felt his balls pulling up, getting ready to release their load. He looked down to where they were joined...and that was all it took. The sight of her bare lips stretched wide around his cock was so carnal, he was coming before his brain registered what was happening.

He thrust as deep inside her as he could, and continued to let loose what felt like gallons of come inside her body. He was sweaty, his arms shaking as the pleasure almost overwhelmed him.

When he came back to himself, he realized what he'd done. That he'd fucked Finley and hadn't even bothered to make sure it was good for her.

His cock was still semi-hard. Brock had a feeling he'd stay like that all damn night. Putting one hand on her ass to keep himself inside her, he rolled, taking her with him.

Finley let out an adorable surprised squeak as she ended up straddling his hips. Her hands braced on his chest as she blinked down at him. "Well, that was...talented," she said with a small smile.

Brock could feel their juices leaking out of her and onto his balls, something he'd never experienced before. It made him more than a little lust-crazed. The thought of her pussy stuffed full of his come made his cock twitch to life even more. "You didn't come," he said. "Show me how you like to be touched."

She frowned. "What?"

"Masturbate for me, Fin."

"Um...here?"

"Yes."

He saw her attempt to suck in her belly, as if she just realized how exposed she was. Her being self-conscious while he was still inside her was unacceptable. He grabbed hold of her thigh and pushed her knee out to the side, taking more of her weight.

"Brock, what are you doing?"

"Relax, Finley. Don't think about anything other than your pleasure."

He then shoved her other leg out, so she wasn't putting any pressure on her knees at all, his cock sliding incrementally deeper inside her.

"I'm too heavy," she complained.

"The fuck you are," Brock growled. "And if you aren't going to show me what you like, you'll have to tell me if I get it right or not." He worked his hand between them and pressed his thumb against her clit.

Finley jolted in his arms, and he watched her nipples harden right in front of him. His mouth watered, and he wanted to suck on her tits, but this was more important. He needed her to come again.

He reached his other hand around her thigh, until he could feel where his cock disappeared into her body. He caressed her pussy lips around his dick as he strummed her clit. It wasn't long before she'd moved back onto her knees and began rocking over him.

He slowed his movements on her clit, and she moaned in frustration.

"Harder," she ordered.

Brock ignored her, lightening his touch even more. Teasing her.

"Brock, please!" she complained.

"Show me how you like it," he demanded.

She was so far gone in her pleasure that she immediately complied. One of her hands moved between her legs and the other stayed flat on his belly, steading herself.

Nothing prepared Brock for the vision in front of him, on top of him. She strummed her clit harshly, using two fingers, while at the same time she began to ride him. His cock came back to life with a vengeance, elongating and hardening as she used him as her own personal dildo.

Eventually, she sat straight up, spine bowed, letting Brock see all of her. And every inch was glorious. Her skin quivered with her thrusts, shiny with a light sheen of sweat. Her tits bounced up and down on her chest as she rode him faster and faster. Way before he was ready for the stunning show to be over, her fingers began a frantic pace on her clit and she let out a long, sexy moan.

He felt her inner muscles flutter and tighten against him as every muscle in her body tensed. Brock couldn't hold back any longer. He grabbed her hips and held her still as he took her from below. Thrusting into her body hard and fast. He fucked her through her orgasm, and just as Finley was coming down from her pleasure, he found his.

He slammed her hips down, their bodies slapping loudly one more time as he came. His cock twitched as he emptied himself inside her for the second time tonight.

Brock felt almost light-headed. They were both sweaty, the scent of vanilla and sex officially one of his favorite smells ever now.

He put a hand between her shoulder blades and urged her to lay down on top of him.

"Too heavy," she murmured.

"No, you aren't," he said, holding on tight so she couldn't shift off him. As of right this moment, his dick was still inside her. Soft now. And Brock knew it was only a matter of time before he slipped all the way out. He wanted to keep the connection as long as he possibly could.

"That was..." Her voice trailed off.

"Yeah," Brock agreed.

After a couple minutes passed, his cock softened enough to ease out of her pussy. He grunted in dissatisfaction, but she didn't make a move to shift off him. He closed his legs, not hating the erotic feel of their juices dripping out of her, onto his thighs.

"Brock?"

"Yeah?"

"What are we doing?"

"Fucking?" he said with a chuckle.

He felt her snort above him. "I mean...I've never had sex without a condom before."

He frowned. Shit. Was she regretting what they'd done? "You want me to call Doc Snow and see if I can get one of those morning-after pills?"

At that, Finley lifted her head to look into his eyes. The overhead light was still on—she was too turned on to care about it earlier, thank God. Brock had loved seeing every inch of her body under and over him. "Do *you* want me to?"

"No!" he said a little too forcefully. Then he sighed. "I meant what I said. If you get pregnant, I'll be overjoyed. Not because I've always wanted kids, which I have, but because I'm having them with *you*. I don't know where you think this is going, but as far as I'm concerned, we aren't a short-term thing." Brock was opening himself up to a boatload of hurt, but he wasn't going to shy away from this.

"Nothing has ever felt as right as being with you. Inside you. That wasn't just fucking. We made love, Finley," he said, almost desperately.

"Yeah," she agreed, and Brock's muscles relaxed.

"I want you so much. I want to spend as much time with you as possible. I want to continue to hang out with you while you bake in the mornings, because we both know I'm no help whatsoever. What gets me through the day is thinking about seeing you when I'm done. Jesus is sick of me talking about you while we're working, but I don't care. What I feel...this isn't casual, Finley...not even close."

"Same," she said with a shy smile.

"Good. I'm not going to tell you I love you, because I'm pretty sure that'll freak you out. But you should get used to the idea, because you'll be hearing it before too long."

Finley grinned tiredly. "All right."

Brock relaxed. "You want to clean up?"

"You mean 'clean up' like we did in the shower earlier?"

"No. I'm talking about me getting up and grabbing a warm washcloth and coming back here and wiping my come off your pussy, then snuggling for a while until I can't keep my hands or mouth or cock off you, so I have to go down on you again before shoving back inside you."

She let out a strangled little laugh. "Um...do I have any other options?"

"No," he said firmly, shaking his head for emphasis.

"Then, yeah, I want to clean up."

Brock couldn't stop smiling. He was a fucking caveman, but she hadn't freaked out on him yet. He'd take it. He eased her off him and slid out of bed before grabbing her hand and helping her stand. "Don't move."

He was back seconds later with clean sheets, since the others were pretty damp, basically used as towels after their shower. He stripped and remade the bed inside of two minutes, then eased Finley back onto the mattress before heading into the bathroom. He returned with a washcloth, finding her covered. He wanted to throw the bedding back and see his come on her pussy, but figured she needed a bit more time before he did something like that. Instead, he climbed under the covers with her and gently wiped her clean. He threw the washcloth blindly toward the corner and pulled her against his side.

She sighed in contentment, and Brock loved the feel of her naked skin against his.

"It's kind of early to go to bed," she muttered.

"We're just resting. We aren't going to bed yet."

"Um...horizontal, in bed...just saying," she quipped.

Brock chuckled as his fingers brushed back and forth on the soft skin of her shoulder. "Shhh. Rest. You're gonna need it."

"Don't forget, I need to get up at four-fifteen to get to work by four-thirty," she mumbled into his chest.

"I won't forget," he reassured her, mentally changing their wake-up time to four so they could shower together before leaving. By the time he was through with her, she'd need that shower...as would he.

As he felt Finley's breaths even out against him, Brock closed his eyes. He was a lucky son-of-a-bitch, and he knew it. The thought of them breaking up or, God forbid, anything happening to Finley was enough to have sweat popping out on his forehead. Thank goodness she didn't have any exes in her life. Or psycho co-workers. Or any stalkers. He couldn't handle Finley going through anything close to what his friends' women had.

No, he was more than all right with them living a perfectly boring life from here on out.

* * *

"Hey, Boss, it's Pete."

"Have you found out what I need to know?"

"Not exactly," Pete mumbled.

"What the hell does that mean?" The Boss asked in a dangerous tone.

"It's just that...she's never alone. Cory and I haven't been able to get to her because she's always with someone else. And you said you didn't want any witnesses."

"You're such a fuck-up!" The Boss raged.

"Seriously! Like today, that homeless guy was with her at the bakery at the ass-crack of dawn. And the mechanic showed up not too long afterward. Then that Hispanic guy got to work and he was with her all day. She stayed late, and we were gonna run her off the road somewhere, but we never got a chance because she stuck to busy streets.

She delivered something to a chick at a bed and breakfast and stayed forever to chat. Then she went home, and before we could think of a way to get inside, she left again. Went out to eat with that mechanic. The waitress spilled a whole fuckin' tray of food on her, and we thought for sure she'd go home then, but instead she went home with that asshole. And she's been there all night."

"Fucking whore," The Boss sighed. "And you two are incompetent. You need to get this done. I've got a goddamn life; I can't be driving to Roanoke every other day to make the pickup. We have to fucking finish this so I can reassure the supplier it's been taken care of. I need to get back to my routine. Do you fucking understand?"

"Yes," Pete said.

"Good. Because if you don't get me what I want, doing jail time for dealing drugs will be the least of your goddamn worries."

Pete swallowed hard. The Boss wasn't someone to cross. There were rumors about what had happened to a few previous dealers when they'd fucked up. He didn't want to disappear without a trace. On the outside, The Boss looked normal...even nice. But it was obvious that, deep down, something was very wrong.

Pete regretted getting involved in this mess. At the time, it seemed like a good way to make money and get the pills he desperately needed. Now, he realized he was good and fucked. He couldn't leave because he knew too much. And if he did try to get out, he'd end up the same way others had...chopped to pieces and dispersed to various landfills around southwest Virginia.

No one knew for sure that was really what had happened to Oscar, Jimmy, and Andrea, but Pete had no doubt The Boss wouldn't hesitate to end anyone who fucked up the cushy operation they had going here in Fallport.

"Did you hear me?" The Boss asked impatiently. "Get the bitch alone and find out what she knows before I have to deal with the situation myself. If that happens, you aren't going to like the fucking consequences!"

"Understood."

The line went dead, and Pete sighed. The call had gone much like he thought it would, but The Boss had been expecting an update. This weekend was Halloween, and the bitch's friend was getting married on a piece of property a little ways outside of town. Pete knew he wouldn't have a chance to get to the fat-ass before then, especially since she was now shacking up with the mechanic, but after...he and Cory would be ready. The second they could get her alone, she'd have some questions to answer.

CHAPTER NINE

Finley felt like she was floating on air. There was something to be said for having good sex—no, *great* sex—every night. Getting up at four in the morning didn't seem to be that much of a hardship when she got to shower with Brock before heading to work. Most of the time their shower turned into either a quickie, or getting each other off orally or by hand.

Brock was an inventive and generous lover. The fact that she was heavier than most people genuinely wasn't an issue for him. After the first time he'd made love to her with all the lights on, she'd lost all her inhibitions. She'd never had as much sex throughout the course of an entire relationship as she'd had with Brock over the last nine days. She'd never believed people could be as voracious as they were in the romance books she'd read, but she under-stood now. All Finley had to do was look at Brock, and she immediately got wet.

But this morning, despite being happier than she could remember being in her life, Finley was stressed. Lilly and

Ethan were getting married today, and there were a million things she needed to do, the most important of which was to get the cake she'd made over to Bristol's house in one piece. Then she had to put it together and hope it turned out as cute as the trial-run cake had been.

"Stop worrying," Brock chided as he zipped the bag they were bringing to Bristol and Rocky's house. It had the clothes they were going to wear to the wedding and reception, along with the gift Brock had insisted on putting both their names on.

"I can't," she whined. "What if they hate it? What if I can't get it to look right? What if it tastes awful?"

Brock came over and pulled her into his embrace and Finley sighed. This was her favorite place in the world to be. Held against Brock's chest so tightly she could hear his heart beating. "Your cake is going to be a hit. I tasted the extra layer you made yesterday and decided not to use. It was delicious. And it'll be even better iced. No one is going to hate it. And it's going to look perfect, but even if it doesn't, Lilly and Ethan aren't going to care. They're just so relieved this day is finally here, it could look like Tony made it and they'd still be thrilled."

Finley knew he was right, but she was still nervous.

"Come on," he said. "The sooner we get there and you can get busy helping others and doing your thing, the less nervous you'll be."

He was right.

As they drove out to Bristol and Rocky's, Finley couldn't help but think back on the last several days. It had been a whirlwind in a lot of ways. She'd spent every night at Brock's house, and the small bag she'd brought over the first day had already expanded to having a week's worth of clothes and all of her toiletries on the counter in his bathroom.

He'd also packed up three boxes of stuff from her kitchen when she'd complained one night about his crappy pans. She'd been kidding, but the next thing she knew, he was unpacking her things and telling her to feel free to rearrange them. They were moving at warp speed...and Finley couldn't find it in her to care. Her clothes were in the dryer mixed with his and both their names were on the new camera lens wrapped in a box on the back seat.

Ethan had told all his friends not to get any gifts for him, but to spoil Lilly instead. It was the sweetest thing Finley had ever heard, and she was so happy for her friend.

Word had gotten around Fallport just as quickly that she and Brock were an item. Probably because the morning after they'd made love for the first time, when Brock was leaving The Sweet Tooth, they'd gotten a little carried away with their goodbye kiss while on the sidewalk in front of the store. When they'd finally broken apart, breathing hard and turned way the hell on, Silas, Otto, and Art had been whistling and catcalling from their spots outside the post office. Finley had been mortified, but Brock had merely smiled and kissed her forehead before saying, "See you this evening."

Now they were on their way to Bristol and Rocky's property. There were still eight hours until the ceremony was supposed to start at sunset, but Finley, along with Elsie, Bristol, and Caryn, were going over early to help out and hopefully to keep Lilly's stress level down.

Lilly and Ethan had chosen not to have any attendants, it was just going to be the two of them standing up in front of their family and friends to pledge their lives and love to each other.

Ethan and Rocky's mom had arrived earlier in the week, and Finley had gotten to meet her when she'd come into the bakery. She was down to earth and friendly, and Finley had adored her on sight.

Lilly's entire family was there as well, and from what she understood from Brock, they were a rowdy, fun group of people that included her dad, along with her four brothers and *their* families. The guest list for the ceremony also included a lot of people Finley had gotten to know from around Fallport, like Whitney Crawford, the owner of the B&B where Lilly had stayed when she'd arrived to work on the paranormal investigations show.

Part of the reason Finley was so nervous about her wedding cake being perfect was precisely *because* so many people from town would be there. This could be an excellent chance to increase her catering sales...but only if nothing went wrong with her very first wedding cake.

The number of people milling around the barn and property when they arrived was kind of surprising, but Brock managed to steer around people carrying chairs and tables, and he backed up right to the front door of the house.

"Come on," he said. "We'll get the cake inside, then I'll go find the guys and see what I can do to help."

Minutes later, before he headed back outside to move his truck and to help out with the setup, Brock hugged her tightly. "Have fun today. Try not to worry. Everything's gonna be perfect."

"I'd settle for fine, not perfect," Finley said dryly. Brock chuckled lightly. Then he studied her with a look she couldn't interpret. "What?" she asked.

He shrugged. "I'm just happy."

Warmth spread through Finley's belly. "Me too."

"Good. If you need anything, just shoot me a text. I'm happy to be an errand boy if necessary. Bobby pins, more alcohol, something you need from the shop...it's not a problem."

Gah. He was the best. "Thanks," she said, her voice cracking.

"I'd do anything for you, Fin. Just sayin'. Now, kiss me and I'll see you later."

She went up on her tiptoes and did as he ordered. The kiss was long and probably way too intimate for their location, especially when there was no way they could do anything about the desire it stirred within each of them.

"Damn, woman," he mock-complained as he ran a thumb over her cheek. "You're lethal."

"I could say the same thing about you," she said.

"Good thing I have to move the truck before finding the guys," he said ruefully, looking down at his crotch.

Finley giggled at seeing his erection pressing against the front of his jeans. "Sorry?"

"No, you aren't. But that's okay. I have no problem with people knowing how much my girl turns me on. Have a good day," he said, kissing her forehead before turning and heading for the door.

They'd been standing in the kitchen, where Bristol had told her to set up everything she needed to finish Lilly's wedding cake. When Brock disappeared down the hall, she heard a throat clearing and whirled around.

Caryn was standing in the living area, and she gave

Finley a crooked smile. "I was gonna ask how things were going between you guys, but I can see for myself that they're good."

Finley blushed, smiling at her friend. "Yeah, you could say that."

"I'm so happy for you both. You deserve each other."

"Thanks. He's..." Finley's words trailed off as she struggled to find the right adjective to describe Brock.

But she didn't need to, Caryn seemed to understand. "Yeah," she said with a nod. "You need any help in here?"

Taking a deep breath, Finley shook her head. "I don't need to start on the cake just yet. It's a little too early. And the last thing I'd want is someone accidentally knocking into it or something. How's Lilly? Is she stressed out?"

"Surprisingly, no. She's pretty calm. I think she's ready for this to just be done."

"Makes sense."

"I came down to grab one of the bottles of caramel apple moonshine I brought with me," Caryn said. "Clyde made a batch just for me for today."

"Cool," Finley told her. "Anything with caramel in it is my favorite."

Caryn beamed. She headed for a box on the floor in the corner of the room, grabbing the bottle.

"Do we need glasses?" Finley asked.

"Nope. There are already some upstairs. Come on... Lilly's getting her hair done, then it's our turn."

"Oh, but I wasn't expecting—"

"I know. None of us were. But even though Lilly doesn't have any bridesmaids, she still wanted to share the day with her friends. So she arranged for us all to have our makeup and hair done."

"That's sweet."

"Yup. But I'll tell you one thing...I'll be more than ready to escape the estrogen overload after a while, so when it's time to come down and work on the cake, please bring me with you."

Finley chuckled. "Deal. Is everyone here already?"

"Everyone but Khloe."

"Oh, I thought she was coming back yesterday. She sent me a text and told me she was returning and I wouldn't need to feed the kittens today." Finley had told the others about how adorable the cats were, and both Bristol and Lilly had already agreed to take one after the wedding was over.

"As far as I know, she's back. And she said she'd try to make the ceremony, but she couldn't come over beforehand," Caryn said with a frown.

"Is she okay?" Finley asked. "I mean, she seems...stressed."

"I don't know. And I agree. Something's up and I hate that she's not talking to us."

"Do you know where she went or what she was doing?"

"No."

"Does anyone?"

Caryn shrugged. "Not that I know of. I mean, she and Bristol are probably the closest, and even she doesn't know where Khloe's been."

"Well, shoot. How can we help her if we don't know what's wrong?" Finley asked. "Maybe I'll make her a double chocolate cake and take it over to her apartment next week. Nothing's as good as chocolate to make someone feel better."

"You're sweet," Caryn said with a smile. "How come I didn't get a double chocolate cake after all my shit?"

Finley stared at her for a second, worried her friend was actually upset with her, but then Caryn laughed.

"I'm kidding! I heard about how you practically dragged poor Brock out of your store when he went to tell you what happened. You were an unstoppable force, demanding he take you to see for yourself that I was all right. I'll take that over a cake any day."

"You haven't tried my double chocolate cake," Finley mumbled, feeling a little embarrassed at how demanding she'd been with Brock that day.

As if she could read her mind, Caryn said, "From where I'm standing, things have worked out perfectly between you and Brock. Glad my plan worked."

"Your plan?"

"Well, *yeah*. I was the one who suggested he go to your shop to tell you what happened that day. And in case you already forgot, I also called him to be your assistant when you sprained your wrist."

"You're awful," Finley said, shaking her head.

"Nope. Just in love, and I want all my friends to feel the same way. Now, come on, I need to get back upstairs with this stuff before there's a riot."

Caryn hooked her arm with Finley's and they walked toward the stairs. She thought about what her friend had said. Was she in love with Brock?

Yes. She absolutely was—and that was scary as hell. She'd fallen hard and fast, and the man had the power to completely break her if he wasn't as serious about her as she was about him. Of course, all signs indicated he wasn't with her just for sex. Hell, he'd told her flat out that he wouldn't mind getting her pregnant. A man who was just with a woman for the sex wouldn't want to jump into fatherhood. No, he'd be going out of his way to make sure there were no long-term consequences of a physical relationship.

But would everything they have fizzle out after burning so bright, so fast?

God, Finley hoped not.

"Stop thinking so hard," Caryn chided as they neared the top of the stairs. "You and Brock are perfect together. He can't take his eyes off you when you're in the same room. And don't forget, I saw that kiss. We're all gonna be celebrating your own wedding sooner rather than later."

"Oh no, this is all too much for me. I just want something small and simple."

Caryn smirked. "Knew you were thinking about it," she crowed.

Finley rolled her eyes. Then she said under her breath, "And there's no reason for a shotgun wedding nowadays."

"Wait—what?" Caryn asked, her eyes huge in her face as she stopped abruptly in the middle of the hall.

"Nothing."

A determined glint shone in Caryn's eyes as she grabbed Finley's arm and pulled her inside a bedroom. Lilly, Elsie, and Bristol—and the woman doing Lilly's hair —all turned to look at them when they entered.

"It's about time. I'm parched!" Elsie joked.

Caryn plunked the bottle of moonshine on a table and turned to the group. "Finley's pregnant!"

Finley choked at her friend's announcement as everyone—well, everyone but the hairdresser—began to speak at once.

"You are?!"

"Holy shit, Brock works fast!"

"Congratulations!"

Finley held up a hand. "Wait, wait, wait! I'm *not* pregnant."

"We were talking about weddings, and you said shotgun weddings weren't necessary anymore. Shotgun weddings are when a woman's daddy forces a man to marry his daughter because he knocked her up. Hence, me reading between the lines and assuming you were preggo," Caryn said, crossing her arms.

"Brock and I have only been *together*-together for a week," Finley protested.

Caryn sighed dramatically. "Right, so it's practically impossible to know if you're preggo after only a week, but...you were the one who said what you said and made me wonder."

It was Finley's turn to sigh. "Fine. The reason I said that is because I'm not on birth control, and Brock and I had a talk, and we decided to just...take our chances. He said no matter what happened between us that he'd take care of any baby I might have."

"That's... Holy shit," Lilly breathed.

"Stupid, I know," Finley said with a grimace.

"No, it's so romantic!" Bristol argued. "I mean, seeing the two of you together...it's obvious that your relationship isn't casual. And if he says he has no problem knocking you up, then he must *actually* want to do that. How do you feel about it?"

"I...I'm not getting any younger. And I'd love to be a mom," Finley said hesitatingly.

"You'd be such a wonderful mother," Elsie said enthusiastically.

"No moonshine for you!" Caryn exclaimed. "Just in case you're already knocked up. But the rest of us are toasting to Brock's super-sperm!"

Everyone laughed—but Lilly blushed as she said, "None for me either."

Finley was kind of glad everyone's attention shifted to the soon-to-be bride. It was kind of embarrassing to talk about her rash decision not to use birth control when she'd literally just started dating Brock, but their support and belief that Brock was definitely serious about her made Finley feel a lot better.

"Are *you*...?" Bristol asked.

Lilly blushed and shrugged. "Good thing my daddy likes Ethan and he doesn't own a shotgun."

Pandemonium erupted as everyone rushed to congratulate Lilly. The questions were fired at her fast and furious, and she held up a hand. "One at a time. Right, so I'm not that far along. Probably too soon to even be talking about it. And I'm freaking out, actually, because I drank the other week when we all got together at Caryn's. Then I peed on a stick last night and it was positive. I know it could be a false positive, but I've been feeling really tired and emotional lately, and I think that's part of why I was so stressed about the wedding."

"That's so awesome," Elsie breathed. "I'm so happy for you," she said as she walked over and gave her friend a huge hug.

"What about you?" Lilly asked.

"What *about* me?"

"I know you and Zeke want more kids."

Elsie frowned. "I want them so bad, but so far...nothing. It's frustrating."

"It'll happen when it's supposed to happen," Bristol told her gently. "You can't stress about it."

"I know, but honestly, it's all I can think about. I want to have Zeke's kids so bad, and I swear I got pregnant with Tony the day I stopped taking my birth control. I'm paranoid that it won't happen," Elsie lamented softly.

"It will," Lilly said firmly.

"I agree. In the meantime, enjoy the act of trying," Caryn said with a wink.

Finley couldn't stop the blush she felt on her face. Luckily no one was looking at her. She thought about how thoroughly and often Brock made love to her, and how the sight of his come dipping out of her seemed to turn him on even more. If she wasn't pregnant right now, she would be soon. She had no doubt.

"Drew and I talked about it, and neither of us want children, but we can't freaking wait to spoil all of yours," Caryn said with a sigh.

"Rocky and I aren't sure either," Bristol added, "but I'll be right by Caryn's side, spoiling the heck out of everyone else's kids."

"We can have sleepovers where we let them stay up half the night and drink soda and eat sugar...then send 'em home," Caryn said with a laugh.

"Let them watch scary movies so they want to sleep with Mommy and Daddy for a week after." Bristol smirked.

Everyone was laughing now. Finley knew her friends would do exactly what they were threatening.

Talk of babies faded away as the morning went on.

Finley headed down to the kitchen after Caryn's hair and makeup was done, to start assembling the cake, and her friend was happy to assist. She texted Brock when they finished, to ask if he'd come help her get the cake out to the barn. He arrived with Tal, and the two of them carefully transported it to the table that had been set up in the barn.

The weather was perfect for a wedding. It was cool, but not cold. Finley didn't have to worry about the cake melting or freezing. Which was a huge relief. Brock kissed her hard before he left to go back to the barn and hang out with the rest of the Eagle Point Search and Rescue team and the arriving guests.

Finley's lips tingled long after they'd parted. She'd never felt pretty before. Had never experienced men whistling at her when she walked down the street. Hadn't been hit on at parties or get-togethers. But with Brock, seeing the desire in his eyes when he looked at her or when he kissed her, she felt beautiful for the first time in her life.

And seeing his face a short while later, after she'd changed into tight jeans and a blouse showcasing ample cleavage, and with her hair and makeup professionally done? Finley had wanted to cry at his expression of lust and longing.

Brock was as handsome as ever, of course, in his black jeans and a crisp white shirt, and Finley felt proud to be by his side.

He held her hand as Lilly exited the house on the arm of her father and walked toward the barn. The ceremony was taking place outside the large barn, where the reception would be held. The sun was low in the sky, and the purple and orange clouds were the perfect backdrop.

Lilly was wearing a white dress that came down past her knees. It was cut low in the front and back, and hugged her chest. It flared out at her waist and the material swished around her thighs as she walked. Her hair was in a fancy updo and her makeup accentuated her bright blue eyes. She was carrying a bouquet of daisies, and she absolutely looked like a fairy princess.

Apparently, Ethan didn't have the patience to wait for her to come to him. He strode across the lawn until he reached Lilly. He went to her other side, and both he and her father walked her through their guests to where the officiant stood waiting. There were no chairs, so everyone was simply standing around in intimate groups, watching.

Brock shifted until he was standing behind Finley, and he wrapped his arms around her waist. He put his chin on her shoulder as he watched his friend marry the woman he loved. Finley had a hard time paying attention to Lilly and Ethan's vows, as she was distracted by Brock's hand resting on her belly. Normally she didn't like when men touched her there. As a fat woman, it wasn't a pleasant thing to have someone draw any attention to her middle. But Brock had proven time and time again that he had absolutely no problem with her shape. And his thumb gently caressing her belly made her wonder if she really could be pregnant already. It wasn't an impossibility.

The ceremony was short and sweet, and before Finley knew it, Lilly and Ethan were kissing after being pronounced man and wife. Everyone cheered as they turned to face their guests and beamed.

As the guests celebrated, Brock turned his head and nibbled on Finley's ear.

"Brock, stop."

"Can't. You're so damn beautiful. I nearly came in my jeans when I saw you. I can't wait to take all those pins out of your hair and see it spread across my pillow as I eat you out."

"Seriously, Brock," Finley complained halfheartedly.

"I want to toast my friend. Dance with you. Eat your amazing cake. Show you off. But as soon as you're ready and want to leave, I'm all for it," he said, his voice a low growl in her ear. "I can't wait to get inside you, Fin. I've never been so damn insatiable with anyone before. I can't go even an hour without thinking about you. About how it feels to come inside you. How you look when you're riding my cock. But it's how you make me feel when I'm with you that really slays me. How you look at me as if the sun rises and sets with me. It feels so good, Fin. Really fucking good —and I'm gonna do everything in my power to get us there."

"Get us where?" Finley asked. She was basically a puddle of goo in his arms. The only thing holding her up was Brock himself. She wanted to tell him she felt the same way about him, but was afraid if she tried to talk further, she'd burst out crying.

"*There*," he said, motioning to where Lilly and Ethan were standing next to a table signing their wedding license with the officiant.

Her heart stopped. Literally stopped.

Craning her head, she looked back at him with wide eyes.

"I wouldn't tell you I wanted you to have my baby if I didn't want to marry you, Fin."

Holy shit. This was faster than fast. Like, lightning fast. Speed-of-light fast.

But she couldn't deny she was right there with him.

"I'm not popping the question right here and now. This is Ethan and Lilly's day. But I wanted to make sure you knew how serious I am about us. I've watched you for what feels like ages, Fin. And nothing I saw made me reluctant to start a relationship with you. Then, when you finally let me in? Fucking dream come true.

"I'm not an idiot. I'm thirty-eight years old and I know a good thing when I see it. I've spent my life watching others meet, marry, have kids, and then fuck up what they had. I vowed that wasn't going to be me. That I was going to wait until I met the one woman who could love me for who I am...fingers stained with grease, rough around the edges, and doesn't give a shit what others think about him."

"You aren't rough around the edges," she protested, turning in his embrace so she was facing him.

He chuckled. "I am. But I don't care."

"I'm serious about you too," Finley felt compelled to say. "I just didn't think I'd ever have a chance with you because you're...*you*," she said with a shrug, frustrated that she wasn't articulating her thoughts very well.

"You're the *only* one who had a chance. Now...shall we go and toast the new couple?" he asked.

She nodded, then wrinkled her nose. "Although I think only water for me."

Brock went so still, Finley was afraid something was wrong.

"Brock?"

"Water? You all right?"

The dang blush was back. She shrugged. "Yeah. I just... we've been...it's the right time in my cycle, and you know we haven't been using anything. Just in case, I don't want..."

"*Fuck*," Brock breathed, resting his forehead on Finley's. "Jesus, Fin. I want you. Right now. So goddamn bad. Want to fill you up again and again. Never wanted to get a woman pregnant, ever—until now."

Finley's nipples tightened under her shirt and she felt how much Brock wanted her as his erection was pressing against her belly. "I'm not saying I am, just that the possibility is there. And if there's a chance, I don't want to do anything that might hurt him or her."

"Of course not." He took a deep breath. Then another. "Give me a second," he whispered, his forehead still on hers.

Finley thought she was going to burst, she was so happy. "Okay," she whispered back.

A full minute passed. Then two. And Brock didn't move. He held her tightly against him as he did his best to regain control over his emotions and his libido.

"Stop makin' out and get over here!" Talon yelled, breaking the spell. "It's time for pictures and Lilly wants to get a pic of the team!"

"Guess that's our cue," Finley told Brock.

He straightened. "Cake. One dance. Then we're leaving."

Finley smiled. "Okay."

"Okay," he said with a nod. His nostrils flared as he took another deep breath. "Best thing that ever happened to me," he said under his breath as he turned, grabbed hold of her hand, and headed toward where Lilly and Ethan were having pictures taken.

Three hours later, after dinner, after Lilly and Ethan

had cut their cake, smooshed it into each other's faces, and everyone had devoured the confection and enthused over how good it was, and after a single dance, Brock was true to his word and told everyone they were heading home. That she had to be up early to open the bakery. Which wasn't a lie, but they both knew why he was in such a hurry to leave.

Finley said her goodbyes as they walked around the barn to get to Lilly and Ethan. Caryn winked at her, while Elsie hugged her and said "go make babies" in her ear.

Lilly thanked her profusely for all she'd done to help her and for the cake. Then she too gave her a long, heartfelt hug. Brock was shaking Ethan's hand and having a conversation with him and Rocky, so Lilly had the opportunity to say, "You look happy."

"I am. Your ceremony was beautiful."

"Thanks. I'm honestly glad it's over. When it's your turn, trust me...elope."

Finley could only smile shyly at her friend.

"I'm so thrilled for you both," Lilly said. "Brock's perfect for you."

"He is," Finley agreed.

"He also looks impatient to get the hell out of here," she joked.

"As does Ethan."

"He's tolerating all this for me," Lilly said with a shrug. "And I love him more for it. But I know he's anxious to get me to himself. I'm kind of jealous you and Brock can leave while I have to stay."

"Why? You're the bride, if you guys leave, no one's gonna say a word. Besides, Bristol and Rocky already said they'd take care of everything here."

"You know what, you're right," Lilly said as she looked over at her husband.

"I know."

Lilly hugged Finley again. This time when she pulled back, she said, "With the way Brock's staring at you, I have a feeling if you aren't already pregnant, you will be by morning."

Finley blushed and opened her mouth to respond when she felt a hand on her lower back.

"You ready?" Brock asked.

Finley had no idea if he'd heard what Lilly said, so she simply nodded.

"See you soon," Lilly said.

"Same. Congratulations again."

As soon as they exited the barn, Brock put his arm around her shoulders and pulled Finley into his side. "Gonna enjoy doing my best to make sure you're knocked up," he said into her ear as they walked.

Finley shivered. Guess he'd overheard Lilly after all.

"If you think I'm gonna complain, you're sadly mistaken," she offered a little sassily. The relief of the wedding being over, the fact that everyone seemed to love her cake, and the way Brock had been eye-fucking her all night gave Finley more confidence than she'd had in a long time.

As it turned out, Brock hadn't been able to wait until they arrived back at his house. He pulled onto a small dirt road not far from Bristol's property and had Finley's pants undone, her back against the passenger door and her legs spread, before she barely knew what was going on. He buried his face between her legs, and because she was so primed, it didn't take long for her to explode.

Smirking, and licking his lips happily, Brock put the truck into gear and headed back to the main road.

Not wanting him to have the upper hand, Finley leaned over and undid *his* jeans.

"Finn, no. I can't—"

But she didn't listen, simply pulling his rock-hard cock out of his pants and going down on him as he drove.

One hand rested on her head as she bobbed up and down, sucking and moaning and trying to give him as much pleasure as he'd given her. He managed to pull into his driveway safely and pulled a lever on the bench seat to shove it backward, giving her more room.

It felt naughty and dirty to be giving him a blow job in his truck in his driveway, but Finley was too far gone to worry about his neighbors seeing them. Apparently, he was in the same frame of mind, because he urged her to go faster, to suck harder.

Within minutes, he was exploding into her mouth, and Finley had never felt as feminine or as sexy as she did right then. She honestly didn't love the taste of semen, but the satisfied look in his eyes, and the way his cock didn't actually soften all the way, was worth it.

Stuffing his cock into his jeans, not bothering to fasten them, he yanked open his door and practically yanked Finley out behind him. She giggled as they rushed toward his front door. The second it closed, they raced to see who could get naked first.

Brock won, of course, since he had less to take off, but Finley still felt as if she was the winner as he picked her up and carried her down the hall. She couldn't remember the last time anyone had carried her like this. Probably because no one ever had. Brock made her feel feminine and dainty and sexy, and she'd already stopped thinking about the extra weight she carried when they were intimate.

He threw her on the bed and proceeded to show her without words, over and over, how important she was to him. How much he loved her body. How serious he was about getting her pregnant.

Finley had never been as happy as she was right that moment. Life was good...very good.

CHAPTER TEN

"I'll meet you there."

Brock frowned as he stood in a bay at Old Town Auto talking to Finley on the phone. It had been just five days since Lilly and Ethan's wedding, and they'd both been crazy busy. Once word got out that Finley had made Lilly's cake, The Sweet Tooth was suddenly slammed with requests for cakes, cupcakes, cookies, and anything else Finley was willing to make for birthday parties, anniversary celebrations...even more upcoming weddings. It seemed that everyone in Fallport wanted Finley to cater their event.

While Brock was thrilled for her, it meant she was working longer hours and they had less time to spend together. By the time she left the bakery in the evenings, she was exhausted. It had been two days since they'd made love, which wasn't what bothered Brock. He loved holding her while she slept. He wasn't with her because of the sex, even though that was out of this world; he genuinely enjoyed simply being near her.

But he didn't like her working herself into the ground. Davis had been stopping by after the bakery closed in the afternoons to help her prep for the next day and to assist in some of the catering orders, but it wasn't enough. Something had to give.

He'd talked to her that morning about not overdoing things. About taking some time for herself. For them. She hadn't hesitated to agree, much to Brock's relief. The last thing he wanted was for her to burn out. She hated to disappoint anyone but accepting every single job someone asked her to do wasn't going to be sustainable in the long run.

They'd planned to try the hiking thing again this afternoon. The weather in the first week of November was perfect for a walk. Cold, but not frigid. The real winter weather wouldn't kick in until December, most likely, and Brock wanted to enjoy the forest while he still could.

There were still just as many tourists coming to Fallport to try to find Bigfoot for themselves as there'd been right after the show aired. Which was great for local businesses, but it meant Brock and his friends were busier than usual as well. They continued to be called out for lost hikers, most thankfully being found within a few hours. Brock was looking forward to a leisurely hike with Finley. Nothing too strenuous, as he was well aware that she could be pregnant.

Her period was late, which she said wasn't actually too unusual, especially since she was more stressed than normal. He couldn't believe how much he *wanted* her to be pregnant. But she'd said she didn't want to jinx anything by taking a pregnancy test, that she wanted to wait. Brock didn't really understand that decision, but he'd decided he was going to treat her as if she was carrying his child already. She'd get pregnant sooner or later, so it wouldn't hurt to be careful now.

But at the moment, she was telling him that she was running late and it would be better if she met him at the Rock Creek Trail.

"It just makes sense," she was saying. "I need to go out in that direction and meet with a woman about what she wants for the cake I'm making for her parents' fiftieth wedding anniversary."

"Why can't she come to the bakery to meet with you like everyone else?" Brock asked.

"Because she doesn't get off work until three, which is when I close the shop. And then her son gets off the bus at three-thirty and she has to be there. It's not a big deal. I'll just go out there, talk to her about what she wants, then I can meet you at the trailhead."

Brock sighed. He would've volunteered to drive her to her appointment, but he was neck deep in the guts of a car someone had brought in and he didn't want to leave it like that. It was better to get as much done as possible. "All right. That'll work."

"Thank you," she said. "I know I've been super busy, but things are already slowing down."

"Because you've already made stuff for half the town," Brock grumbled. He wasn't sure why he was so grumpy.

"Not quite," Finley said with a laugh. "But I think the novelty will wear off quickly. I'm thankful for the business, but I'm not sure being *that* busy is something I really aspire to. And it's not anything I can sustain, as you pointed out this morning. I'd rather make less money and have more free time than be slammed every day and make bank."

Brock was perfectly all right with that line of thinking. Anything Finley wanted, he'd be more than able to provide. Though he also knew how important it was for her to have her own money, to be successful.

"So, what time do you think you can be there? Remember, it's getting dark earlier and earlier."

"Three forty-five? That should be enough time, I think."

Thirty minutes past the original time he'd planned to pick her up. Brock would have to live with that. "Okay."

"I'll let you know if I'm running late," she said.

"The cell service is spotty out that way," he warned.

"Right. I'll text before I leave my client's house then."

"Sounds good. Be safe," Brock said.

"I will. You too."

"See you later."

"Bye."

Brock hung up and turned back to the vehicle he'd been working on before Finley had called. They wouldn't be able to hike as long as he'd hoped, but the fresh air would be nice regardless. Especially since he wouldn't be on the job. He truly loved being out in the woods, but it was hard to appreciate it when he was looking for a lost person.

"Hey, Brock, can you come look at this real quick?" Jesus asked from under the hood of the car in the next bay.

Doing his best to put his worry for Finley out of his mind so he could get some work done, Brock headed for his friend.

* * *

Adrenaline coursed through Pete's veins. Finally! It was totally unnatural that the bitch was never alone. He'd been following her for a week straight and she was *never* by herself. It was infuriating and frustrating. And The Boss was getting more and more pissed. The supplier refused to come to Fallport until he knew the baker wasn't an issue, so The Boss had to keep driving to Roanoke. Certain people were beginning to question all the trips to the city, and The Boss was fucking livid.

But *finally*, the baker was alone. She'd driven out to some house and met with a woman, and was now on her way back to town.

"Ram her," Cory insisted as they followed her down the two-lane road that led back to Fallport.

"I'm gonna. Shut up already!" Pete bitched. "I need to find the best place to do it. Somewhere she can pull off and we won't be seen while we find out what she knows." The shoulders on both sides of the road were deep, and he had to hit her hard enough so she'd stop, but not so hard that she'd lose control of her vehicle. The last thing they needed was the cops showing up because of a big accident.

Just when Pete was about to make his move, her brake lights came on and she slowed down.

"What's she doing?" Cory asked.

"How the fuck do I know?" Pete retorted.

"Fuck, she's pulling into that trailhead parking lot," Cory said. "Go in after her."

"What? No! There are always a ton of people around there."

"Look, we don't have a choice. The Boss expects us to

get answers and she's by herself. We have to do it *now*."

"Fuck," Pete muttered but obediently pulled into the parking lot.

"Is she meeting someone?" Cory asked.

Looking around, Pete didn't see anyone who seemed to be waiting for her. "It doesn't look like it."

"Good. We'll follow her into the woods a bit, then grab her. Take her off the trail so if anyone comes by, they don't see us." Cory smirked. "We might have to convince her to talk, if you know what I mean." He grabbed his crotch with a grin.

Pete nodded. "Yeah, man. We deserve that shit. She's led us on a chase for too goddamn long."

"Although she's pretty fuckin' fat. Not sure I can get it up," Cory muttered as he turned to open his door.

"Pussy is pussy," Pete said with a shrug. "Besides, that guy she's with doesn't seem to mind."

"Must have a magic pussy," Cory agreed. "Come on, I'm actually kind of excited about this now. We'll get off, make sure the bitch knows if she tells anyone about what happened, she'll fucking regret it, find out what she saw in that alley, then get the hell out of here. The Boss'll be happy, we'll be happy once we're paid, and things will go back to normal."

Pete held up a hand, and Cory high-fived him as they tried to look nonchalant while following the bakery bitch toward the trail.

* * *

Brock had gotten to the trailhead a bit early, only to find a woman in the parking lot looking extremely stressed. Not able to ignore her, he asked what was wrong. She told him that she'd gone hiking with her parents, and her mom had sprained her ankle on the trail. Her dad was helping her back to the trailhead, but she'd hoped to call for an ambulance to meet them. She couldn't get her cell phone to work.

Brock had informed her that it wasn't unusual, and he offered to head up the trail to meet the couple. The woman had been thankful, and he'd set off. The couple was supposed to be less than half a mile from the parking area, and thankfully, Brock ran into them relatively quickly. Finley wouldn't mind him helping someone, of course, but this was supposed to be their time to decompress.

He was pleasantly surprised to see that the woman was actually moving quite well. She was limping a little, but she said that after a while, her ankle had actually felt a bit better.

Brock walked with them and learned they were from South Carolina and, like everyone else, had come to Fallport because of the paranormal show, but not to search for Bigfoot. They just thought the town had seemed so charming.

As he neared the parking area, Brock saw Finley walking down the trail toward them. He smiled widely at her.

"That your young lady?" the older man asked.

"Sure is," Brock said.

"She's pretty. Take care of her."

"She is. And I plan to. Doc Snow should still be in his office when you get back to town. He'll take a look at that ankle and make sure nothing's terribly wrong."

"Thank you for coming to help us," the woman said.

"Of course."

Brock said goodbye to the couple and waited for Finley to catch up to him on the trail. He took the time to soak in the sight of her. She'd changed since he'd seen her that morning. She had on a pair of hiking boots, long cargo pants, and a long-sleeve T-shirt. She also had a sweatshirt tied around her waist. He approved wholeheartedly. Wearing layers was important this time of year because while it wasn't terribly chilly at the moment, when the sun went down, it would get colder. And while he didn't plan on them being out that late, being prepared in the woods was imperative.

He had a backpack with water, snacks, and a small first aid kit. He didn't expect anything to happen, but with his and Finley's history with "dates," he wasn't taking any chances.

"Hey," she said as she approached.

"Hi," he returned warmly. When she got close enough, he reached out and wrapped an arm around her waist and pulled her into him. He inhaled deeply. "Nutmeg," he said as he buried his nose in the space between her neck and shoulder.

She giggled. "You're good at that."

"You always smell good enough to eat," he said with a leer.

Finley rolled her eyes and shook her head at him. "You're bad."

"You love it."

"I do," she said in a serious tone.

Brock's heart began to beat faster. They hadn't said the words, but he felt her love every time he was around her, just as he hoped she felt his. He immediately wanted to steer her back down to the parking lot and take her home, but they both needed this break in their routine. A nice easy walk would do them good.

Then he could bring her home and take her to bed.

He turned and headed back the way he'd come a moment earlier with the couple. They made small talk as he told Finley about the woman's ankle and how he was pretty sure it was just a light sprain.

He'd just opened his mouth to ask her how the meeting with the potential customer went when Finley let out a surprised *oof*.

Acting instinctively, Brock moved to catch her, assuming she'd tripped over a tree root or something—but she hadn't lost her footing.

Someone had grabbed her from behind, and she'd made the noise when she'd stumbled backward, landing against the man.

Brock's eyes widened when he saw two men, probably in their early twenties and looking very nervous, standing in the middle of the trail. The one with black hair had an arm around Finley's chest, holding her against him...and the other hand held a sharp-looking knife against her throat.

Brock froze.

"Don't fucking move," the guy with the knife barked.

Brock had no intention of moving. He could've taken both these punks down, easily. But the tip of that knife was way too close to Finley's jugular. His mind immediately spun with different scenarios on how to get her away from that asshole without her being hurt in the process.

"What do you want?" Brock growled, his hands clenching into fists.

Instead of answering, the guy holding Finley said, "Empty their pockets. Take his backpack."

They weren't too far from the trailhead, but of course when Brock was desperate to spot one of the tourists who always seemed to be around, they were nowhere to be found.

"You heard him, give me your phone, wallet, and take off that backpack," the brown-haired asshole growled.

When Brock hesitated, the black-haired man tightened his hold around Finley, and Brock saw a drop of blood slowly began to roll down her neck. She didn't scream. Didn't cry out. She simply kept her gaze on Brock.

He saw trust there. Complete confidence that he would get them out of this.

Not giving a shit if these guys robbed him—nothing was more important than Finley—Brock did as he was ordered. He shrugged out of his pack and dropped it on the dirt at his feet. He threw his wallet down on top and pulled the satellite phone out of a pocket along his thigh.

"Shit, man, that thing looks like it came from the nineties," the brown-haired man said with a laugh.

"Right? I think my old man had one of those car phones back in the day," the other guy scoffed.

What a couple of idiots. They obviously had no idea the satellite phone was the only way to communicate in this part of the woods.

"Now hers," black-haired guy said.

It took everything within Brock not to fucking kill the asshole who took great delight in sticking his hand into Finley's pockets. He was sure he copped a feel while he was there, but again, Finley didn't protest, didn't do anything but stand completely still as he took out her cell phone.

"Right. Now let's go," the man holding Finley said.

"You've got our shit, let her go," Brock ordered, furious when the man turned Finley and started walking with her in front of him...off the trail.

"We ain't done with her yet."

The words sent ice shooting through Brock's veins. No way in hell was he going to stand by while these assholes raped his woman. Thoughts of her sparkling eyes that morning when she'd teased him in the shower sprang to his mind. The noises she made when he went down on her. How hard she gripped his biceps when she came.

No, these two weren't going to fucking touch his woman. Weren't going to do a damn thing to change how uninhibited she was, in bed and out.

"If you do anything, I'll shove this knife into her fucking throat," the man told Brock, obviously sensing his rising anger.

"Don't hurt her," Brock said between clenched teeth.

"I won't...as long as you both do exactly as I say."

"Someone's coming," the brown-haired guy warned.

"Go," Black Hair said, gesturing in front of him. "Don't want you behind me. Start walking. I'll tell you when to stop."

Frustrated beyond belief, but deciding for the moment he was better off doing as ordered, Brock stepped off the trail and began bushwhacking in the direction the guy indicated. He bent tree branches out of his way and shuffled his feet, leaving clues for his team. He had no idea what these two fuckers had planned, but eventually someone would come looking for him and Finley, and he was leaving a trail a five-year-old could follow.

"It's getting dark," Brown Hair Guy said. "The clouds have moved in. It's probably gonna rain."

"I know, shut the fuck up, Cory."

Cory. Brock noted the name.

"We need to just question her and get the hell out of here," Cory insisted, his voice almost a whine.

Brock had thought this was a typical robbery, but it was clear the two men had a different agenda. He racked his brain, trying to figure out what the hell was going on, what they could possibly want to question Finley about.

"Please, I don't know what you—"

"Shut up, bitch!" the guy holding her seethed.

Brock turned to see him punctuate his words with the press of the fucking blade against Finley's throat, and he was nearly blinded with fury. It took every bit of discipline he'd learned as a customs officer to not jump the man right that second.

"I don't want to hear you fucking whining. When I want you to talk, you'll know it. Understand?"

Brock could barely hear her whispered, "Yes," but apparently it was enough for the man holding her hostage.

"Good. Now keep walking."

Brock did as he ordered, his frustration rising with every step.

"Pete, it's really getting dark. We've been walking forever, man. I think this is good."

The guy holding Finley, the man obviously in charge, was Pete.

Brock's lips pressed together. They were going down. He'd fucking kill them both if he had to, and have no remorse doing so. But at the moment, he couldn't do a damn thing with that knife at Finley's throat, and Pete knew it.

Since they weren't on a trail, walking was rough going on the uneven, debris-filled ground, and the asshole wasn't even trying not to hurt her. There were a few nicks and shallow cuts on Finley's neck now, the small trickles of blood looking obscene against her white skin. The Pete guy never moved the blade off of her neck. He clearly wasn't an idiot, well aware that if he gave Brock even a small opening, he was a dead man.

"God, you're such a fucking pussy," Pete seethed in response to Cory's complaint. "Fine. Stop walking, asshole, and go over there to that tree," he ordered Brock, motioning to a large tree about twenty meters away.

"No," Brock said, not willing to be that far away from Finley.

"No?" Pete echoed, pressing the blade harder against her neck. She went up on her tiptoes to try to get away from the pressure of the knife, but it was no use. Her back was plastered against Pete's and his arm was a tight band around her chest, holding her secure.

Brock held up his hands in capitulation. He'd never felt so helpless in his life. "Fine! I'm going. *Stop* fucking hurting her!"

"I'll do whatever the hell I want to do with her," Pete growled.

Brock slowly backed toward the tree, each step making him more and more nauseous. He was too far away. If Pete decided to actually use that knife, there wasn't a damn thing Brock could do to stop it.

Cory laughed. "*He's* the fucking pussy," he taunted

Brock. "Goddamn grease monkey, good for nothing but tinkering with cars. Pathetic."

Brock didn't give a shit what these men thought about him. He'd much rather their attention be on him than Finley.

"Keep your eye on him," Pete warned his friend.

Brock noticed for the first time that Cory also held a knife, but he wasn't scared of the weapon or the man. He could easily wrestle the thing out of his grip, or even slam a hand down on his wrist, making him drop it, hopefully breaking a bone or two. But while he was busy doing that, Pete would have a chance to hurt Finley.

His body practically vibrated with impatience as he stood there, waiting for an opening. A distraction. All he needed was a split-second diversion, and he'd be able to cross the space between him and Finley and get her away from that fucking blade.

"Now," Pete said with a note of anticipation in his tone. "*You*, bitch. You're going to tell us what we want to know or you'll fuckin' regret it. I'll start with taking a pinky finger. Then maybe your thumb. Then I'll carve up your face an inch at a time."

"What do you w-want?" she asked. Brock could tell she was trying to sound brave, but the small stutter let him know she wasn't as calm as she was desperately trying to be.

"*Fuck*, she's fat," Cory said from where he was standing not far from Brock. "We could fuck the answers out of her like we talked about, but who wants to see that body naked? Gross."

Brock saw red. He actually took a step toward Cory, but Pete's words stopped him.

"Don't be a hero," he warned.

Brock froze once more, glaring at the man threatening his woman.

"Good boy," he mocked, turning back to Finley. He dropped his arm from around her chest and turned her, grabbing for her left hand as he did. He held the knife at the base of her pinky and said, "You ready to talk?"

Brock sized up the situation. The knife wasn't at Finley's throat anymore, which gave him more options. He had no doubt Pete would do as he threatened and cut off her pinky, but losing a finger was better than having the blade sink into her jugular vein. The thought made him want to puke, but he took a deep breath as he prepared to move.

"What do you want to know?" she asked, lifting her chin bravely.

Brock was so fucking proud of her, despite being pissed they were in this situation in the first place.

"I need to know *exactly* what you saw when—"

Movement out of the corner of his eye caught Brock's attention.

To his utter astonishment, a woman ran out of the trees toward Pete and Finley.

She was dressed in what looked like a knee-length brown dress that blended into their surroundings perfectly. It was torn in places, and absolutely filthy. She was barefoot, and her auburn hair was long, down to her butt. It flowed slightly behind her as she ran.

He couldn't tell how old she was in the split second before Brock himself was moving.

The mystery woman ran past Pete, quiet and quick on her feet. As she did, she threw a handful of what Brock assumed was dirt right into his face. Since he'd been talking, the dirt went straight into his mouth and eyes, and he immediately dropped Finley's hand, frantically brushing at his face as he sputtered and choked.

It was exactly the opening Brock needed.

Crossing the space between them in seconds, he grabbed Finley around the waist and spun her away from Pete and that damn knife. He desperately wanted to pound the man into the ground and find out exactly what the hell was going on, but it was more important to get Finley to safety.

"Run!" he ordered, pushing her toward the trees. But he needn't have bothered. She was already moving.

"Fuck!" Brock heard Cory shout. "Come back here!"

He had no intention of going back.

Pete was still coughing and swearing. The woman who'd thrown the dirt had excellent aim. She'd never stopped moving either. The last Brock saw of her, she was disappearing back into the trees as if she hadn't been there at all.

Brock cursed the lack of leaves on the trees around them, but was thankful for the clouds that had moved in, accelerating the darkness that was descending on the area. This late in the year, the second the sun sank below the horizon, it got dark in a hurry, especially in the forest.

He could hear Finley breathing hard, but she didn't stop running. Brock listened as they ran, and he couldn't hear their kidnappers following, but he wasn't going to take any chances. He couldn't get the sight of that damn blade against her throat out of his mind.

Giving directions to Finley as they ran was difficult, it would be easier if he took the lead, but he wasn't going to leave her vulnerable to either Pete or Cory rushing up behind them and taking her out.

He had no idea how long or far they'd run when he realized Finley was slowing. Her breaths were loud in the silence of the evening, and Brock knew she needed to take a break.

They'd just run down an incline, and there was a small stream directly in front of them. The sound of the water moving over the rocks would mask their voices and harsh breathing. He hadn't been more than two feet from her the entire time, and now Brock reached out and took hold of her arm. "Stop, Fin."

She did immediately, and something shifted inside Brock. She'd followed his every command as they'd run, trusting him to know where to go and how to get away from Pete and Cory. She hadn't questioned him once. Hadn't done anything during the entire incident that would put her, them, in more danger. He was so damn proud of her.

He spun her around and wrapped her in his arms. She not only went willingly, she practically threw herself at him, latching on as if she was never going to let go again.

Looking around, it was hard to see more than the shapes of the trees now. Brock tilted his head and heard nothing but the water running and Finley's pants against his chest.

Satisfied for the moment that they could safely take a break, Brock walked them to his left, toward a large boulder that looked dark in the waning light. He crouched behind it, on the side facing the creek, so if anyone did come down the hill they'd just traversed, they wouldn't immediately see them. Then he shifted to his ass and

Finley adjusted herself so she was sitting on his lap, her knees straddling his hips.

Finley didn't say a word, just clung to him tightly as she attempted to catch her breath. So much adrenaline was coursing through Brock's veins that he was literally shaking.

"You're okay. You're good. I'm so proud of you. Fuck, Finley, you did so good." He kept murmuring to her as he buried his nose into her hair and held her tightly.

It was several moments before her breathing and heartbeat finally slowed. Then she began to shake. Almost violently. Brock's arms tightened around her, and he closed his eyes as emotions threatened to overwhelm him. Anger. Fear. Confusion. Relief.

"I've got you. You're safe," he told her.

Finley nodded against his neck, and he felt her take a deep breath. Then another. Then she slowly pulled away from him and said softly, "I'm okay."

"Fuck," Brock said, closing his eyes. "Fuck, fuck, *fuck*." Having Finley safe in his arms was almost overwhelming.

He felt her hands on either side of his head right before her lips landed on his. It wasn't a passionate kiss, this wasn't the time or place for that, but feeling her warmth, knowing she was doing her best to comfort him despite what she'd just gone through, went a long way toward Brock pulling his head out of his ass.

It was almost too dark to see much of anything by now, but he could still see the lines of blood on her neck. He lifted a hand and brushed his fingers over her skin with a feather-light touch. "Does it hurt?"

"No."

Brock wasn't sure if she was lying or not, but the fact

that she was downplaying her injuries made him both proud and furious at the same time.

"Who was that woman?" she asked after a moment.

Brock frowned. "I have no clue. Come on, we need to find a place to hunker down."

"Hunker down?" she asked.

"Yeah."

"We aren't going to go back to the trailhead?"

"No. I have no idea where those guys might be. The last thing I want is to run into them again. And I'm not going to risk your health, or mine, by walking around in the dark either."

"Okay."

"Okay?" he questioned.

"Uh-huh."

"You aren't going to complain about spending the night in the dark? In the cold? In the woods?" he couldn't help but ask.

"Brock, I'm not gonna lie, when that guy grabbed me, it scared the shit out of me. But knowing you were there, and you were going to get us out of whatever was happening, made everything not quite as frightening. If I was by myself? I would've been a mess. If I was out here in the woods alone? I'd be freaking out. But I'm *not* alone. You're here, and you're the most competent person I know when it comes to the forest. Am I thrilled? No. But lucky for you, I've got lots of natural insulation."

Brock knew she was trying to lighten the mood, but he didn't like it. "Don't joke about that, Finley. I mean it."

"I'm sorry. All I'm trying to say is that I'm scared, I'm gonna be sore as hell tomorrow because running isn't my jam at all. But you're here, and I know you aren't going to let anything happen to me. I'd rather be here in the middle of the woods, on the run from two men I've never met, than anywhere else by myself. So no, I'm not going to complain about spending the night in the dark, in the cold, here in the woods, because I'm with you."

"I love you," Brock blurted.

He felt Finley gasp. Then he heard a quiet sob.

"Don't cry," he ordered.

"I'm s-sorry. I just...I love you so much, and I don't understand what happened or why, but I'm just so relieved you're with me."

Brock palmed the back of her head and drew her back down so she was resting against his chest once more. He closed his eyes as he attempted to relax his muscles.

"I'm thinking this dating thing *really* isn't for us," she said after a minute.

Brock frowned. They'd just said they loved each other, and now she was saying she didn't want to date him? Then it hit him what she meant, and he snorted. "Told you."

"You were right."

Brock grinned. Fuck. How could he be smiling at a time like this? But he knew. It was because of the woman in his arms.

They sat there for several minutes before Brock stirred. "We need to move, sweetheart. I need to find us a place to lay low."

"Do you know where we are?" she asked.

"I have a general idea, but until tomorrow when I can see clearly, I won't know for sure. But it doesn't matter."

"Why not?"

"Because the second you don't show up at your shop tomorrow morning, Davis is gonna raise the alarm. Simon will call Ethan, who will rouse the others. They'll find our cars at the trailhead, and will quickly see the signs of where we went off the established trail. We'll be back home in a warm shower by ten at the latest."

"What if Davis doesn't come tomorrow?" she asked.

Brock shrugged. "Then when Liam shows up and the shop's empty and still locked, *he'll* call Simon. And before you ask, I can definitely find my way back to the trail and our cars on my own, but it's safer to just stay put and let the team come to us."

"Because those guys might still be out there?" she asked quietly.

"Yes."

"I don't know what they wanted me to tell them."

"Shhh, let's find a place to sleep, then we can talk," Brock said. "Can you stand?"

"Of course," she said a little huffily, and Brock was never so glad that his Finley was as strong as she was. He thought back to just weeks ago, when she couldn't even meet his eyes when he came into her shop. The difference between that woman and the one in his lap right now was almost shocking. But then again, maybe it wasn't. She'd simply gotten comfortable with him—finally—and gained more confidence the longer they were together.

Brock held onto her hand as she scooted backward and stood. When she swayed, he was right there with an arm around her waist. "Fin?"

"I'm okay," she insisted. "My legs are just a little Jell-O-y after all that running. Fat girls don't run, you know."

He didn't hear any self-deprecation in her tone, so he let that one go. "You did great, Fin. Seriously." He untied the sweatshirt from around her waist, extremely grateful it hadn't fallen off, and held it out to her. Once she'd pulled it over her head, he said, "Come on, follow me and watch where you step. Don't let go of my hand either."

"Wasn't planning on it," she mumbled.

The second they were up and moving, a light rain began to fall. It was cold, and being wet in the woods in November, without shelter, wasn't a good combination. But again, Finley didn't complain, she simply gripped his hand tighter and followed him without a word.

They'd walked along the small stream for about half a mile when Brock found what he suspected would be there. He'd told Finley he wasn't positive where they were, but even in the dark, he'd had a good idea. And he was right. "We're here," he said quietly. He was fairly sure they were the only two people in this part of the forest, but he wasn't going to take a chance that he was wrong and Pete and Cory were lurking around trying to find them.

"Where's here?" she asked tiredly.

"There's a massive flat rock to our left. The top juts out just far enough from the base for us to crawl under it and get out of the rain."

"A cave?" she asked.

"Not exactly. But it'll get us out of the elements, and I guarantee no one will see us in there if they happen to stumble by."

"Okay."

Brock led them over to what he and his team had dubbed Umbrella Rock and gestured for Finley to crawl under the low overhang.

She did so without a word of complaint.

He hated that they were both wet, but taking their

clothes off wouldn't actually help them stay warm right now.

Brock followed her under the overhang, reclined on his side with his back to the opening, and pulled Finley's back against his front. He was between her and the world, and he couldn't imagine ever being anywhere else.

"You're so warm," she said softly as she snuggled against him.

Brock took one of her hands in his as he held her close. As usual, her fingers were much colder than the rest of her. He pushed his other arm under her head so she was using him as a pillow. There wasn't an inch of space between them now, and he prayed the warmth of his body would keep her from being too cold throughout the night.

After a couple minutes, he felt her sigh against him. "I have so many questions about what happened."

Brock resisted the urge to snort. He had just as many. "I need you to think, Finley. What would those guys have wanted you to tell them? Has anything odd happened lately? Anyone come into the bakery who gave you or Liam bad vibes? Did you see something that maybe you shouldn't have?"

At his last question, he felt her stiffen against him. Bingo.

"What? What did you see?"

"I didn't think anything about it the first time. Khloe asked me to feed the stray kittens while she was gone. I went over every morning before I opened the bakery."

Brock growled. He knew about her feeding the kittens, but he'd hated that she was in the back parking lot of the library so early, in the dark, even for just a few days. Once she'd started spending the night with him, he'd gone with her to feed the kittens until Khloe returned.

Finley turned her head and, even though it was dark, Brock could practically feel the daggers she was shooting his way. "I'm a grown woman, Brock. And this is Fallport. So yes, at four in the morning, I went over to feed those kittens by myself before you started accompanying me."

"I just...fuck, Fin. I just worry about you."

She heaved out a sigh and settled back against him. Brock rested his chin on top of her head.

"I know, and I appreciate it. It wasn't a big deal. Anyway, I was sitting by the dumpster and playing with the kittens after they ate and a black pickup truck pulled up behind The Cellar. I wasn't alarmed or anything, and I knew they couldn't see me sitting on the ground, since it was so dark. Someone came around the corner of the building and leaned into the passenger-side window. They spoke for a moment, then the guy took a backpack and walked away. I honestly didn't think too much about it. But then when I was there with the kittens a few days later, the same truck came back. Seeing it once didn't register, but twice? It was weird."

"And you didn't tell me about it?"

"Brock, we weren't *together*-together then, and honestly, even though it was weird, it wasn't as if there was a shootout or huge bundles of cocaine being exchanged. The whole thing happened really fast. But..."

"But?" Brock asked when she paused.

"I felt weird enough about it that I did write down the license plate."

Brock sighed against her. "Good girl. What'd you do with it?"

"Well, I still wasn't convinced I was seeing monsters when there weren't any. I wrote it down when I got back to the shop and put it in my recipe box."

"We'll take it to Simon as soon as we get back to town tomorrow," Brock said firmly.

"Do you really think that's what this was all about?" she asked.

"Can you think of anything else odd or weird that those two men might want to question you about?" he asked.

He liked that she didn't immediately say no. That she took the time to really think about his question. Then she shook her head. "No."

"Then yes, I'm guessing that was it. Probably a drug deal going down and whoever was in that truck wants to know what you saw or who you told about it. You saw the two people exchange something?"

"Yeah. But like I said, it was just a backpack. Not a huge crate with the word DRUGS stamped on the side. Do you really think that Pete guy would've cut off my fingers if I didn't tell him what he wanted to know?"

Brock shuddered. "Yes."

Finley whimpered, and Brock regretted being so blunt. "But you're safe now," he reassured her.

"Which brings us back to that woman. Who *was* she, Brock? I mean, she showed up in the middle of nowhere, looking like she'd been raised in the woods, threw that dirt at Pete and disappeared!"

"Bigfoot's woman?" Brock joked.

"I'm serious," Finley protested.

"Sorry. I know you are. And I have no idea who she was. But I'm thankful as hell she was there. I couldn't do anything while that prick had a knife against your throat."

"You could've taken him," Finley said firmly.

"You're right. But again, I wasn't going to do a damn thing that would risk you being hurt or killed. You're everything to me, Finley. I don't give a damn how fast it's been, I know how I feel," he said almost defensively.

Her hand gripped his as she turned her head toward him once more. "I know. It's so crazy, but I feel as if I've waited my whole life for you. You don't see me like everyone else does."

"Because they're idiots. And their loss is my gain."

She sighed in contentment against him. Then shivered.

"Damn, you're cold," Brock said, tightening his arms around her.

"I'm okay," she told him immediately.

He snorted.

"Okay, I'm a little chilly, but overall I'm thankful to be alive, to have all my digits, and for that random forest woman who saved us. We have to find her," she said softly.

"Won't be easy if she doesn't want to be found," Brock said. "It looked as if she's spent quite a bit of time in the woods."

"She didn't have any shoes on, Brock," Finley said. "And it's cold. She needs our help."

"Maybe she doesn't," Brock mused.

"She does," Finley insisted. "I don't know what happened to her or why she's living in the woods, but it can't be good. She's obviously been out here a while. She's probably scared. But she still did what she could to help me. *Us.*"

"You're right. I'll see what I can do."

"Thank you."

"You don't have to thank me for that. I want to make sure she's okay too," Brock said.

After a few minutes had passed, Brock thought Finley might've fallen asleep, but then she whispered, "Do you think those guys are gone? That they aren't looking for us?"

"I do. They were amateurs. Had no idea what they were doing in the woods. I'm guessing they realized their best course of action was to retreat."

"But they didn't get the answers they wanted."

Brock pressed his lips together. "I know."

"If I go to Simon and tell him what I saw and give him that license plate number, what I saw won't be a secret anymore. So I shouldn't be in any more danger...right?"

"Honestly? I don't know," Brock said. Her reasoning was sound. There should no longer be a reason for anyone to come after her to find out what she knows after she talked to Simon. Those guys would have bigger problems to deal with than Finley. But that didn't mean someone wouldn't be pissed and want revenge. If she *had* seen a drug deal in action, and the info she told the police disrupted the flow of drugs coming into Fallport, someone wouldn't be happy.

"You'll keep me safe," she said without a shred of doubt.

Her trust in his abilities made Brock feel good, but it didn't make the worry for her go away. "I will," he said firmly.

* * *

"Shit. Damn! *Fuck!*" Pete bitched as they made their way back to the trailhead.

"Do you know where we are?" Cory asked.

"We're in the fucking forest," he said sarcastically.

"I can't see a damn thing," Cory bitched.

"At least you didn't get dirt thrown in your fucking eyes," Pete countered as he almost tripped over a tree root.

"Who the fuck was that, anyway? And where she'd come from?"

"No clue."

"It was like she disappeared in a puff of smoke," Cory went on. "One second she's there, and the next she's gone. Maybe it was a ghost."

"It wasn't a fucking ghost," Pete said in disgust. "Ghosts can't throw dirt."

"How do you know?"

This was the most ridiculous conversation Pete had ever had, and he was fucking done with it. He pulled out his cell phone, knowing The Boss wasn't going to be happy with what happened, but also knowing that if he didn't call, he'd regret it later.

"Damn it," he swore when he didn't get a signal after he clicked it on.

"What?"

"Damn phone doesn't work," Pete said.

Cory pulled his own phone out and shrugged. "I don't have any bars either."

"Give me that asshole's backpack," Pete ordered.

Cory stopped and shrugged it off and handed it over. Pete put it on the ground and fumbled with the zipper before pulling out the comparatively huge cell phone the asshole had on him. "Maybe one of theirs will work," he said as he clicked the monstrosity on.

When he heard a tone in his ear, he sighed. At least something was going right. He quickly dialed The Boss's number and waited.

"You get the info?" The Boss asked as a greeting.

"There were complications," Pete started.

He winced as The Boss let out a long litany of swear words. "What the fuck happened *now*?"

Pete explained how they'd finally gotten the bitch alone and had followed her into the woods. But then she'd met up with the fucking mechanic, and Pete had been pissed enough to grab her anyway. He explained that he was on the verge of getting the info he wanted when some crazy jungle bitch helped them get away.

"Did you go after her?" The Boss demanded.

"We tried, but I had dirt in my eyes and it was dark," he complained.

"Fucking worthless," The Boss seethed.

"We'll get her next time," Pete said.

"No, you won't. You're done. I don't ever want to see or hear from you again. And if I get wind of you blabbing to anyone about what happened, you'll fucking regret it. My suggestion is that you and your buddy get the fuck out of town and never come back," The Boss said.

"But what about our payment? Our pills?"

"You're not getting a damn dime, and no one's gonna sell shit to you in this town again. Get the hell gone, asshole. You're done."

Pete scowled. He wanted to argue, but deep down, he knew he'd fucked up. And The Boss had already given him plenty of chances to get the job done. The smartest thing he could do was exactly as ordered. Leave town. The alternative was ending up like the other dealers who'd disappeared.

Being kicked out of Fallport was actually the best outcome he could hope for. And leaving wouldn't exactly be a hardship. He hated this fucking place. He'd go somewhere he could get lost in the crowds, where he could score drugs without worrying about some asshole breathing down his back. "Fine."

"Where are you right now?" The Boss asked.

"In the middle of the fucking woods," Pete grumbled.

"How are you calling me?"

"The mechanic had a fucking ancient cell phone on him. It's as big as my head. But the damn thing works when both mine and Cory's didn't."

"Jesus, you're such a fucking idiot. That mechanic is on the Eagle Point Search and Rescue team. That's a satellite phone. And now you've compromised me. You don't think the cops won't check the phone records when they find out you took it from him, you fucking imbecile?"

Pete hated being talked down to, but he wasn't willing to piss off The Boss any more than he already had. "I'll get rid of it."

"Yes, you will, but that's not gonna change the fact that now I've got to cover my damn tracks and get rid of this burner I've been using, *and* the others I bought at the same time. If I ever see or hear from you again, you're a goddamn dead man."

"Sorry," Pete said. "You won't. I'm out of here."

The phone went dead in his ear, and he sighed, feeling as if he'd narrowly escaped his own death by the skin of his teeth. "We have to get the fuck out of here," he said.

"I know, we're trying to find the trail," Cory bitched.

"No, out of Fallport. Out of Virginia."

"Man, I need a hit," Cory whined.

"Give me that," Pete growled, sick of Cory's shit. He couldn't wait to get away from him. Away from *everything*. He grabbed the backpack out of his accomplice's hand and stuffed the satellite phone inside. Then he looked around, squinting in the dark, and walked over to a small tree. He got down on his knees and grabbed a nearby stick. "Don't just stand there, come help me dig a hole. We gotta ditch this shit. *Now*."

Cory obviously heard the urgency in Pete's tone, and he didn't complain as he got to his knees and helped dig.

Ten minutes later, a light rain started to fall. The backpack and all the stuff they'd taken from the bitch and the mechanic was now buried a foot under the ground. No one would find that shit, especially since it took them another fifteen minutes to finally find the trail.

Pete half expected the mechanic dude to jump out from behind a tree at any moment, but they made it back to the parking area, and Pete climbed behind the wheel of his car. He and Cory didn't speak as they drove back to Fallport. When he pulled in front of Cory's shithole apartment, Pete said, "Get out."

Cory did, and without a word, Pete drove off. He had to make a quick stop at his own place, grab what he could, and then he was gone.

He thought about the fat bitch when the light rain changed to a steady downpour. "I hope you're fucking miserable and you die of hyperthermia," he muttered under his breath.

CHAPTER ELEVEN

Finley woke up at some point in the middle of the night. She was chilly, but not freezing. She listened to the hard rain outside their little hiding spot and was doubly grateful for Brock. She'd turned at some point and was now lying with her nose pressed against his chest. The cuts on her neck stung, and the muscles in her legs hurt like a son-of-a-bitch. But she was alive. And safe. Nothing else mattered.

The next time she woke up, the sun was beginning its ascent into the sky. She figured it was around seven or so in the morning. She shifted against Brock, and his arms tightened.

"Are you awake?" she whispered.

"Yes. Have been for hours," he told her.

Lifting her head, she saw dark circles under Brock's eyes. "Are you all right?" she asked.

"No."

That was it. One word. "What's wrong?"

"I just can't stop thinking about what could've

happened. How all I could do was stand there and watch as that asshole held a knife to your neck."

"I'm fine," she said firmly. "And you did exactly what you should've done."

"How can you not blame me for not acting sooner?"

"Because I was the one with the knife at my throat. If you'd done anything, he would've used it. Brock, I knew we had to bide our time. Assess the situation. And I was also sure that as soon as you could, you'd get me away from him."

"Why are you so trusting?" Brock asked.

Finley put a hand on his cheek and said clearly, "Because I love you."

His eyes closed as he inhaled deeply through his nose.

"And you were about to do something when the mystery woman ran by, weren't you?"

"How'd you know?"

"Because when Pete turned me around, I saw you move. It was subtle, but the second that knife wasn't against my throat, you were about to act."

"He could've cut your finger off before I got there," Brock said miserably.

"So?" Finley asked.

"*So?* I can't believe you just said that," Brock retorted a little angrily.

Finley was feeling a little angry herself. She was tired, sore, hungry, had to pee, and she was stiff from the cold. "I could've lived without a finger," she barked, "but not with my fucking throat slit!"

They stared at each other for a moment before Brock broke. His eyes watered, and even when he shut them, tears leaked from behind his closed lids.

Her anger leached out immediately. "I'm *okay*, Brock. We're both okay. You got me away from there, found us this safe place to hide. We're good."

She leaned up and kissed his cheeks, swiping away his tears as she did so.

He opened his eyes...and she stilled at the intense look in them. "I can't live without you, Finley."

"Then it's a good thing you don't have to," she said as calmly as she could.

Brock moved a hand to her nape and kissed her. It was a sweet kiss. Passionate, but not hard. He worshiped her mouth, letting her know without words how relieved he was that everything turned out the way it had.

Then he pulled back, licked his lips, wiped his eyes with his shoulders and said, "I need to get a look at your neck, now that it's light."

Finley wanted to protest, but if the roles had been reversed, she would've wanted to see for herself that Brock was all right, so she merely nodded. He scooted backward out from under the outcropping of rock and took a moment to stretch. Putting his hands on his hips and bending backward.

He was so damn gorgeous, and Finley had to pinch herself that he was hers.

"Come on, I'll help you up," he said, holding out a hand.

Finley gratefully took it, moaning as her muscles protested her movement.

Brock gently tilted her head up, and a growl vibrated deep in his throat. Finley couldn't help but grin.

"What are you smiling about?" he clipped.

"You sound like a beast," she said. "All growly and alpha-y."

"You'd make the same noise if it was me standing here with dried blood all over my neck and staining my shirt."

That sobered Finley immediately. She reached up and grabbed his wrists. "I'm all right, Brock. Promise. I'm guessing that it probably looks worse than it is. I can barely feel it." That last part was a little white lie, but she'd never add to Brock's obvious distress by admitting that moving her head back and forth was painful.

He grabbed her hand and turned, leading her to a large rock not too far from where they'd spent the night. "Sit," he ordered.

"I need to pee," Finley said, knowing she was blushing.

Brock sighed. "Right. After, will you sit and let me take care of you?"

"You've been taking care of me since the day you came to The Sweet Tooth to help me bake when I hurt my wrist," she said evenly.

It was the right thing to say, she could see some of the tension in Brock's shoulders relax. He leaned down and took her hand again, helping her stand. "Come on, I'll find you a place you can do your business."

"And something to wipe with?" she asked.

He chuckled. "Yes, that too."

"Thank you," she said, the two words for so much more than just finding her some makeshift toilet paper and a place to pee.

He turned to her and said, "You don't have to thank me for giving you everything you need or want. It's my pleasure."

Finley couldn't speak around the lump in her throat.

This man. She had no idea how she'd gotten so lucky, but she wasn't going to let a day go by without making sure he knew how much she loved and appreciated him.

After she'd taken care of her business, Brock sat her back down on the rock once more. He ripped a strip off the bottom of his T-shirt and cleaned her neck. The water from the stream was ice-cold, but she didn't complain, simply let Brock do what he so obviously needed to do. Then he found some late-season wild berries that he promised were safe to eat to try to assuage their empty bellies.

Afterward, he sat on the ground next to where she was still seated on the rock, wrapped his arm around her legs, and leaned his head against her thigh.

"Maybe we should start heading back for the trail," she said after a good ten minutes had passed.

"Nope. The guys'll be here soon."

"You sound so sure."

"I am."

The confidence in his tone was reassuring, so Finley mentally shrugged and did her best to relax.

It was probably less than twenty minutes later when Brock lifted his head and looked to his right. He stood and brushed the dirt off his butt. Finley was about to ask him what was up when she heard voices through the trees.

"Told you they'd be here soon," he said with a smile, holding out his hand. Finley took it and let him help her stand.

Within seconds, Ethan, Zeke, and Tal emerged from around a bend in the creek.

When they saw her and Brock, all three broke out into a jog.

"Damn, it's good to see you!" Ethan exclaimed.

"You just *had* to take a walk in the woods in the middle of the night in a rainstorm, huh?" Zeke joked.

"What the hell happened? Finley, are you all right?" Tal asked, no humor in his tone at all.

"I'm fine," she reassured them, wondering how bad she must look for Tal's expression to be so murderous.

Ethan's gaze went to her blood-stained shirt. All joking gone from his tone now, he ordered, "Start talking, Brock."

He calmly told them everything that had happened the night before. How he and Finley had started off on a relaxed and easy hike, only to be kidnapped and taken deeper into the forest. He gave his friends the names of the men who'd taken them, told them about their belongings being stolen, the knife Pete had used to keep him from acting, and finally, he told them the incredible story of the mystery woman who'd helped him and Finley to escape.

When he was done, the other three men were vibrating with anger.

"Simon called me this morning at five. Davis was concerned when he got to the bakery and you weren't there," Ethan informed them.

Finley glanced at Brock, and he said, "Told you so."

She could only smile in return.

"Anyway, we called Jesus to see if he knew where you might be, and he told us you had planned on meeting Finley for a hike. So we drove out here, saw both your cars in the parking lot, and immediately started looking for you," Ethan explained.

"We knew something happened because you hadn't

called," Zeke said. "Rocky and Drew are following the beacon, and we followed your trail."

"Using the fucking clear-as-day path you left us," Talon added. "Assuming you didn't go back to the car park because of the guys you got away from?" he asked.

"Exactly," Brock said. "I wasn't going to risk running into them again in the dark. Finley was my first responsibility."

"Wait...beacon? What beacon?" Finley interrupted.

"The satellite phones Bristol bought for the team actually have homing beacons," Zeke explained. "So if they're accidentally dropped or something, we can find them. Those suckers are expensive as hell, and anything we can do not to lose them is a good thing."

"It's still here in the forest?" Brock asked.

"Yeah," Ethan answered.

"Does that mean Pete and Cory are still out here looking for us?" Finley asked in a tremulous voice.

"I doubt it," Ethan said easily. "The beacon was stationary. And Brock's right, it would be stupid for them to hang around this long."

"They probably ditched our stuff," Brock said, putting an arm around her shoulders.

"So I might get my cell phone back?" Finley asked.

"Maybe," Brock said. "Why?"

"Because I've got some recipes I saved from the internet on there. And I took a picture of you the other night while you slept that I didn't move to the cloud yet."

"Was it X-rated?" Brock teased.

"What? No!" Finley exclaimed. "Jeez."

"I want to know more about this woman who helped

you," Tal said. "Who was she? Where is she now? Is she okay?"

"I don't know, man," Brock said. "She appeared out of nowhere. I had no idea she was even there until she was halfway across the clearing. She wore a torn brown dress, no shoes, and she looked pretty rough."

"Rough how?" Talon asked.

"Just rough. Dirty. Tangled hair... As if she'd been out here camping for a while. Or even living out here."

Tal scowled. It was obvious he was deeply disturbed at the thought of a woman being out in the woods alone.

"Where's Raid?" Finley asked. The rest of the team had been accounted for, but Raiden hadn't been mentioned.

"Khloe's sick," Zeke said. "He and Duke are over at her apartment taking care of her."

"What?" Finley asked, frowning. "She's sick? She's *never* sick. We need to get back to town so I can check on her," she demanded. "Why are we standing here? Let's go."

Brock chuckled.

"This is not funny," Finley said, frowning harder. "Why are you laughing?"

"I'm not," Brock denied, but it was weak since he most certainly had been laughing. "It's just that I'm not surprised you're more concerned about your friends than you are about yourself, or about the fact you've just spent the night in the woods, in November, after being kidnapped."

Finley was trying *not* to think about those things. She was very aware of how lucky she and Brock had been. "I'm fine. You're fine. Khloe is *not* fine. And you know as well as I do that she and Raiden rub each other the wrong way. I don't know why, but if he's over there, then she must be *really* sick."

"I talked to Raid, and he asked Doc Snow to stop by. He thinks that she's just run down. That she's pushed herself too hard lately and hasn't been taking care of herself. You know, not eating the right things, not sleeping enough, too much stress. She's going to be fine, Finley," Zeke said gently.

"And I'm thinking we need to get you to Doc Snow as well," Ethan said, eyeing her neck.

Finley brought a hand up to the cuts on her neck, but Brock stopped her before she could touch them. "Your hands are dirty, Fin. Leave them."

Looking down, she could see her hands were covered in dirt. She even had dirt under her fingernails. She smiled up at Brock and held her hands out, palms down. "Look, we match," she said.

Brock rolled his eyes. "Only you would be happy about having black shit under your nails. Come on, let's get the hell out of here. Need to feed you, have Doc Snow check you out, get you in a shower, and then maybe we can both get some real sleep."

"Oh, but, my shop—" Finley started, as they all began walking along the stream back the way the other men had appeared.

"Liam's got it under control," Ethan told her.

"But there's nothing to sell," she said in confusion.

"Of course there is. Davis took care of it."

"Oh." The weight she felt rolling off her shoulders was immense. It wasn't as if she hadn't closed her shop in the past when it had been just her, and she needed to be with her friends when tragedies struck. But she'd always felt guilty for not being open, even if it was the right thing to do. Knowing her employees had things covered was a huge blessing and relief.

Finley was sure the walk back to the trail took a lot longer than it probably took the three men to find them, since her slow pace slowed them down, but no one complained. Her muscles protested each step and if it hadn't been for Brock's firm hold on her hand, she would have face-planted more than once. It was another huge relief to finally step foot on the well-marked and relatively flat trail.

When they arrived in the parking area, Rocky and Drew were there. Brock's backpack, covered in mud, was sitting on the hood of Drew's Jeep.

Both men walked toward them, and when Rocky got close enough, he scowled and asked, "What the fuck happened to your neck?"

"I'll catch you up," Ethan told his brother. "Brock needs to get her to the doc, then they need to go home and rest."

"You're all right?" Drew asked Finley.

She nodded, more grateful than she could express that she had such good friends who were so concerned about her.

"Expect a visit from Caryn later," Drew warned. "She's not gonna be happy to hear about this."

"Bristol too," Rocky agreed.

"I'm guessing your house is gonna be full of our women," Ethan told Brock.

"And they'll be welcome, but give us a few hours," he replied.

"I'll do my best. No promises though," Rocky said.

"Is my phone in there?" Finley asked, nodding at Brock's backpack.

"Yes," Rocky told her.

"I'll text everyone and reassure them I'm okay. Maybe everyone can come over for dinner? I can make homemade pizza or something," Finley said.

"Dinner sounds good. But you aren't making a damn thing," Drew said firmly.

"I'll call Sandra. She'll take care of it," Rocky promised.

Once again, Finley was almost overwhelmed with gratitude for these men.

"Thanks," she said, doing her best not to burst out into tears.

"Can one of you get her car back to my place?" Brock asked, obviously sensing she was at the end of her rope.

"Of course," Zeke said. "Go."

"I'm gonna stay here and check things out," Talon said, not quite pulling off the nonchalant tone Finley was sure he was trying to project.

"What? Why? You think the guys who took them are still out there?" Drew asked.

"No, I'm sure they're long gone. Probably out of Fallport, if they know what's good for them."

"Then what are you looking for?" Drew asked, his brows furrowing.

"I'm guessing a ghost," Ethan said. "I'll fill you guys in on that too," he added, when Drew turned to him with a questioning look.

Finley took the time to hug each of the men before Brock ushered her toward his truck. As soon as she settled into the passenger seat, he took her hand in his. "Close your eyes, Fin, we'll be at the clinic in a few minutes."

"I'm okay, Brock. I just want to go home."

"Not happening. I know you're tired and want a shower, but I need to make sure you're really fine. That your wounds aren't infected."

Finley wanted to protest. Now that she was safe, and could feel the warmth of the heat coming through the vents, she was exhausted. But she couldn't deny Brock's concern made her feel warm and fuzzy inside. "Okay."

"Thank you." He brought their clasped hands up to his mouth and kissed the back of her hand.

* * *

Two hours later, Brock stared down at a sleeping Finley. Doc Snow had written a prescription for antibiotics, just to be safe. The cuts on her neck were superficial, but the sight of them still enraged Brock. He'd also called Simon to report what had happened. He'd described Pete and Cory, and the police chief seemed to know exactly who they were...which hopefully meant they'd be found sooner rather than later.

He'd brought Finley back to his house and they'd showered together. Neither felt amorous as they soaped each other up. Brock spent a good amount of time trying to get the dirt out from under Finley's fingernails. She might not mind having hands that looked like his, but he did.

He wrapped her up in one of his robes that swam on her and sat her at his small kitchen table. He heated some soup, and after they both ate, he took her back to his bed and tucked her in. He was going to leave her alone, needing some time to decompress and come to terms with his rage over what could've happened, but when Finley grabbed his hand and said "stay," he couldn't bear to disappoint her.

So he shucked off his sweatpants and boxers and climbed under the blankets. They were both naked, and nothing felt as good as her soft curves against him. Brock knew he was holding her too tightly, but she didn't complain, simply held on to him just as closely.

She was out in minutes, but even as exhausted as Brock was, he couldn't sleep. He kept running everything that had happened through his head. He could've lost her. *Had* almost lost her.

Then a thought occurred to him, and his hand moved to her belly.

He had no idea if she was pregnant, but there was certainly a good chance. He'd filled her over and over again with his come, and as far as he knew, she hadn't had her period since she'd practically moved in with him.

Closing his eyes, he realized there'd been a chance he could've lost her *and* their unborn child.

His teeth clenched and his eyes popped open once more. No one was going to hurt a hair on her head. No fucking way. And if anyone dared say one derogatory word to her about her weight, how fast they'd gotten together, or anything else, they'd fucking regret it.

Brock was aware he was overreacting, but he didn't care. The thought of Finley being pregnant with his child, and having that knife at her throat, was repugnant. "Never again," he muttered fiercely.

His words roused Finley, and she snuggled against him. One of her legs was thrown over his thigh, her head was on his shoulder, and her arm was around his belly, clutching him to her. "My Brock," she muttered, then went still once more.

The rage he'd been feeling disappeared like a puff of smoke at her words.

He *was* hers. Body and soul. He'd do whatever it took to keep her, and any child she might be carrying, safe from here on out. She was moving in with him. Having his baby. And she was going to marry him.

Finally, Brock allowed himself to relax. His Finley wasn't going to agree to living together or marriage simply because he demanded it, but she loved him. Both those things would happen, sooner rather than later.

He fell asleep with the scent of vanilla in his nose, and the bone-deep satisfaction that his woman was safe.

CHAPTER TWELVE

"You're smothering me!" Finley told Brock in frustration.

He ran a hand through his hair, obviously just as frustrated as she was. "I'm trying to keep you safe," he returned.

Finley took a deep breath. "I know, and I appreciate it. But it's been a *month*. We've talked to Simon multiple times, he's still working with the Roanoke Police Department to track down whoever stole that truck. Pete's car was tracked by a toll booth camera in New York, and Cory was in Georgia when he got that speeding ticket. They're nowhere near me. It's all good. I'm fine. Nothing's happened."

"Yes, but Pete and Cory *are* still out there somewhere. Just because they were last seen in other states doesn't mean they can't come back. I just want to make sure nothing happens to you."

"And I love you for that, but I can't live the rest of my life in a bubble," Finley said. "I *can't*."

Brock pressed his lips together and stared at her. He wasn't happy, but Finley wouldn't let this go.

"Please. I actually feel *more* worried with you hovering and your friends following me around. It makes me feel as if there's something I *have to be* afraid of. And I can't live my life like this."

"I can't...I just..." Brock stuttered.

Finley walked up to him and hugged him hard. "I know. If something happened to you, I don't know what I'd do either. But this isn't living, Brock. Constantly looking over my shoulder, questioning everyone who walks into The Sweet Tooth. It's stifling."

Brock stared down at her for a full minute before he sighed. "Okay."

"Okay what?"

"I'll try to stop being so paranoid."

"Good. And?"

Brock's lips twitched. "I'll call off the guys."

"Thank you," Finley said, satisfied. It wasn't that she didn't appreciate everyone looking out for her, she just needed to at least attempt to live her life, and that was hard to do when she knew everyone expected the boogeyman to jump out from around every corner. She trusted Simon and Brock to keep her safe. And to tell her if there was any proof she was actually in danger. Pete and Cory were out of the picture as far as she was concerned, there was no way they'd come back to Fallport. Not with everyone looking for them. And even though that truck had been stolen, leaving them with no clues about the unknown driver, Finley wasn't worried about him either. It would be stupid of him to resume deliveries with the police on the alert.

She needed to move on. Couldn't spend the next weeks or months, however long it took for the police to figure out who was involved in the drug drop-off, living in fear.

"Maybe I can give you something else to think about," she told Brock. This wasn't the time or place she'd planned on doing this, a picnic in The Circle in the middle of the town square wasn't exactly private, but when Brock had shown up to take her to lunch, she hadn't been able to deny him.

"Yeah?" he asked.

Finley nodded and didn't beat around the bush. "I'm pregnant."

Brock stared at her for a full ten seconds, before grinning. Huge. "I know."

"*What*? How?"

"Fin, you've been living with me for a while, and you haven't had your period even once. And I know your body better than you do by now. If you think I haven't noticed the subtle changes, you're crazy."

"Like what?" she asked, shocked that he somehow knew she was pregnant before she did.

Brock leaned into her. They were sitting next to each other at the picnic table in the middle of the gazebo. He wrapped his arm around her hips and lowered his head to nuzzle at her ear. "Your breasts are way more sensitive. Remember the other night? I made you come with just my mouth on your nipples and my fingers in your pussy."

Finley blushed. He so had. And the way he'd taken her hard and fast afterward had been hot as hell.

"And given how many times I've filled you with my come, I'm actually surprised it's taken this long. How far along are you?"

"Not far enough to tell everyone yet," she pouted.

"Right," Brock said, sobering. "The chances of a miscarriage are higher in the first three months than any other time. And you're almost forty. Maybe you should consider taking some time off—"

"No," Finley said, trying to stay calm.

"You don't know what I was going to say," Brock protested.

"Of course I do. You want me to stay home, sitting on my ass for the next eight and a half months. Not going to happen. First of all, I'd be bored out of my head. Secondly, you'd drive me crazy hovering over me, and third—no. Just no."

Brock frowned. "I just want you and Little Bean to be healthy."

"Me and Little Bean *are* healthy," she told him. "And we're gonna stay that way too."

"I'm a worrier," Brock informed her, as if she didn't know.

Finley laughed. "Really?" she said sarcastically.

His lips twitched. "You're just going to have to get used to it."

"I honestly don't mind you worrying about me because I worry about you all the time too. But we can't live our lives in fear, Brock. We have to *live*. I've waited too long to find you, I don't want to miss out on a second of the life we could have together because I'm afraid of what *might* happen."

She could tell she'd finally gotten through to him. He sighed. "You're right."

"I know," she teased.

"But you need to stay alert. Don't take any chances. If

something feels off, trust your instincts. And if you feel sick, listen to your body and get off your feet."

Finley nodded immediately. "I will."

Brock stared at her, then said, "I'm going to do my best not to hover, but you're going to have to cut me some slack. It isn't every day the woman I love is carrying my child."

Finley almost melted on her seat. "As long as you're trying, I'm okay with you being protective."

"Good. Now, is there any chance I can convince you to head home for the rest of the day?"

She smiled. "Nope. I have four dozen cookies to make for a birthday party tomorrow afternoon and a cake I need to start on for tomorrow as well."

Brock sighed. "Right. Can I ask something else?"

"Of course."

"Will you move the rest of your stuff to my house?"

Finley's eyes widened.

He quickly went on. "I know it's a big step to move in with me officially, but we've already moved most of the stuff from your kitchen to mine, and your plants, and all of your winter clothes. We haven't spent a night apart since that first night you gave yourself to me. I can't imagine not coming home to you in my house, or waking up without you by my side. If you don't like the house, I can find another one. In fact, I should probably do that anyway, since Little Bean will be arriving next year. He or she is going to need their own room because there's no way I'm making love to you in front of them. It would scar them for life. But I—"

Finley stopped his babbling by putting a finger on his lips. "Yes," she said simply.

"Yes?"

"Yes," she confirmed.

Brock lifted her hand from his lips and kissed her palm. "You're being very agreeable all of a sudden."

Finley shrugged. "Why would I say no when I'm deliriously happy living with you?"

"Right. I'm not gonna push my luck and ask you to marry me right now, but it's coming, sweetheart."

Finley's heart skipped a beat. She loved Brock and knew he loved her back. All her life, she'd wanted to find someone who could appreciate her exactly how she was, curves and all. There was nothing she wanted more than to marry this man. Make Brock hers officially. She wanted to tell him to ask her. Right this second. But she could wait. She was carrying his baby, and she'd be moving in with him. Her bakery was doing remarkably well, and she had some amazing friends.

Adding one more thing to her "happy" list would probably be pushing her luck.

"All right."

Brock grinned at her. "When do we get to do an ultrasound so I can meet my Little Bean?" he asked.

"You want to go with me?"

"Hell yes, I want to go! I want to experience every part of the process when it comes to our child."

She chuckled dryly. "Not sure you want to share in the morning sickness."

"Wrong. I'll hold you while you puke, make sure your hair doesn't get in the yuck. I'll have a toothbrush ready and waiting, and I'll rub your belly or back until you feel better."

Finley frowned and poked him in the arm. Hard.

"Ow, what was that for?" Brock asked, clutching his arm where she'd poked him.

"I'm just trying to make sure you're real, and not a cyborg or something."

"I'm real," he promised. "And I'm sure there will be days when you find me so annoying, you want to smack me. I'm not perfect, but for you, I'm trying to be."

"I don't want or need perfect," she reassured him. "I just need you to accept me the way I am."

"I do," he said gruffly. "Just as you accept me."

Finley tilted her head, studying him for a moment, then said, "You know what? I can probably deal with the cookies and cake tomorrow morning."

"What?"

"I *am* feeling a little tired. Maybe I'll go home and crawl into bed. Naked. Then to help me take the edge off, I might touch myself...give myself an orgasm so I can sleep better."

"Right. And I'm thinking I need to make sure you get home and settled in our bed, safe and sound."

Finley nodded. "Yeah, I agree." She brought his hand to her belly and smiled. "I'm also thinking we should celebrate your super-sperm making this Little Bean."

His pupils dilated and he was on his feet, cleaning up what was left of their lunch, before she said another word. Satisfaction and anticipation coursed through Finley's veins. There were some downsides to having an alpha boyfriend, but there were way more positives. Including midday sex whenever she wanted it. Like today. Right now.

He grabbed hold of her hand and began towing her toward his truck, parallel parked outside the post office.

"Where's the fire?" Otto called as they got near.

Finley chuckled but Brock didn't bother to reply. He simply held open the door for her to climb up and over to her side. He did wave at the three old men, who were laughing as he started the vehicle. She heard Silas call out, "Have fun!" before they were on their way.

"I probably should've stopped and told Liam I wasn't coming back to the store," she said.

"You've got three minutes to text him and let him know," Brock practically growled. "Then you're mine."

Finley didn't hesitate to pull out her phone.

* * *

The hardest thing Brock had ever done was not yell to the rooftops that he was going to be a father. He was both excited as hell and worried about something going wrong with either Finley or their Little Bean.

The day after he'd learned about the pregnancy, the SAR team was called out to find a hiker who'd gotten separated from the rest of his group. Brock wanted to spill the baby news to his friends the second they reached the trail-head, but he honored Finley's request to wait.

Duke and Raiden had taken point on the missing hiker, and they found the twenty-eight-year-old tourist within thirty minutes. He was at the bottom of a ravine, where he'd fallen and twisted his ankle.

Other than being a little embarrassed and sore, he was going to be all right. He managed to hobble out of the woods using Ethan and Talon as crutches, and his fellow hikers promised to take him to a twenty-four-hour clinic when they got home.

"Any luck?" Brock asked Talon as they all gathered

around to shoot the shit before heading their separate ways.

"Luck with what?" Raid asked.

"Finding the mysterious woman who saved me and Finley," Brock said.

"I'm not really looking for her," Talon said with a shrug. But they all knew he was lying.

"Right, so...on that note, I was talking with Silas, Otto, and Art the other day," Rocky said, "and I mentioned what happened. How this woman appeared out of nowhere and then disappeared just as silently and mysteriously. And Silas said something that was intriguing."

All eyes were on Rocky as he spoke.

"What'd he say?" Tal asked impatiently.

"Apparently, there was a little girl who went missing. Long before we moved to town, obviously. She was eight at the time. A neighbor said she thought she saw her getting into a green two-door car around the time she was supposed to get home from school. The townspeople and the police searched and searched, but there was never any trace of the little girl or clues to who might have taken her. The parents were beside themselves and ended up getting a divorce because of the stress and moved away."

"And?" Zeke asked when Rocky paused.

"Heather Brown was her name. She had red hair and was somewhat of a tomboy. Silas said at the time of her disappearance, there was some sort of religious group living on the edge of the woods. Liked to call itself 'The Community'. The women all wore long dresses and weren't allowed to talk to anyone outside the group, especially men. The police investigated them at the time, but they didn't find any evidence of Heather out there, or a green car. The leader of the place died over a year ago, and as far as the locals know, the sect disbanded and everyone left Virginia. The area where they lived is now deserted and falling apart."

"You think our mystery woman could be this missing little girl?" Brock asked skeptically.

"You said yourself that the woman had red hair and looked as if she was completely comfortable in the woods. What if she *was* taken by someone in that sect? And when the leader died and everyone left, she stayed behind? She'd be twenty-eight or so now, and probably very comfortable living off the land."

"If it *is* her, why wouldn't she have come forward by now? Eight is old enough to remember her life before she was kidnapped. And it's not as if there haven't been hundreds of people in the forest lately," Raid argued.

"She was probably scared out of her mind when she was taken," Tal said quietly. "And I'm sure she was threatened. Possibly abused. She might've been terrified and confused and did whatever she had to in order to survive. Twenty years..." he said with a shake of his head. "That's also a long, long time to brainwash a child. She very likely doesn't know a different life beyond the one she's had. When everyone up and left, if she was taught to distrust outsiders...maybe she was too scared to come forward to ask for help. So she stayed where she was. Doing what she knew. Sometimes the hell you know is less frightening than taking a chance on the unknown."

"We don't know it's her," Zeke reminded him.

"We don't know it's *not* her," Tal countered.

"For the sake of argument—if she's stayed hidden since the group disbanded, what makes you think you can find her and convince her that she's safe?" Brock asked.

His friend met his gaze. "She risked being seen, being *caught*, to help you and Finley. That tells me she knows the difference between right and wrong. And I'm guessing she wants to make a change, but isn't sure who to trust or how to go about it. She doesn't have a vehicle. Who knows what kind of education she's received. Those piece-of-shit cult members, or whatever they were...they probably didn't bother to teach her a damn thing except how to serve their leader. It's easier to oppress people if they're uneducated. But regardless, she still risked herself to help you."

Brock nodded. "I'll stay and walk with you," he said. "It's the least I can do for what she did for me."

"What about Finley? You want one of us to watch her for you while you're out here with Tal?" Drew asked.

Brock wanted to say yes. Wanted to tell his friends to keep an even closer eye on his woman, now that she was pregnant. But he'd promised to try to loosen up. To not be as paranoid about her safety. One of the hardest things he'd ever done was to shake his head. "No. It's been a month. I talked to Simon just yesterday, and although he knows there's an issue with drugs in Fallport, he doesn't think Finley's in any danger. Not after she gave him the info on what she saw and that license number."

"They find the truck?" Zeke asked.

"Unfortunately, no," Brock said with a sigh.

"Damn."

Brock nodded. "As much as I don't like it, Finley's right. I'm smothering her. She's a grown adult and she's promised to be careful."

"Well, then...want me to have Elsie invite her to On

SEARCHING FOR FINLEY

the Rocks for dinner when she's done at the bakery today?" Zeke asked slyly.

Brock smiled. "Yes."

"And maybe she'd like to come over and check out our wedding pictures Lilly finally got back tomorrow?" Ethan suggested with a grin.

"I'm sure Bristol's dying to show off the latest stained-glass piece she's making for a hotshot actress out in Hollywood."

Brock loved his friends so much. He wouldn't be breaking his promise to Finley to tell the guys to back off, but if their women wanted to hang out with her in the afternoons before he got off work...who was he to stop them? "Thanks, guys."

"Not that I think she's in any danger, but it's better to be safe than sorry," Drew agreed.

It was on the tip of his tongue yet again to tell his friends that Finley was pregnant, but he bit the words back at the last moment.

"I'll see if I can find any pictures or more info about Heather Brown," Rocky told Tal.

"Appreciate it. Even if the woman isn't her, I still want to make sure she's safe. The weather's getting colder and it's gonna snow soon. I can't stand thinking about anyone out here on their own," Tal said.

"If it *is* her, she obviously knows how to take care of herself," Zeke reminded him.

"She was barefoot. And I..." Talon shook his head. "I just need to find her."

Brock clasped his friend's shoulder. They all knew Tal's last mission with the Special Boat Service had gone horribly wrong, and he'd quit as a result. They also knew whatever happened had involved women and children...but he'd never given them details and they hadn't pushed. "Come on. We can go out to where this 'Community' used to live and see if we can get any clues there. If we're lucky, we'll find Heather. If not, we'll go over where you've already searched, including where Finley and I were taken by those assholes. See if we can't find any evidence of a trail, or better yet, where she's been living or hiding."

"Thanks," Tal said.

"Call if you need us," Ethan said.

"Will do," Brock told him. Then he and Talon headed back toward the trail they'd recently come down while escorting the young man with the sprained ankle.

CHAPTER THIRTEEN

Two days later, Finley stepped back from the counter and tilted her head as she examined the cake she'd just finished decorating. It looked pretty damn good, if she did say so herself. It was for a four-year-old who was into the show *Paw Patrol*. Since Marshall was her favorite character, she made the cake in the shape of a firetruck.

Pulling out her phone, Finley took a picture and texted it to Caryn, who she knew would get a kick out of it. She wasn't disappointed when she immediately messaged back.

Caryn: That's awesome!!!!! You're so making me one of those for my birthday!!!

Finley chuckled and carefully picked up the cake and moved it to the large refrigerator. After securing the cake for the mother to pick up later today, she arched her back and stretched. Her back was sore from decorating the cake, but she was also fairly sore all over. Brock was not a gentle lover...not that she wanted him to be. He wasn't afraid to manhandle her where he wanted her, hold her tightly, and fuck her hard. And Finley loved every second. She also gave as good as she got, digging her nails into his arms or butt, and telling him exactly what she liked and wanted.

She felt like a completely different woman when she was with him. Sexy. Beautiful. Desired.

She had no problem with the lights being on now. How could she feel anything but pretty when he couldn't keep his gaze or his hands off her?

"Please tell me the way you're rubbing your belly means what I think it does," Bristol said from the doorway of the kitchen, scaring the shit out of Finley.

She hadn't realized she'd just been standing there, staring into space and caressing her stomach. She smiled at the diminutive woman. "Hi."

"Don't 'hi' me," Bristol scolded with a smile. "Please tell me you're pregnant."

Finley shrugged. "I'm pregnant."

Bristol squealed and rushed into the room. Her leg was finally healed after her ordeal with a stalker, and she was relishing the freedom of being able to move around without the knee walker she'd been using for months.

She hugged Finley tightly, then stood back and assessed her. "You look good."

The compliment settled deep. She'd never been the kind of woman who received spontaneous compliments. She'd totally take it. "Thanks."

"How far are you?"

"Not even two months yet," Finley said. "Which is why

we haven't said anything."

Bristol nodded. "I get it. But I have to say, I'm pretty thrilled I'm one of the first to know. Have you told Brock?"

"Of course. Although, he said he already knew."

"Let me guess, because of the changes in your body?"

Finley blushed. "Uh-huh."

Bristol beamed. "I'm so happy for you guys."

"Me too. I mean, I hadn't thought much about kids. I've always liked and wanted them, but figured it was too late for that to happen. Not to mention I had to find a guy first," Finley said dryly.

"Brock is definitely not messing around," Bristol said.

Finley snorted. "Understatement of the century."

"Does it bother you?" she asked with a tilt of her head.

"Does what bother me?"

"How fast things are going with you guys? I mean, you're living with him, pregnant, and I can't see Brock not wanting to put a ring on your finger before your baby is born. He's pretty much super alpha, like Rocky and all the other guys."

"Honestly? It doesn't *feel* like we've moved as fast as we have. I mean, I've had a crush on Brock for ages. How could I not? He's everything I've ever wanted in a man. But I kept my feelings to myself. At least...I *thought* I had."

"He knew you liked him," Bristol said. "He was trying not to rush you. To give you time to get over your shyness with him."

Finley nodded. "Yeah. So when I finally did let down my guard, take a chance, I already knew him pretty well. And apparently he knew me too."

"Of course. We'd been talking you up as much as we

could whenever we were around him."

"We?" Finley asked.

"Lilly, Elsie, Caryn, and me."

"Caryn practically threw him at me," Finley said without heat. "When she was found out at that moonshine cabin, she immediately sent Brock to tell me what happened."

"Yup. She's pretty sneaky," Bristol agreed with a smile. Then she sobered. "You two are more right for each other than any couple I've ever met. And that includes me and Rocky. You just click. It was obvious from the start. Your sweetness balances out his rough edges."

"I'm not that sweet," Finley grumbled.

"Riiiight. You give free cookies to all the kids who come into your shop. You supply cupcakes to kids at the elementary school whose parents can't afford to do anything for them on their birthday. You—"

"Okay, okay, I'm the sugar plum fairy," Finley said with an eye roll.

"All I'm saying is that you and Brock work. Really well. I'm so happy for the two of you...sorry...three of you," Bristol said with a smile.

"Me too."

"So...when's the wedding?"

Finley laughed out loud. "We just had Lilly's and yours is less than three weeks away. Everyone has to be wedding'd out by now."

"Are you kidding? No way! What kind of wedding do you want? A big shindig? Something small? Or do you want to do what Elsie and Zeke did and just get it done quietly at the courthouse?"

Finley shrugged. "I haven't thought about it much.

Besides, he hasn't even asked yet. I'm not putting the cart before the horse." That was a little lie. She *had* thought about it. And while she'd loved every second of Lilly's wedding, and knew Bristol's would be just as awesome, that wasn't for her. She didn't like being the center of attention. And with her size, just the thought of wearing a huge, poufy wedding dress gave her hives. Of course, it didn't have to be huge and poufy, but still.

"He's gonna ask. Like I said before, there's no way Brock Mabrey is gonna let that baby be born without you wearing his ring."

Finley's hand went to her belly again. "I want this baby," she whispered. "So much."

Bristol came closer and put her hand over Finley's on her stomach. "It's gonna be fine."

"I'm almost forty," Finley whispered. "Women have miscarriages all the time. I just...I don't want to lose this Little Bean."

Bristol smiled at the nickname but didn't comment on it. "I wish I knew the right thing to say here. I'm probably going to muck this up, but here goes. You can't control Mother Nature, Finley. Losing a child has to be one of the most devastating things a woman could ever go through. But you have to trust that whatever happens is what's *supposed* to happen. You're healthy, you don't take risks. I hope and pray that everything turns out all right with your baby, but you know what? If the worst happens, Brock will *always* be by your side. He'll hold you when you cry and celebrate your victories. All you have to do is trust him to be there for you."

"Thank you," Finley whispered.

They hugged once more, and Finley did her best to

control her tears. That was another thing that had changed when she got pregnant. She cried at the drop of a hat. She also got mad much more easily as well. In fact, all her emotions seemed supercharged. Of course, when she complained about it to Brock, he simply shrugged and told her it was a part of her charm.

"When you feel comfortable, and after you share with everyone, I'm totally throwing you a baby shower. Complete with all the silly games people play at those things. Wait—Lilly's preggo too! You guys are only...what? A few weeks apart? This is gonna be *so* awesome! Double baby shower! Your kids will grow up together. Maybe they can date and end up getting married someday!"

Finley couldn't help but roll her eyes. "Slow your roll there, Bristol."

They both laughed. Then Bristol asked, "Are you going to find out the gender?"

"Oh, um...honestly, I hadn't thought about it. I'll have to ask Brock what he wants."

"He's gonna want to know," Bristol said firmly.

"You think?"

"Oh, yeah. He's gonna need some time to process if it's a girl. Can you imagine how overprotective he's gonna be? His daughter will have him wrapped around her finger for sure."

Bristol wasn't wrong. Finley could imagine Brock's reaction to having their Little Bean being a girl. She'd be a total daddy's girl...one who would probably be able to put an engine together by the time she was four. She smiled.

"Right. I'm so happy for you, Finley. Seriously. You and Brock are utterly adorable together."

Adorable. Finley almost laughed at the word. A

memory from yesterday flashed through her mind. Brock had been behind her while she'd been on her hands and knees in front of a huge mirror he'd bought days earlier. He'd been taking her hard—and he'd slapped her ass.

Apparently, he'd felt her delighted reaction around his cock, because he'd done it again. And again. Then he'd used his thumb to caress her ass while his other hand rubbed her clit as he fucked her—all the while, staring at their erotic reflection in the mirror. After she exploded, he pulled out and came all over her ass, rubbing it into her skin as he praised her. Telling her how beautiful she was and how he was the luckiest man alive.

Yeah. Adorable was the last word she'd use to describe her man. Intense, sexy, demanding, insatiable? Yes. Adorable, no.

Bristol chuckled as if she could read Finley's mind. "I said *together* you two are adorable. Now get your mind out of the gutter."

Finley laughed.

"I did have a reason for stopping by," Bristol said with a smile.

"Yeah?"

"Uh-huh. A photographer from *National Geographic* is coming to town to take pictures of the stained glass I made for Sunny Side Up. I got with Sandra, and she's going bring back her Bigfoot-themed menu. She agreed to donate one hundred percent of the proceeds for the day the photographer is here, to an animal charity in Africa. One that's trying to keep rhinos and elephants safe from poachers who want their tusks. Anyway, I wondered if you might be willing to make some Bigfoot cookies to sell as well?"

"Yes!" Finley said without having to think about it. Then she frowned. "But I'd have to research how to decorate them so they'd look cool and not stupid."

"Your cookies could never look stupid," Bristol said.

"Ha. You're sweet, but trust me, baking is actually a lot easier than decorating."

"I have faith in you."

They spent a few more minutes talking about the details, how many cookies she should make, when the pictures of her stained glass would be featured by the world-famous magazine, and more about the charity the money would go to. By the time they were done, Finley's mind was spinning and she'd decided to make elephant and rhinoceros cookies, as well as the Bigfoot ones.

When three o'clock rolled around and the shop closed up, Finley was more than ready to leave. She couldn't wait to talk to Brock about the photographer coming to town and her ideas for the cookies. She had two more custom orders she needed to get done by tomorrow afternoon, but her desire to see Brock outweighed her desire to get a head start on the projects. She'd still have plenty of time to get them finished before her clients came to pick up the goodies.

Liam walked Finley to her car when she was ready. She was well aware that Brock had talked to her employee and asked him to make sure she made it to her vehicle safely, whenever Brock couldn't. He'd backed off his hovering ever since she'd told him he was suffocating her, but deep down, she didn't mind him wanting to make sure she was safe.

Thinking about what could've happened in the forest with Pete and Cory was scary. It had been a close call, and

Finley was more than happy for something like that to never happen again. Her friends had all proven to be extremely tough, but deep down, Finley knew she wasn't like that. If she'd been in any of the situations that Lilly, Elsie, Bristol, or Caryn had been in, she probably would've freaked out and definitely not handled it nearly as well as they had.

So Brock asking Liam to walk her to her car made Finley feel protected in a less-paranoid way. Having one of the Eagle Point SAR team members sit outside her shop all day, as if they were afraid the boogeyman was going to leap out from behind a rock, was suffocating. She was glad Brock finally understood the difference.

Finley waved at Liam and pulled out of the parking lot and headed for Old Town Auto. Another change thanks to the little life forming deep within her womb was that Finley was horny all the time. She'd gone online to see if what she was feeling was normal, and was relieved to find that it was. Most of the women on the forums she'd found said their libidos seemed to taper off eventually as their pregnancies progressed.

Of course, Brock had no issues whatsoever with her increased sexuality. He reveled in it. Encouraged her to let loose in their bedroom...and anywhere else in their house, for that matter. And she knew that anytime she wanted sex, day or night, he was more than willing to accommodate.

Squirming in her seat, Finley pulled into the auto shop. She should really leave Brock alone. He was working. She could go home and masturbate. But she didn't want to do that. She wanted her man.

Taking a deep breath, she climbed out of the car and

headed for the open bay. Brock was bent over the front of a vehicle, his perfect ass outlined in the overalls he wore, and she could see his left arm flexing as he did something under the hood.

Her nipples tightened and wetness flooded her panties. She didn't even have a chance to get embarrassed by her arousal. As if he could sense her standing there, Brock's head popped around the side of the hood.

He took one look at her and turned his head to yell, "Jesus!"

His partner stuck his head out of the door to their office, off to the left. "Yeah?"

"I'm headed out," Brock said as he wiped his hands on a rag hanging over the side of the car.

"Okay!"

"I'll finish up the Abernathys' car in the morning."

"Ten-four."

Then Brock stalked toward Finley, and all she could do was stare at him and do her best not to drool. When he reached her, he leaned down, and Finley could smell oil, sweat, and a hint of the soap he'd used in the shower that morning.

"You need your man?" he asked huskily.

Her belly clenched and she nodded.

He lifted a hand and wrapped it around her nape, pulling her against him roughly, and Finley let out a small *oof* as she hit his rock-hard body. "You're so fucking gorgeous. You have flour in your hair and you smell like," he lowered his head to the crook of her neck and inhaled deeply, "sugar."

She smiled as she wrapped her arms around his neck

and surreptitiously rubbed her breasts against his chest. "I should, since I've been frosting cookies all afternoon."

His free hand smoothed down her back to her ass, and he clutched the ample flesh there firmly. "Hard and fast, or soft and slow?" he asked against her lips.

Finley flushed. She was practically panting as she said, "Hard and fast. I need you, Brock."

Without another word, he grabbed her hand and pulled her toward the side of the building, where his truck was parked. Finley grinned as she did her best to keep up with him. She loved when he got like this. She wouldn't have minded a quickie right there at his shop, but he'd told her in no uncertain terms that he would never disrespect her by fucking her where someone could walk in and see them. She was his alone, and *no one* was going to see what was his.

The drive to his place took way too long, despite being less than five minutes. Finley squirmed in her seat the entire time. The second he turned off the engine in his driveway, Brock pulled her across the seat and toward the house.

Two seconds after the door shut behind them, he pounced. He stripped her right there in the entryway, shoved his pants down just far enough to expose his rock-hard cock, and entered her in one deep thrust.

Finley screamed with pleasure. She'd been ready for him, but he was still big, and when he filled her, the slight pinch only increased her desire. He took her right there against the wall, making her feel small and petite as he towered over her.

After they'd both come, he picked her up and carried her into the living room. He settled her on the couch, then went to his knees in front of her. He shoved her legs apart with his shoulders and stared at her pussy for a long moment.

"Brock?" Finley panted.

"You'll never know how damn sexy this is," he told her as he used a finger to swipe at his come that was leaking out of her body. "Knowing we made a life together? I can't explain how in awe I am." Then he straightened on his knees, pulled her ass to the edge of the couch, and eased himself inside her once again.

"That first one take the edge off, baby?" he asked, as he lazily pumped in and out of her.

Finley nodded.

"Good. I need a shower."

She smiled up at him. He did. But she loved him like this. All sweaty and manly. His stained hands on her body. He was so different from her, and she loved that. He used to overwhelm her with his raw masculinity. She thought she could never be enough for someone like him. But now she realized that their differences complemented each other perfectly.

"After," she panted as he began to thrust faster.

He grinned at her, then got serious as he did his best to make sure she was satisfied.

Later, after he'd made her come twice more, filling her to the brim again, after a shower, and after he'd insisted she sit on the couch and relax while he grilled some pork chops for dinner, she was snuggled up against his side while a football game played on the television.

"Brock?" she asked.

"Yeah?"

"Do you want to know the gender of our baby?"

He looked down at her. "Do you?"

"I think it might be kind of cool for it to be a surprise. But that's a pain. We wouldn't know what to put on a baby registry, and we'd have to think up two names just in case."

"As far as the baby registry goes, does it really matter if it's a boy or a girl?" he asked. "We can put green, yellow, purple, magenta, and who the hell else cares what color clothes and toys in there. The baby isn't going to give a shit what color their pajamas are. They're just going to sleep, eat, and poop."

"You wouldn't care if your son wore pink?" she asked.

"Fuck no. Clothes don't make the man, or woman," he said with uncanny insight. "My daughter can wear whatever color she wants. Blue, purple, pink, or yellow with orange polka dots. If my son wants to play with dolls and be a ballet dancer, I don't give a fuck. All I want is for him or her to be a good person, and to be happy. All I want is for *you* to be happy."

Tears filled Finley's eyes.

"Don't cry," he ordered.

She smiled. "Can't help it. You're being awesome."

"Of course I am, that shouldn't be a surprise."

She laughed at that, and he smiled at her. "There. Better," he said when her tears dried up. Then he caressed her cheek with the backs of his fingers. "If you want Little Bean's gender to be a surprise, that's what we'll do."

"But what do *you* want?" she insisted.

"Like I just said—I want you to be happy. I want you to give birth safely without any complications. I want us to be a family. I want world peace, but that's not something I have any say in, so I'll have to be content with making sure my woman and Little Bean are both as safe and happy as they can be."

"Brock," she whispered.

"We'll keep it a surprise for now. If you change your mind anytime in the next several months, then we'll ask Doc to let us know."

"Okay," she said.

"Okay."

Finley snuggled into him and sighed happily. This was what she'd always wanted. To love and be loved. Loved for who she was, and not because of what she looked like or what her profession was or anything else. She had a feeling Brock felt the same way.

Picking up one of his hands, she kissed each of his stained fingers before resting her head back against his chest. He squeezed her tightly, then relaxed into the cushions.

* * *

Hillary Kendall, simply known as "The Boss" to the small-time dealers she worked with and the junkies she sold to, paced back and forth in her living room.

She was pissed. Infuriated. So angry she couldn't see straight.

That dumb fucking bitch *ruined* the good thing she'd had going!

Five years ago, when Hillary had knee surgery, she hadn't thought the procedure would be a big deal. After several complications, and months of painkillers, her knee had finally healed. But not before she'd become dependent on the pills her doctor had prescribed.

At first, it was difficult to sneak around behind her husband's and kids' backs to get the pills she needed to function. Long drives to Roanoke to meet with shady people in dark alleys. But before long, she'd made better connections, and she only had to drive to the rest area east of Fallport, by the interstate.

Then she'd been offered a chance to sell pills in Fallport herself.

She'd jumped at the opportunity.

Ever since, she'd lived a double life. PTA member, highly involved with her daughter's classes, volunteering at the school, coaching her son's little league team. Even while running her own small drug empire and making money hand over fist, she hadn't missed a football game in the two years since Robert had entered high school. And her daughter Nevaeh was the most popular kid in seventh grade.

Her husband still didn't suspect a thing. Didn't care *what* she did, as long as dinner was ready when he got home, the house was clean, and his kids excelled at school.

But everything was on the verge of collapse. All because of that stupid baker bitch.

All Pete and Cory had to do was scare her badly enough so she'd keep her fucking mouth shut. But they'd failed spectacularly. The day after she and that greasy mechanic had been rescued from the woods, she'd gone straight to the police with the license plate number of her supplier's truck.

Pete and Cory both left town, but it was only a matter of time before the cops tracked them down. She had no doubt they'd sing like canaries. Snitching on her and the entire operation. Dumbass Pete had used that satellite phone, and while no one had come knocking on her door wanting to know why a druggie who'd kidnapped a woman and threatened her life had called a phone she'd bought a year ago, she wasn't stupid. She knew how forensics and phone tracing went. She watched all those crime shows on TV.

She'd done her best to cover her tracks when she'd bought the phones, using cash, buying them in Roanoke... but she couldn't do anything about the cameras at the convenience store where she bought the burners. And the fucking cell towers the phones pinged off. It was only a matter of time before the police chief tracked back far enough and came knocking on her door, wanting to talk to her.

But Hillary wasn't going down before getting revenge on the bitch who'd made her entire life crash and burn.

Her supplier in Roanoke was pissed that he'd had to ditch the truck he'd stolen, that the people she'd hired had been so stupid and careless. He'd cut her off completely. All her customers had found someone else to buy from, but worse...she wasn't getting the pills *she* needed to function and keep up appearances.

Two weeks ago, she'd been in Roanoke, trying yet again to find another source, when someone had offered her heroin. She knew she shouldn't do it...but she'd been utterly desperate.

The peace that had filled her that first time was euphoric. Like nothing she'd ever known. Ten times better than the feeling she got from pills.

She'd bought what she assumed would be enough to hold her over until she could get to Roanoke again.

She'd used all of it in less than three days.

Hillary seethed as she paced. She was now one of *those* people. A scumbag drug addict. While taking pills, she'd found a warped sense of comfort in the fact that she was using legal drugs. Something that had been prescribed by her doctor.

But now that she'd been doing heroin several times a day, every day, for the last two weeks, drained several grand from their bank account—which her husband would notice soon—missed two football games, and had forgotten to pick up Nevaeh from school three days in a row because she'd been scouring Fallport to find someone who'd sell her some heroin, Hillary knew she was on the brink of losing everything. Her husband would divorce her, she'd lose custody of her kids, and she'd have to resort to living on the streets like that pathetic fucker Davis Woolford.

And it was Finley Norris's fucking fault!

The bitch was going to *pay*.

She thought her life was so perfect? She was about to find out how quickly a perfect life could fall apart...just like Hillary's had.

Grimacing, she stopped pacing and turned to head toward the garage. She had a meeting with a guy who'd promised her the best black tar heroin she'd ever get her hands on. She didn't give a shit about the quality, she just needed the high.

Ignoring the pile of laundry that needed to be done, the dishes in the sink, and the empty dog dish, Hillary left the house. Fuck it. She wasn't a slave. Her family could do shit for themselves for once! She had people to meet...and revenge plans to make.

CHAPTER FOURTEEN

Brock kissed Finley in the kitchen at The Sweet Tooth. He'd come in with her, as usual, to spend time together as she was getting ready for the day. Things between them had never been better. She was carrying his child—a fact Bristol discovered yesterday, so he couldn't wait to tell the rest of their friends—had officially moved in with him already, and no matter how much time they spent together, he still couldn't get enough.

His Finley was funny, sweet, and even still bashful at times. He loved corrupting her. Turning what she thought was embarrassing into something carnal. Making her beg for him to play with her ass, fuck her harder, or eat her out after he'd come inside her. But he wasn't with her because of all the sex, as hot as it was. He genuinely *liked* her. She was such a good person. Even to those who didn't deserve it.

She always made excuses for people who were assholes to her or Liam when they came into her shop. When he raged about someone being rude, she simply shrugged and said they were probably going through something in their lives that others knew nothing about, and she was willing to cut them a break.

That wasn't Brock's philosophy in life...if someone was an asshole, if they didn't have the decency not to take their own personal problems out on someone else, they deserved to be taken down a peg. But her kind heart was only one of the many reasons why he loved his Finley so much.

She was his reward. He didn't deserve her, and he knew it. She could do so much better than him. But now that she was carrying his child and had said she loved him, he wasn't letting her go. Ever. He'd do whatever it took to keep her.

This morning, she was stressed because she had to get three catering orders together, as well as fill the cases in the store for walk-ins. Brock was proud as he could be that her catering business had taken off like it had, but he also worried about the stress it put on her.

"You know, you don't have to accept every single job that comes in," he told her as he held her close. Davis had left thirty minutes earlier, but he said he'd be back around lunch to help finish up anything she hadn't been able to complete. The man had been invaluable, and even though he was still reserved and didn't come by every day, he was an important reason why The Sweet Tooth was doing so well.

"I know," she said. But his Finley was too nice to turn anyone down.

"What if you made it clear that you only accept two custom jobs a day? Period. First come, first served. That would give you some breathing room...especially once you're further along in your pregnancy. And it would create scarcity."

"What do you mean?" she asked.

"I mean, if people know that they can't just wander in and get a custom cake whenever they want, that they actually have to plan, it would make your time and work more valuable. Not to mention, you could probably charge more than you are."

"I don't want to take advantage of anyone," she protested.

"And you wouldn't be. But your time *is* valuable. And your skill is out of this world. You think Bristol accepts every request for her to make a window?" He didn't give her time to answer. "No. She charges out the nose because her pieces are rare and she knows people will pay to own one. And she gets to choose which projects she wants to do. It's simple economics, Fin."

She sighed. "But I'd feel awful if someone needed something and I said no."

"It's a cake, hon. Not a gold-plated engagement ring."

She still looked unsure.

"What if you stocked some of the most popular cakes and cupcakes in a special case in the front? If someone needs something last-minute, they can choose from the selection, and you can teach Liam how to write shit like 'Happy Birthday' or 'Congrats on Being an Asshole' on the top."

She giggled.

He loved that sound. "All I'm saying is, running around like a chicken with your head cut off isn't going to work once you're in your last trimester. Or when our Little Bean is here. You want to spend every day from four-thirty in the morning until six at night here in the store once he or she is born?"

Finley frowned. "No."

"Right. You need to make changes now, so when that time comes, it's not a shock to your customers."

"You're right." Then she lifted a hand and put it over his mouth. "And don't say 'I know.'"

She knew him too well. Brock licked her palm, tasting flour from where she'd rolled out some dough for more cinnamon rolls right before he said he needed to get going.

He loved the shiver that went through her at the feel of his tongue on her skin. Of course, that made him think about putting his lips and tongue on other places on her body.

"No," she said with a shake of her head and a smile. "Don't even think about it. I have stuff to do."

Brock smiled back as she lowered her hand. "I love you," he said.

"I love you too."

"Don't work too hard today."

"I won't."

He rolled his eyes.

"I could say the same about you," she countered.

She wasn't wrong. Brock did work hard, but now he did it so he could support his soon-to-be family, not because he was bored out of his skull and didn't want to go home to an empty house.

"Call me when you're done here," he said. "I'm gonna pick up dinner from On the Rocks, and I want to time it so it's still warm by the time you get home."

"Okay."

Brock smiled again and couldn't help but run his gaze

down her body. She was so damn lush. Her curves made him half mad with lust. And she was all his. Anyone who turned up their nose at plus-size women didn't know what they were missing.

"I have cinnamon rolls to finish," she said firmly.

Brock sighed. "I know."

"Is this normal?" she asked. "I mean, how we can't keep our hands off each other?"

"Don't know, don't care," he said immediately. "Our relationship is exactly how it should be."

"I think so too," she said—then licked her lips sensually.

"Hold that thought," Brock said with a chuckle, then he kissed her hard. He didn't linger, because it was difficult enough to tear himself away. Kissing her the way he wanted to would lead to both of them being unsatisfied.

He brushed his thumb over her cheek, then grinned as he backed away. "See you later."

"Later."

He forced himself to turn and walk out of the kitchen. He gave Liam a chin lift as he went and said hello to a few people in line that he knew.

As he walked toward his truck parked in front of the building, Brock had the thought that his life was absolutely perfect.

On its heels, an insidious voice whispered that nothing perfect lasted forever.

He climbed behind the wheel of the truck and shivered. No, nothing was going to happen. He and Finley were great. They were going to have a child. Get married. Live happily ever after. Nothing and no one would fuck with his life. He wouldn't allow it.

Taking a deep breath, he started the engine and headed for Old Town Auto. He had an engine to rebuild.

* * *

Around four o'clock, Brock's phone rang. He'd been expecting Finley's call.

"Hey, sweetheart. How was your day?"

"Busy," she said with a laugh. "Yours?"

"Same. You on your way home?"

"Kind of."

"Kind of?" he asked. "How can you *kind of* be on your way home?"

"Well, I was all set to start wrapping things up when I got a call."

Brock groaned. "Please tell me you said no."

Finley sighed. "I couldn't! She needs a cake for her daughter's thirteenth birthday party tonight!"

"Finley," Brock said in exasperation.

"I know, I know. And I thought about what you said this morning, and I think it's a good idea. But I couldn't say no. She planned on making the cake herself but her oven quit working. The woman said it literally blew up or something. So now she's dealing with trying to air out the house before ten teenagers show up. She said it didn't need to be fancy or anything, and she's paying me double. *And* she's going to give me a hundred bucks to deliver it. Aren't you at least proud of me for charging her more for the late notice?"

Brock sighed in frustration. "I am. But...you need a better method for taking orders. Like, a form online, or a special phone number that you aren't allowed to answer.

Let Liam take the requests. You can't say no to a single hard-luck story, Fin."

"I know," she said. "Are you mad?"

"Of course not. I can be there in about fifteen minutes. I need to finish what I'm doing and clean up a bit, then I'll be there to pick you up."

"Oh no, I need to get going right now. I'll call Elsie and put in our order so the food's ready for when you get here. The lady's house is only like eight minutes from town. We can probably get home around the same time."

Brock didn't like it, but he remembered her begging him not to smother her. "All right. But I don't think it's a good idea for people to get used to you making deliveries after hours."

"This is a one-time thing. And I know the woman. I mean, I've seen her. She's been in the shop before. She's involved in the PTA and has a high school boy on the football team and her daughter is a cheerleader or something. It's fine."

"Just because someone looks safe on the outside doesn't mean they are," Brock felt compelled to say.

"I know, but Hillary's harmless. I'm just going to drive the cake out there, then head home. Now, what do you want me to order you for dinner?"

When Brock hung up a few minutes later, he wanted to call Finley right back and tell her that he'd changed his mind. That he'd leave right now and pick her up to deliver the cake. But he sighed and shook his head. No. He'd promised not to go overboard with his protective tendencies.

He halfheartedly cleaned up his work area and was ready to leave in half the time it should've taken him. The food wasn't ready when he got to On the Rocks, and he chatted with Zeke as he waited for his and Finley's dinner.

He was disappointed when he beat Finley home, but grabbed a quick shower after he put their dinner in the oven to stay warm. When he got out of the shower, she still wasn't home.

Looking at his watch, Brock saw that thirty minutes had passed since he'd last talked to her. It was possible she'd lost track of time talking to the woman she was delivering the cake to...

But uneasiness swam through Brock's veins, and he pulled out his phone. He clicked on Finley's name and listened to the ringing in his ear. She didn't pick up and the call went to voicemail.

"Hey, Fin. It's me. Just wanted to call and check on you. Call me as soon as you can. Love you."

He hung up and tapped the phone on his chin. Brock paced the house as another five minutes crawled by. He tried calling Finley again, and once more it went to voicemail.

Something was wrong. He knew it deep in his bones.

He also knew he was a paranoid son-of-a-bitch...but he had the same feeling now that he used to get when shit was about to hit the fan while searching for someone who'd crossed the border illegally.

Mentally kicking himself for not asking Finley for the address of the home she was going to, Brock dialed Simon.

"Fallport PD. Chief Hill speaking," he answered.

"Hey, Simon. This is Brock Mabrey."

"What's up?" the chief asked.

"I'm hoping nothing. Finley was supposed to deliver a cake and be home twenty minutes ago. But she's not here."

"Hmmm. There haven't been any accidents reported in the last half hour or so," the chief said.

Brock swallowed hard. Not that he wanted Finley to have been in an accident, but that would be preferrable to the nightmare scenarios going through his head at the moment. "Something's wrong," he said. "I want to go to the house where she was supposed to deliver the cake, but I didn't think to get the address when I talked to Finley."

"Do you know anything about where she was going?"

"The woman who ordered the cake has two kids, the girl is thirteen and it's her birthday. The boy plays football on the high school team. The customer's name is Hillary. I don't know her last name."

"Kendall," Simon said without hesitation. "Hillary Kendall. Her daughter's name is Nevaeh, which is Heaven spelled backward," he said with a chuckle. "Her son's a good ball player for sure. He should be able to play in college, if that's what he wants to do."

"You know their address?"

"Of course. But you aren't going out there on your own. I'll be at your place in two minutes. Can you wait that long?"

Brock wasn't sure he could, but having an officer with him would make things much easier. He couldn't exactly barge his way inside the woman's house without any proof that Finley was there. "I'll wait," he clipped.

"On my way," Simon said, then hung up.

Nausea churned in Brock's belly. Why was he even thinking about having to push his way into someone's house, anyway? That shouldn't even be a thought in his head.

But it was. Because he knew Finley would never worry

him like this if she could avoid it. She'd been very good about letting him know where she was and what she was doing. He wasn't being controlling; he didn't care who she hung out with or where she went, he just needed to know she was safe.

And his instincts were screaming that she was anything but safe right now. Not answering her phone, not texting him to let him know where she was, being—he looked at his watch—thirty-five minutes later than expected.

As he waited for Simon to arrive, Brock called Talon.

"Hey, Brock."

"Finley's missing."

"What?"

"She's missing. She was going to deliver a cake then come home. She's not here."

"Where?"

Brock gave his friend the name of the woman who'd ordered the cake. "Simon's coming to get me to go to her house."

"I'm calling Raid, we'll be right behind you."

"Thanks," he said, seeing a car pull up outside the house. "Simon's here."

"Stay strong. We're coming."

Brock hung up, and even though he was relieved his friends were coming to have his back, unease still churned in his gut. Finley needed him. He knew it as well as Rocky had known when Bristol was in trouble, and as his other friends knew their women were in danger.

He jumped into Simon's cruiser and they were moving before Brock had a chance to buckle his seat belt. Once the chief told him where they were heading, he texted the address to Talon.

"Has the crime lab gotten back to you with the trace on the number called from my sat phone?" Brock asked. He'd been lax in talking with Simon for the last couple days about what was going on with the men who'd kidnapped him and Finley in the woods. "Any word on Pete and Cory?"

"The lab's backed way the fuck up. Budget cuts and all that shit," Simon said tersely. "Cory's still in the wind, but Pete was found."

"He was?" Brock asked. "Why didn't you tell me?"

"I just did," Simon said calmly.

"What'd he say? Who were they working with?"

"He was dead," Simon told him. "Overdose."

"Fuck," Brock muttered.

"Yeah, but when I called a few days ago to chew someone's ass out at the lab, I was promised I'd have the information by the end of the week."

Brock silently fumed.

"You think this has something to do with that?" the chief asked.

"What else am I supposed to think?" he retorted. "Finley's the nicest person ever. She smells like fucking vanilla and cinnamon. She has a permanent smile on her face and she's never had a harsh word for anyone, even the assholes who deserve it."

"Maybe she had a flat tire," Simon suggested. "Or she stayed to help Hillary with the party."

Both of those things were possible, but Brock shook his head. "She would've called."

"Yeah," Simon agreed.

It only took five minutes to reach the house Hillary Kendall lived in with her family. It was a middle-class neighborhood, the kind that would be full of kids playing in all the yards during the summer. It was too cold for that now, but the homes were well-maintained and it looked perfectly harmless.

Simon pulled into the Kendalls' driveway, and Brock frowned. "There's supposed to be a party going on here."

"Maybe everyone has already dropped off their kids," Simon suggested as he got out of the car. "Stay calm, Brock," he ordered. "And stay behind me."

Brock nodded as the police chief walked up to the front door. He rang the doorbell and both men waited impatiently for someone to answer.

After what seemed like hours but was probably only twenty seconds or so, a teenage boy opened the door. "Can I help you?"

"Robert, right?" Simon asked.

The boy nodded.

"Is your mom home?"

He shrugged. "No."

"No?" Simon asked in surprise.

"She's always gone these days," the boy said.

"What about your sister?"

"She's got a thing at school. Don't know what. Why?"

Brock turned and kicked a dead plant sitting on the walkway to the porch as hard as he could. It went flying across the lawn just as Tal and Raid arrived.

He heard Simon asking the boy if today was his sister's birthday, and the kid's confused response was that, no, her birthday was in April.

"She here?" Tal asked as he approached.

"No. It's not the kid's birthday and the woman who ordered the cake isn't here."

Simon returned to his side. "Call Liam," he ordered Brock.

He looked back at the house. The boy was still standing at the front door, looking confused and a little worried.

"You going to search the house?" Raid asked the police chief.

"No need. She's not here. The boy's not lying. He's the only one home."

Brock already had his phone to his ear. As soon as Liam answered, he said, "I need the address of where Finley was going to deliver that cake this afternoon."

To his credit, Liam didn't ask questions. Didn't demand to know why Brock sounded so curt. "Hang on...I looked it up on Google Maps for her to find out how far it was."

Brock held his breath as he waited for Liam to find the address. He rattled it off, and Brock repeated it for the men around him.

"Is she okay?" Liam asked.

"She will be," Brock vowed. But of course he didn't know that. Just this morning, he'd had the thought that his life was perfect—and now he could literally lose everything. The woman he loved, their child...

Determination rose within him. No. He wasn't going to fucking lose Finley. Not when he'd just found her.

As if Tal could read his mind, he put his hand on Brock's shoulder. "We'll find her."

Brock nodded and jogged toward Simon's car. Damn straight they were going to find Finley, and when they did, anyone who'd lain a finger on her was going to pay. He had no qualms about hurting a woman. He knew as well as the rest of the men on his team that women could be just as evil as men. And if Hillary Kendall was the person behind Finley's kidnapping, she obviously had no problem hurting others to get what she wanted.

As they sped toward the address Liam had given them, Brock realized that he didn't give a shit *what* Hillary might want. He had no idea why she'd lured Finley out of her shop. The bottom line was, none of that mattered. He'd keep Finley and their Little Bean safe, or die trying.

CHAPTER FIFTEEN

Finley frowned as she pulled up at the address Hillary had given her.

"This can't be right," she muttered as she glanced around the rundown neighborhood. Many of the houses were boarded up, and those that weren't had a look of neglect about them. There was no way Hillary Kendall lived here. There must've been a mistake.

Just as Finley reached for the gear shift to reverse her car, her driver's side door opened and the barrel of a pistol was shoved against her head.

"Get out of the car," a high-pitched voice ordered.

Finley immediately put her hands up and said, "Don't hurt me. Take whatever money I've got. And the car."

"I don't want your fucking money. Or your car," the woman said. She shoved the pistol harder against her skull. "Get out."

Finley's heart was beating a million miles an hour. This couldn't be happening. All she could think about was the life in her womb. If she was shot, her and Brock's Little Bean would never have a chance to be born. Would never know how much he or she was loved.

Whoever was holding the gun to her head obviously wanted something. Otherwise, she would've shot her already...right? Finley prayed that was going to be this woman's mistake.

Very slowly, she slid out of the car and got her first look at the person threatening her.

"Hillary?" Finley said in disbelief.

"Yeah, it's me, bitch. Walk!"

Confused, Finley did as ordered. She desperately wanted to make a break for it, but she had no idea if anyone was with Hillary, and she definitely didn't want to get shot in the back as she ran.

Panic almost overwhelmed her. She wasn't some soldier or commando. Wasn't an officer like Brock. When they'd been in the woods and she'd had that knife to her throat, she hadn't panicked because Brock had been with her, and she knew he'd know what to do. But now it was just her. And her unborn child. A tiny little human who was relying on her to get them out of this.

Finley had no idea what to do or how to get them both to safety.

Hillary forced her to walk into the dilapidated house. As soon as she entered, Finley gagged a little at the stench. Something had died and was rotting in there. She could only pray it wasn't a human body.

The house was clearly old, the kind built long before open-concept was a thing, with a small foyer that fed into a hallway. Hillary marched her down the narrow passage to a large entryway on the right. A living room. "Sit," she ordered, pointing to a lone wooden chair in the middle of the room.

Finley walked over to the rickety chair and held her breath as she sat. With her luck, the damn thing would break under her weight. Luckily, it held, although the creaking when she sat had her holding her breath for a moment.

Feeling much better now that the weapon wasn't right against her head, Finley took a deep breath. Of course, that didn't mean Hillary wasn't still pointing the damn gun at her. She was.

"Lean over and use those zip-ties to attach yourself to the legs of the chair."

Looking down, Finley saw two white plastic zip-ties lying on the floor at her feet. There was no way they were going to fit around both her ankles and the legs of the chair. She looked up at Hillary to tell her as much, but the woman was glaring at her so hard, Finley swallowed the words.

She grabbed a zip-tie and inched up the leg of her cotton pants. They were kind of like scrubs...nice and roomy. She liked wearing them to bake in because they didn't constrict and were very comfortable.

Finley wrapped the tie around her ankle and, just as she'd thought, there was no way she was going to be able to get the damn thing to fasten around the leg of the chair. Her breathing increased as she momentarily gave into panic. Then she took a deep breath.

"What's taking so long? Hurry up, bitch!"

Finley looked up and asked, "Why are you doing this?"

"Because you fucked up my life!" Hillary spat.

Surprised at the venom in her tone, Finley said, "I don't even know you. I think you've only come into the bakery once."

"That was to scope things out. To come face-to-face with the cunt whose life I was going to ruin, just like she ruined mine!"

Flinching at the absolute hatred in the woman's expression, Finley was relieved that she'd at least diverted her attention. As the woman went on and on about how bad her life was, Finley leaned down again and did her best to make it look as if she was wrapping the zip-tie around the chair and her ankle. In reality, it was only around her ankle, fastened in the back. If she didn't move her feet away from the chair, she could pray that Hillary might not notice.

The noise the tie made as the plastic zipped closed made the other woman cackle in glee. "Now the other one."

Dropping the hem of her pants leg over the zip-tie to hide it, Finley held her breath as she did the same with her left ankle.

Hillary was so busy pacing while saying something about her knee and Roanoke and heroin, she still didn't notice that her captive wasn't actually attached to the chair.

Finley's heart was beating furiously in her chest. Her arms were shaky with adrenaline, but she couldn't think of anything to do next. Yes, she'd gotten one over on her captor with the zip-ties, but if Hillary was going to shoot her, there wasn't much Finley could do about it.

To her utter relief, the thought that she was now

bound seemed to make Hillary let down her guard. The pistol she'd been pointing at her the entire time lowered.

"It's all your goddamn fault! If you'd just kept your fucking mouth *shut*, this wouldn't be happening to you! You had to go and blab about my supplier's truck! He freaked out and refused to come to Fallport anymore, so I had to go to *him*. And driving to Roanoke every other day is a pain in the ass and hard to miss. Then my clients got spooked after what happened with Pete and Cory, so they aren't buying from me now—and there went all my money! My supplier refused to sell to me. I had to find other means to get my high. That *means* was heroin, you bitch! I'd avoided hard drugs for so long and now I'm a fucking addict—all because of *you*!"

She continued with her tirade, but Finley tuned her out. The woman was obviously crazy. She'd have never even said anything about the damn truck if Pete and Cory hadn't kidnapped her. If the hell that was Hillary's life was anyone's fault, it was her own.

Finley let Hillary rant on as she furtively searched the room to see if there was anything she could use as a weapon. She could probably use the chair she was sitting on, bash it over Hillary's head, but with the way it creaked and groaned as she shifted, it would probably break into a million pieces and do little damage.

She needed to get hold of the gun, but she'd never shot a weapon in her life. What if she couldn't figure out how to work it? And she really didn't want to have to kill Hillary. She just wanted to get away.

"Are you listening to me?" Hillary screeched.

Finley looked up at her and nodded. "Yes," she said in a much firmer voice than she'd expected to hear. Inside, she was quaking; outwardly, she seemed as calm as if she was meeting a good friend for lunch.

"You'd better be! Because I'm the last voice you're ever gonna hear. No one will know what happened to you. The fire will burn through those zip-ties and everyone will just think you were in the wrong place at the wrong time!"

Finley frowned. Fire?

Before she could ask Hillary what she was talking about, and possibly beg for her life—because at this point, that seemed to be the only option she had for getting out of this—Hillary spun away.

Finley tensed. This was her chance.

But the other woman had turned around again before Finley could even move. She was holding two one-gallon jugs Finley hadn't even noticed...and they were filled with some sort of liquid.

"What, you aren't going to beg for your life?" Hillary asked with a huge grin on her face.

Finley *had* been about to do just that, but she didn't get a word out before Hillary went on.

"It won't do you any good. And now you know who I am, so I can't let you go anyway." As she drew closer, Finley braced. Hillary put one of the jugs on the floor, and unscrewed the cap of the other. She was still holding the pistol, so some of the liquid splashed out of the container.

"Shit!" Hillary swore as the liquid splattered her shirt and hands.

Finley's insides froze as a familiar smell hit her nose.

Gasoline.

She knew exactly what this insane woman had planned for her.

As if reading her mind, Hillary upended the contents of the first jug over Finley's head.

Gasping in shock, Finley immediately began to cough violently as she inhaled fumes from the gas. Any idea of fighting back receded as the only thought in her head was getting some much-needed oxygen into her lungs. Her ears began ringing, and she vaguely heard Hillary laughing maniacally.

Before Finley could catch her breath, Hillary was pouring the contents of the second jug onto her lap, soaking her clothes.

It hurt to breathe and some of the gas leaked into her eyes, making them burn viciously. Everything around her wavered as her eyes overflowed with tears, her body instinctively trying to flush out the toxic liquid. This situation had gone from bad to worse.

Rivers of tears were still streaming down her face as Hillary threw the second jug to the floor, then backed away a few feet, a triumphant look on her face.

"Please, don't do this!" Finley choked out. If this woman wanted her to beg, that was what she'd do. She'd do anything to live.

Desperately, she thought again about jumping up from the chair and using it as a weapon, but her vision was shit from the gas and it was still almost impossible to breathe through the fumes. Hillary stood between her and the entrance to the living room. If she failed to incapacitate the woman, she'd be shot immediately.

She'd waited too long to fight back. A mistake that was going to result in her death.

And the death of her and Brock's child.

"It's too late. You're gonna burn. Fat makes a fire burn

hotter too," Hillary seethed. "There's not gonna be anything left but ashes by the time someone calls the fire department. There aren't any neighbors around here to give a shit. I should know—I've sold enough pills to the losers who live in these houses. You should've minded your own business, bitch."

Hillary smiled then. A truly evil smile, as she raised the pistol and pointed it at Finley's head. "Want me to shoot you instead? Make this nice and fast?" she asked.

Finley wanted to say yes. The thought of being set on fire was enough to literally make her pee her pants. She was so scared. Terrified. One of her hands went to her belly...

No, if Hillary shot her, she'd be dead immediately, without even a sliver of a chance to save herself and Little Bean.

"No? Fine by me. I'd rather watch you burn." She took something out of her pocket and smirked.

A book of matches.

She awkwardly tore a match from the pack; it was apparently tough to point a gun while manipulating a book of matches at the same time.

"Time to say goodbye, bitch!" Hillary said as she backed away a little more, clearly intending to toss the match from a safe distance. She struck the match on the strike pad.

Everything seemed to happen at once.

The second the match burst into a flame, a large whoosh sounded—and Hillary let out a screech.

The fumes from the gas on her hands and clothes caught fire.

Finley acted without thought. She leapt from the chair,

desperate to get away from the fire that was engulfing Hillary's clothes.

She dropped to the floor, frantically trying to stifle the flames. The screams of pain and terror coming from the woman would haunt Finley forever—but she didn't pause. She was covered in gas; if she got anywhere near Hillary in an attempt to help, she'd share her fate.

Racing to the front door, Finley was instantly swamped in dismay to find it locked. There was an old-fashioned dead bolt that required a key. She vaguely remembered Hillary pocketing something after they'd entered the house and she'd locked the door behind them.

She wasted a precious second wondering how in the hell her captor had the keys to an abandoned house, before panic almost overwhelmed her again. She could hear keening wails from the living room, louder than ever, as well the crackling of flames as the gasoline spilled on the floor fueled the growing inferno.

Finley ran toward the back of the house, tripping over a loose board in the hall and landing hard on her face. Blood welled up in her mouth, but she ignored it. All she could think of was the trail of gas she was leaving in her wake. The liquid was dripping off her clothes and hair, and almost deliriously, she couldn't help thinking of the old cartoons where fire raced along a trail of gas on the ground. She had no idea if that was actually possible or not, but she didn't want to find out.

Sobbing, Finley found herself in a small kitchen, or what *used* to be a kitchen. There was a disgusting sink and a space for a refrigerator and stove. She saw the carcass of some sort of animal in the corner, which explained why the house smelled so bad. There were flies on what was left of the animal, and all over the kitchen.

Nausea rose within Finley. She had no time to be sick. She had to get out. The worst thing about this room was that there wasn't a door.

But there *was* a small window over the sink.

She didn't even hesitate. Climbing onto the counter, Finley tried desperately to figure out how to unlock it. Thick smoke began to waft into the room. Finley gave up on the lock and sat on her ass, aiming a foot at the window. She kicked as hard as she could.

To her surprise, it broke easily. Pain arched up her leg from where the glass cut her calf, but she was too relieved to have a way out of the house of horrors to care.

The rest of the glass was easy to kick out, and it was at that moment when Finley had second thoughts. She wasn't sure she could even fit out of the window.

Then she thought about the baby inside of her—and determination welled. She would fit. There was no *way* she was coming this close to escaping, only to fail now.

Taking a brief second to look out the window, she saw it opened to an overgrown backyard that was completely fenced in. There was a doghouse in the back corner, and what looked like another animal carcass near it. Her heart breaking for the poor dog who'd obviously been left to fend for itself at some point, Finley took a deep breath.

It was about six feet or so to the ground from the window. She didn't really want to go out head first, but that seemed the best way to maneuver herself out the window and have some sort of control.

Hearing something behind her, Finley turned to the kitchen door...

And stared in horror as Hillary stumbled into the room.

Her face looked like the stuff of nightmares, burnt almost beyond recognition, the flesh seemingly melting before Finley's eyes. There was a deep gurgling sound coming from her throat that Finley could hear even over the crackle of the flames engulfing her body and every surface she touched.

Her arm came up slowly and she reached a hand toward Finley.

It was *impossible* that the woman was still walking! But obviously adrenaline, hatred, drugs, her need for revenge...*something* was keeping her upright.

Finley was out of time. If that burning zombie bitch touched her soaked clothes, Finley was done for.

She turned and dove out the window. There were still a few small shards of glass stubbornly sticking to the windowpane, but Finley didn't feel them bite into her skin as she escaped. For a split second, she thought she wasn't going to make it. That she was too fat. But she wiggled frantically until her hips and stomach slipped through. She fell to the ground in an undignified heap, biting her tongue for the second time in five minutes.

Turning over onto her butt, Finley scrambled away from the window. Keeping her eyes on the gaping space, praying Hillary wouldn't—couldn't—follow her, she held her breath as she made her way across the yard toward the farthest back corner, where she'd seen the dog house.

She didn't see any more of Hillary, but before too long, flames were licking out of the open kitchen window. Finley forced herself to her feet and searched for a back or side gate so she could get out of the yard and away from the burning house.

There wasn't one.

She shoved at the fence, but its boards didn't budge. She let out a hysterical laugh. Figured she'd find herself in the only yard in a dilapidated block that had a fucking impenetrable fence. Looking down at the sizable carcass, she could only assume the previous owners had reinforced their fence because they had a very large, powerful dog they didn't want escaping.

She tried to shove the dog house closer to the fence so she could stand on it and climb over, but the stupid thing wouldn't budge. Kneeling on the ground, she dug at the packed dirt, trying to free the structure, only to realize whoever had built the strong fence had also reinforced the doghouse. Again, probably because the dog was big and powerful.

Increasingly desperate, Finley looked once more for an escape route and *finally* found a gate—at the front. Right next to the house.

The now wildly burning house.

There was no way in hell she was getting anywhere near it. She had no idea how close she had to be for the fumes of her clothes to ignite, and she wasn't willing to risk it.

Just as she had that thought, her skin began to burn.

Squealing frantically, she looked down, half expecting to find her body on fire, but it seemed it was the feel of the gasoline on her skin finally registering.

Whimpering, Finley tore at her shirt, whipping it over her head and throwing it as far as she could. She did the same with her pants. She felt a little better with the gasoline-soaked clothes off, but her hair was still drenched.

Backing into the corner of the yard, as far away from the burning house as she could, Finley prayed hard that someone would call in the blaze. The possibility that the fence could catch fire was an increasing threat.

"Brock," she croaked, her gaze fixed on the house. He'd get to her as fast as he could. She had no doubt.

CHAPTER SIXTEEN

Brock stared at the house in absolute horror as they approached. It was one of the poorer neighborhoods in Fallport, and there were flames shooting out of every window of the house and from under the eaves. He heard Simon on the radio calling for the fire department, but all Brock could see was Finley's car parked in the driveway. The tires were smoking from the heat of the fire that was only feet away.

She was here. And if she was inside, there was absolutely no chance of her still being alive.

That didn't stop him from leaping out of the car and running toward the front door.

He was roughly tackled from behind. Tal and Raid held his arms as he struggled with every bit of strength he had. "Let me go!" he cried desperately.

"You can't go in there!" Raid shouted.

"Fin's in there!" Brock yelled back, his voice cracking.

All movement stopped when, a split-second later, the roof on the second floor collapsed.

An inhuman scream left Brock's mouth as any hope of saving the woman he loved with every molecule in his body was crushed.

This wasn't going to end the way it had when Caryn had rescued Lilly from a house fire. It was too late.

He was too late.

In the distance, he heard sirens, but Brock couldn't take his eyes off the inferno. He'd taken too long to act when Finley hadn't come home when she should have. He'd gotten complacent with a loved one's safety for the first time ever—and the only person he'd ever vowed to love and protect had suffered the consequences.

Brock shut down. His entire body went numb. Nothing would be the same again. He'd have to leave Fallport. How could he stay? He couldn't. He wasn't strong enough to drive past The Sweet Tooth and know his Fin wouldn't be there. To regularly see Lilly, Elsie, and the others.

Then another thought struck him, and the pain literally made him clutch his chest.

Their child.

Not only had he lost Finley...his chance to be a father had literally gone up in flames.

A sound he didn't recognize erupted, eclipsing the roar of the flames, and he realized seconds later the noise was coming from him. A combination whimper, moan, and desperate keening. He couldn't stop. Despair filled him. He'd failed not only Finley, but their Little Bean too. He'd never forgive himself. Ever.

Tal and Raid sat back slowly, recognizing the threat of him running into the burning building had passed. They all knew it was too late.

Then, through the fog that had descended over Brock, another sound penetrated.

He tilted his head in confusion, trying to hear it better over the crackling of the flames consuming the building and the increasingly loud sirens. He stood abruptly.

The fire engine turned down the street, and then all Brock could hear was the siren echoing off the other houses, making his ears ring. But he was already moving. He knew what he'd heard.

His name.

Adrenaline coursed through him as he frantically looked around, trying to pinpoint where the sound might have come from.

He took off running before Tal and Raid could grab him again. But he wasn't heading for the now completely engulfed house. No, he went straight to the wooden gate on the right side of the yard. The wood was smoking, but it hadn't caught fire yet.

"Brock, what—"

Raid didn't get another word out before Brock was pulling frantically on the wood. "Help me!" he ordered.

Bless his friends, they didn't ask any questions. Didn't ask what the hell he was doing, they simply joined him in trying to open the gate. It was obviously padlocked from the inside, but that wasn't going to stop Brock. He'd heard what he heard, and for the first time since arriving to find the home shrouded in flames, hope filled him.

The men resorted to kicking the planks of wood. First one board finally broke. Then another. When Raid knocked a third one out, Brock wasn't waiting any longer. He got on his knees and shoved his head and shoulders through the opening. It was a tight fit, but he didn't even feel the scrapes of the jagged wood against his back as he forced himself into the yard. Didn't feel the heat of the flames burning just feet from his face.

The weeds were long, probably around a foot high, but as if his entire being knew exactly where to look, Brock's gaze locked onto a figure huddled at the far back corner of the yard.

"Bloody hell!" He heard Tal exclaim as he made his way through the same hole Brock had just vacated.

Brock was already on the move. He was running through the yard toward Finley. He dropped to his knees in front of her, noticing immediately that she was practically naked, wearing nothing but her bra and panties...and, ominously, zip-ties around her ankles. The very sight of the tiny strips of plastic had his guts churning.

Her clothes and shoes were in a heap several yards from where she huddled, her knees curled in front of her and her arms clasped around them.

"Finley!" he croaked.

"Don't touch me!" she shouted, clearly panicked.

Brock froze. "What?"

"I'm covered in gas! If you touch me, you'll get it on you too. I can't watch you die, Brock! I can't! All it'll take is one of those sparks and I'll go up in flames like she did!"

It was obvious Finley was in shock, but Brock immediately understood the seriousness of the situation. Her hair was wet, and only now did the pungent scent of gasoline register. He didn't think a spark would cause the liquid to ignite, but he wasn't going to take any chances. He placed a hand on Finley's knee—he needed the contact—and shouted to Raid, who was doing his best to break down more of the gate.

"Get a hose back here!" he yelled, then turned back to Finley without waiting to see if Raid was listening. He sat next to her, then picked her up and placed her onto his lap. She fought him for a few precious seconds...then seemed to melt against him.

As soon as his hand cupped her nape, she burst into tears. They were huge, wrenching sobs that tore Brock's heart out. His own eyes filled with tears, and he wasn't ashamed when they spilled over and fell down his cheeks. He thought he'd lost everything, and now here he was, holding a scared-to-death but alive Finley in his arms.

He wanted to ask what happened. How the hell she'd ended up covered in gas in the backyard of this dilapidated house, but that could wait. Reassuring his woman that she was all right couldn't.

"She's bleeding," Tal said gently after a moment. "Brock, let me take a look at her."

At his words, Finley clutched Brock tighter.

"She's okay," he said softly. "You're okay," he told Finley. "Aren't you?"

It took a moment, but he felt her take a long, deep breath before she nodded. She lifted her head and looked at Tal, who was crouched beside them. "Cut my arms and calf getting out the window."

"And your hips too," Tal added.

Finley frowned. "I did?"

"She's in shock," he said, standing and glaring at the side of the house, as if that would make the firefighters magically appear.

But it seemed as if Tal's impatient glare actually did the trick. Raid appeared and pointed toward the corner where Brock and Finley were sitting.

Two firefighters pulled a hose through the yard.

"She's covered in gasoline. I don't want to risk taking her anywhere near the house until that shit is rinsed off," Brock explained to the firefighter holding the nozzle. He recognized him. It was Oscar. He'd been assigned as captain of the Fallport Fire Department after the former captain, and several of his close friends, were fired.

"Smart," he said. "This will be cold," he warned.

Brock nodded and turned to Finley. "Hold your breath," he told her.

She nodded, and Brock motioned for Oscar to proceed.

He gently opened the nozzle until a light stream of water came out of the hose. When fighting a fire, the immense pressure of the water exiting the nozzle could actually be very dangerous, but Oscar was careful not to let it get out of hand.

Brock shivered as the water cascaded over both him and Finley. She jerked in his arms when the water hit but didn't try to get away.

"Get her hair good." Brock heard Talon order.

After about fifteen more seconds, the water turned off. "That should be good enough to get her to the ambulance," Oscar said.

Brock nodded. "Thank you." He reached a hand up toward Tal. His friend took it, and Brock felt a hand on his bicep. Raid, standing on his other side. Then he was standing with Finley in his arms. He set her on her feet gently, running his eyes down her body, noting her wounds. She was shivering, probably more from shock and reaction than from the cold.

She looked up at him, then quickly at Tal and Raid, and her gaze hit the ground...the way it used to before they'd gotten together. When she thought there was no way he could ever want her because of her size.

Brock turned to Raid. "Shirt," he ordered.

Without hesitation, Raiden stripped off his T-shirt and handed it to Brock.

"Hang on, sweetheart. I'll have you covered in a second." He draped the material over her still dripping hair, and she immediately lifted a hand to find the arm hole. As soon as she was covered, she swayed slightly.

Brock swore and wrapped an arm around her waist. His clothes were soaking wet, and now the dry shirt would be as well, but he didn't even think twice about it. Glancing at the house, he saw Oscar and the other two firefighters were using the hose to pour water on the side nearest the gate, which was now lying completely demolished on the ground.

Eyeing the fire, and deciding it was more important to get Finley out of this yard than wait for another exit to be created, he urged her forward.

"Brock, no!" she protested.

He stopped and turned her toward him. "Do you think I'd let anything happen to you? I swear to God, I would've walked into that burning house to get to you if I thought there was even a one percent chance you were still alive."

He watched the fear swirl in her eyes, but he also saw trust. In him.

"Okay," she said, voice shaky. "But if we burst into flames, don't blame me."

Fuck, he loved this woman. He had no idea what had

happened in that house—it was bad, whatever it was. But somehow, she'd managed to escape. She was bleeding, obviously traumatized, but alive. And still able to make a joke.

"At least this didn't happen while we were on a date," he replied. He wasn't really in the mood to joke back, but if she could, then he'd follow her lead.

She snorted, and the sound was so Finley, something that had tightened within Brock finally eased.

Situating himself on her right side, with Tal in front of them and Raid at their backs, Brock held Finley close as they quickly walked past the side of the house that was now simply smoking instead of engulfed in flames.

He felt Finley sigh in relief as they made it through the gate. Brock steered her toward an ambulance that was sitting behind the firetrucks.

"Finley, you all right?" Simon asked as he approached.

"I'm alive," she told him with a weak smile.

"I'm gonna need to know—"

Brock cut him off. "Not now," he said firmly. "She's bleeding. And was doused with gas."

"Fuck. Okay," Simon agreed quickly. "But...is there anyone else in the house?" he asked.

Finley's steps faltered, and Brock wanted to punch the police chief for upsetting her. He felt the love of his life straighten her spine.

"Hillary. Last I saw her, she was in the kitchen."

"Okay, thanks. I'll be by the clinic to talk after Doc Snow takes a look at you."

"We might be headed to Roanoke," Brock warned.

"No," Finley said. "I don't want to go to the hospital."

"But the baby..." Brock said gently.

"Baby?!" Raid and Tal said at the same time.

"Guess it's not a secret anymore, huh?" Finley said dryly. Then she sighed. "If Doc Snow thinks I need to go, for the baby's sake, I will. But *I'm* fine."

Brock could live with that. "All right. Come on, I'll help you up into the back," he said as they neared the ambulance.

Within a minute, she was sitting on the stretcher in the back of the well-lit truck and the paramedics were bustling around her. Brock turned to Tal and Raid. "Thanks for being here."

"Of course. The others are on their way," Tal said. "They're gonna be pissed they *weren't* here."

Brock glanced at his watch, surprised to see that not even fifteen minutes had gone by since they'd arrived at the fully engulfed house.

"I didn't have time to call Ethan until after we found Finley," Raiden apologized.

"It's fine. But maybe you can tell them we're on our way to the clinic?"

"Will do," Raid said.

"I'll let you know what they find in the house," Tal said.

"Appreciate it. Finley's gonna be locked down until I know everyone even remotely connected to that fucking bitch is behind bars," Brock said in a low, harsh tone.

"Don't blame you," Raiden said.

"You'll call and tell us what happened after she talks to Simon?" Tal asked.

Brock nodded, dreading hearing the story. It was bad

enough just imagining what she might've gone through. Hearing her talk about it firsthand might break him.

He climbed into the back of the ambulance. He didn't give the paramedics a chance to tell him he wasn't allowed. He wasn't letting Finley out of his sight. Probably not for a damn long time.

"You tell them you're pregnant?" he asked Finley gently as a medic started an IV in her arm.

"Yes," she said softly, one hand going to her belly protectively.

"Don't worry, we'll get her hooked up to a monitor here in a second."

"We good to go?" another paramedic asked from outside the vehicle.

"Yeah, let's roll."

When it was just the three of them in the back of the ambulance, the paramedic asked, "How far along are you?"

"I'm not really sure, but at max, eight weeks," Finley said softly.

"Ah. It might be too early to hear your baby's heartbeat if you're less than six weeks along, but let's check it out."

Brock held his breath as the paramedic lifted Finley's shirt and held a wand to her stomach.

At first, nothing happened as he moved the wand around a bit. But then a soft *thump thump thump* came through the speakers of the machine behind him.

Brock froze. The thought of Finley being pregnant had been exciting. But this was the first time it truly, fully sank in. The fast-beating heart was his child. *Their* child.

Finley closed her eyes and sighed.

"Fin?" he asked.

"I was so scared," she whispered as the paramedic turned to put the equipment away.

"I'm incredibly proud of you," Brock whispered, leaning over her. He was sitting on a bench seat next to the stretcher and he took hold of her hand.

"I didn't do anything. All I could do was sit there and pray she didn't shoot me," Finley said, the agony clear in her voice.

"You got away," he murmured.

"Only because she fucked up. I didn't do anything to protect our baby! I should've fought harder. Shouldn't have gotten out of the car... I should've done *something*!"

"Shhh," Brock soothed. "You're safe. Our baby's safe. If anyone is to blame, it's me. I shouldn't have waited so long. I knew when you didn't come home in fifteen minutes something was wrong, but I tried to convince myself you were just chatting with your client. And when you didn't answer your phone, I should've done something right then."

Finley shook her head. "No, it wasn't your fault."

"And it wasn't yours either," Brock said firmly. He wasn't ever going to forgive himself for not acting sooner, but he'd do whatever it took for Finley to let go of any blame or regret she had about what happened.

Tears leaked from her eyes as she cried. Brock rested his cheek on her belly as he gripped her hand firmly. He needed to be close to her. To their baby. And while he obviously couldn't hear or feel their Little Bean, he felt closer to him or her like this.

The drive to the clinic didn't take long and before he was ready, he was sitting up and letting go of Finley's hand. Doc Snow was waiting for them, thank God, and he quickly and efficiently got Finley settled into one of the rooms.

He didn't even try to tell Brock to wait outside, which was a good thing, because there was no way he was leaving her.

To make sure things were all right with their baby, he did a transvaginal ultrasound, and the thumping of their baby's heartbeat was even clearer and louder than it was in the ambulance as it filled the room.

"Normal," the doctor said with a small smile. "Your baby's just fine."

Brock closed his eyes in relief.

"Now, will you please let me take care of those cuts?" he asked with a grin.

Brock was nodding even before Finley. She'd refused to let him do anything about the multitude of cuts on her body until he'd checked out their baby.

There were three cuts that needed a couple of stitches, including the one on her calf from breaking the window with her foot, and they were taken care of quickly and with a minimum of fuss. She still smelled like gasoline, but the dousing at the scene had done a decent job of rinsing her skin of the caustic liquid.

"You can shower when you get home, but you need to cover those stitches. Just put a piece of plastic over them and tape it down. Remove the plastic when you're done so the wounds can breathe. Take it easy—meaning, stay off your feet. I don't think your baby is in any danger, but you just went through something extremely traumatic, and your blood pressure needs time to come down and stress isn't good for pregnant mommies. Or daddies," he added with a look at Brock.

"She'll take it easy," he vowed.

Finley didn't laugh. Or even smile. Brock hated to see her so upset. He'd hoped once she found out from the doc that their baby was okay, she'd breathe easier, but that hadn't been the case. She was most likely thinking about her upcoming interview with the chief. And having to recount everything that had happened to her.

"Simon's here," Doc Snow said. "You want me to send him in?"

When Finley tensed, Brock knew his thoughts were correct. He wanted to tell the police chief to wait. That Finley needed some time to come to terms with everything that happened, but that wasn't the right course of action. She needed to get it out, once and for all, *then* they could move on. If she needed counseling, he'd make sure she got it. But waiting to talk about Hillary fucking Kendall wasn't the right thing for her.

Brock nodded at the doctor when Finley didn't look up from her hands clasped in her lap. She'd exchanged Raid's shirt for a hospital gown. He couldn't wait to get her home, in bed, and in one of *his* shirts.

The doctor left and Simon entered. He pulled up a chair next to Finley's bed. Brock reached for one of her hands and clasped it tightly.

"Would you feel better if I left?" he forced himself to ask. He didn't want to leave her. No way in hell. But he'd do whatever it took to make this easier on Fin.

"No!" she exclaimed almost frantically. "Don't leave."

"Shhh," Brock soothed. "If you want me to stay, I'm staying."

She nodded firmly.

Brock lifted their clasped hands to his mouth and kissed her fingers reverently.

"Start anywhere that feels right," Simon said as he pulled out his phone, set it up on a small table next to the bed where it would record video and audio of Finley, and hit record.

She took a deep breath, then spoke.

CHAPTER SEVENTEEN

"She offered me a hundred bucks to deliver the cake. She sounded so desperate. It wasn't a big deal for me to bring it to her house on my way home," Finley said, her voice sounding hollow as she recounted the events that took place.

"As soon as I pulled up to the address she gave me, I knew something was wrong. I figured I just wrote it down wrong or something. I was about to pull away when my door opened and a gun was pressed to my head."

Brock's hand tightened painfully around hers, but Finley welcomed the slight ache. It was difficult to talk about what happened, but it had to be done. Brock's tight hold kept her grounded, made her feel safe. "I didn't know what to do. I should've thrown the car in reverse and left."

"If you'd tried, she would've shot you right then and there," Simon said gently. "What happened then?"

Finley went through Hillary's next steps. She told the police chief and Brock about the zip-ties—which Doc Snow had cut off—about Hillary ranting, about how surprised she'd been when the enraged woman dumped gas over her head. How scared she was, positive she'd be set ablaze while still alive. When her hands began to shake, Brock simply tightened his hold on her fingers yet again.

"I guess the gas she'd spilled on herself ignited when she lit the match. I remember being oddly surprised she had an old-fashioned book of matches," Finley said with a shrug. "Although, I suppose it doesn't matter what she was going to use to set me on fire."

"It was very smart of you to pretend to attach your legs to the chair," Simon told her. "So...after...you ran into the kitchen?"

Finley nodded. "Yeah. The gas felt as if it was burning my skin, but I knew if I didn't get out of there, it wouldn't matter if Hillary hadn't thrown that match on me or not. I'd go up in flames as easily as she did. I'd knocked out the window and was ready to crawl through when she came stumbling into the kitchen." Finley shivered and her voice lowered to a whisper. "It was awful. Her face looked like it was melting. I don't know how she found the strength to walk. Maybe she was just that determined to see me die."

Finley jerked when Brock's hand touched her face. She'd been so intent on telling her story that she hadn't realized she was crying. He gently wiped the tears from her face with his free hand.

Brock took up the story then, explaining how he'd discovered where she was, how he, Tal, and Raid had broken into the backyard and found her.

"Was all this really about me seeing that black truck?" Finley asked Simon.

"Yes and no," Simon said. "After looking into Pete and Cory's histories, and now that I know Hillary was behind what happened to you...I can extrapolate and guess that Hillary Kendall was addicted to the pain pills she was selling, and she'd managed to work her way up the chain from just a user to the local supplier. Probably got involved just for easy access and free pills...at first. But like these things usually go, the further you're embroiled in the drug trade, the more desperate and power hungry you become.

"I'm fairly certain you saw *her* supplier delivering pills to a contact here in Fallport. That contact would then get the drugs to Hillary, who'd package them up and get them to her clients either herself or with the help of small-time dealers."

"Like Pete and Cory," Brock said.

"Yes. But from what you've told us," he said to Finley, "you obviously spooked her supplier. He refused to drive to Fallport, so she had to go to him. I talked to her husband before coming here. He said recently, she'd been going to Roanoke all the time. Was never home anymore. When we get the records from your satellite phone back, I'm positive they'll lead back to her somehow, indicating that she was the one who sent Pete and Cory to find out exactly what you'd seen and who you'd told. In her mind, if she could reassure her guy that you hadn't seen anything— or if you had, that you were too scared to tell anyone—he'd resume their previous arrangement. But...that didn't happen."

Finley shook her head. "Yes, I saw the truck and wrote down the license plate, but if she hadn't sent those guys after me, I would've forgotten all about it."

Simon nodded. "She didn't know that though. Anyway, I'm thinking things went downhill from there and she was cut off altogether. She was desperate for the drugs and turned to heroin, as you mentioned. And she blamed you for her little empire falling apart."

"She's dead?" Finley asked tentatively.

Simon nodded.

"What about her family? Will they be all right?"

She heard Brock make a noise, and she turned to him. "What?"

He merely shook his head. "I'm not surprised that, even after everything that happened, you're worried about a drug dealer's family."

"They're innocent in this. At least, I'm assuming they are. And it won't be easy living in a small town and dealing with the fallout of her actions."

"I'll keep my eye on them. Make sure they're good," Simon said.

Finley rested her head on the pillow behind her and closed her eyes. "Thank you."

"Go home," Simon ordered gently. "Let Brock take care of you. You did good, Finley. I'm proud of you."

His words echoed in the room, but strangely they made Finley feel sad. He might be proud of her, but she wasn't proud of herself. She should've done more to get herself out of that awful situation. She did almost nothing...just as she did nothing when she and Brock were in the woods. She waited for *him* to act.

Maybe if she hadn't, her life and the life of her child wouldn't have been threatened. Hillary might not be dead, and she could've gotten the help she'd obviously needed.

Finley's hand went to her belly. She thought of Hillary's two kids, how they didn't have a mother anymore. Maybe the woman hadn't been the best mom in the world, but she was the only one those teenagers had...and now she was gone.

Guilt weighed heavily on her shoulders, and Finley just wanted to sleep, to block it all out.

Simon stood. He shook Brock's hand and patted Finley gently on the calf before he walked out of the room.

"You ready to go home?" Brock asked quietly.

Finley nodded, but she didn't open her eyes. She was tired. So damn tired.

* * *

A week later, Brock stood in his kitchen. He braced himself on the counter and stared down into the sink, frowning. He'd just made breakfast for Finley, and she'd only eaten a few bites of the omelet before saying she just wasn't hungry and pushing it away.

She was here, but she wasn't here. She'd barely gotten out of bed since the fire, and it was clear she wasn't dealing with what happened. Brock had talked with Doc Snow about getting a psychologist to come to the house to see her, and they were working on making that happen, but in the meantime, his spunky, glass-half-full woman was a mere shell of who she'd been before the kidnapping.

Brock was at a loss as to what to do to help her, and it was eating him up inside. All the other women had been by to see her, but it was obvious she wasn't ready to talk. They only stayed for a short time, worried when Finley wouldn't speak or outright refused to see them. Each of them promised to keep coming back, to do what they could to help Finley feel better.

But with every day that passed, Brock could feel the

woman he loved slipping through his fingers. She spent as much time as possible sleeping, and when he tried to gently coax her to get up, to open her bakery, to get out of the house, she argued that she wasn't feeling up to it. That she wanted to stay off her feet for the baby's sake. He was terrified to push too much.

Brock felt helpless, and he hated it. At night, Finley held him almost desperately, but in the morning, more often than not she wouldn't meet his eyes and was barely going through the motions of living.

A knock on his front door made Brock sigh. People had been arriving nonstop since the fire, and while he appreciated it, his refrigerator and freezer were already overflowing and it was hard to carry on a conversation with someone when the woman he loved was slowly disappearing into herself.

Brock *had* to do something.

And he would...as soon as he got rid of whoever was at his door.

When he opened it, Brock was shocked to see Khloe Moore standing there. At only five foot four, she was a tiny little thing...but at the moment, she looked ready to do battle.

"I'm here to see Finley," she announced.

"She's not feeling up to visitors," Brock said quietly, repeating what she'd told him every time someone had stopped by to see her in the last few days.

"Tough," Khloe retorted, pushing past Brock into the house.

He stood there, shocked for a moment, before slowly closing the door and following Khloe into his living room.

"Seriously, Khloe, she's struggling hard, and she doesn't want to see anyone."

"I don't care, Brock. She's seeing me."

He couldn't help but feel a twinge of relief. He had no idea how this visit was going to go, but maybe Khloe's approach would be the catalyst for him to finally have a heart-to-heart talk with Finley. She needed to get out of bed. Start living again. What happened to her was awful, and he'd always hold guilt in his heart that he hadn't found her faster. That he hadn't taken the threat against her more seriously. That he hadn't figured out who was behind Pete and Cory's actions in the woods that day.

Without waiting for him to tell her where Finley was, Khloe turned and practically stomped down the hall toward his bedroom, the movement even more pronounced thanks to her slight limp. Brock debated whether or not to stay. He wanted to ensure Khloe didn't upset his woman...but he grudgingly admitted his approach of not pushing, of catering to her desire to stay in bed all day, had failed hard.

"I'm going to go mow the lawn. I'd appreciate anything you can do to help bring back my Finley...but if she's even more worse off when you leave, I'm not going to be happy."

She turned, and for the first time since he'd met her, Brock saw deep pain in the other woman's hazel eyes.

Whatever Khloe Moore had been through in her life, it had deeply affected her.

"I'll handle her with care...and tough love," Khloe promised before turning to his bedroom door.

Brock stared down the hallway, hoping with everything

he had that Khloe would be able to do what he hadn't... pull Finley out of the depression she'd fallen into.

* * *

Finley was in that weird space between sleep and wakefulness when the door to the bedroom opened. She rolled over, expecting to see Brock. No matter how shitty she felt, she couldn't *not* want to see him.

But it wasn't the man she loved. Khloe was closing the door behind her. She strode over to the side of the bed, studied Finley with her hands on her hips, and finally declared, "You look like shit."

For a second, Finley could only gape at her friend. Then she chuckled. The sound was rusty, but it was still a laugh. "Wow, why don't you tell me what you really think," she quipped.

"I plan to," Khloe informed her. "But not until you get your ass out of bed and make me a cinnamon roll."

Finley's brows furrowed. "What?"

"I'm hungry, and I want a cinnamon roll. Since The Sweet Tooth is closed, I haven't had one all week. So get up and get into the kitchen and make me one."

Finley should've been surprised at the complete gall of Khloe's request—no, *order*—but for some reason, she wasn't. Emotion was beyond her. "Today's not a good day," she said with a shrug. "Sorry."

"When *will* be a good day?" Khloe returned. "It's been a week, Finley. You need to get back to your life."

"A week? You think that's enough to get over almost being set on fire and burned alive?" Finley shot back.

"The operative word in that sentence being *almost*," Khloe replied.

"I can't...I just...I *can't*," Finley said lamely.

"Bullshit. You can, you're simply wallowing. You need to snap out of it."

For the first time in a week, Finley felt an emotion begin to stir—anger. "You think it's that easy?"

"It's never easy," Khloe returned. "It's hard as hell. Maybe the hardest thing you'll ever have to do. But you're *alive*, Fin. What happened sucks. Big time. You were kidnapped not once, but twice. But you've got friends who love and support you, a man who thinks the sun rises and sets for you, and you have a business to run."

"I'm not sure I want to anymore," Finley admitted.

"Right. I get that. But what about Liam? And Davis? What about the people who've come to look forward to your baked goods every morning? Liam would literally do anything for you. Yes, the money he's earned has changed his family's life, but more than that, he respects and admires you. And he's so damn thankful you gave him a chance, especially since so many other people didn't.

"And Davis? Shit, Finley, he's so much better than he was. He's always going to have his demons, but feeling as if he's needed? As if he's contributing? That's something no counselor has been able to do for him since he left the military. But *you* did. Simply by accepting him exactly as he is. You gonna throw all that away?"

Finley felt sick inside. "That's not fair," she whispered.

"I know. It really isn't. But I'm not sorry for using Davis or Liam against you. You need someone to kick you in the ass, and Brock won't do it because he loves you too much. I envy you, Finley."

She snorted. "Envy me? You've got to be kidding."

"I'm not."

Finley sat up, all the rage and pain she'd been trying to suppress swirling up from deep within her. "I sat there and let a crazy woman do whatever she wanted! I wasn't attached to that chair! When she poured gas on me, I should've attacked her. Should've done something to try to protect myself and my baby. But I *didn't*! I sat there and watched her light that damn match, knowing she was about to throw it at me, and I'd burst into flames. I want to be strong, like everyone else, but I'm *not*!"

Khloe sat on the edge of the bed and put her hand on Finley's arm. "There is literally no right or wrong way to act in a dire situation. If you bum-rushed that bitch, she could've shot you. I heard through the grapevine that she kept that pistol pointed at you the entire time. You bided your time until you could get away.

"Do you think Bristol should've fought her kidnapper? You think there's a day that goes by that she doesn't wonder what if? What if she'd done more to escape? What if she didn't lie there docilely and let him believe she wanted to stay with him? And do you think Elsie doesn't beat herself up for letting Tony go with her ex when, deep down, she knew something wasn't right with his sudden appearance? Or Lilly isn't embarrassed that she didn't realize her co-worker was a freaking *murderer*?

"And if you think I don't feel like complete shit because I was the one who asked you to look after those kittens while I was gone, that *I'm* the reason you saw that drug deal to begin with, you're crazy.

"Being strong and brave isn't about going all kung fu on

someone. It's about using your brain to decide when to bide your time, and when to fight back."

Finley had never seen Khloe like this, and all she could do was sit there and listen.

"Life is full of shit, Finley. But it's also filled with so much beauty and goodness, it's almost painful at times. People who will be your friend even when you've given them absolutely no reason to like you. Small-town parades where people laugh and find joy in seeing how far they can spit a damn watermelon seed. Innocent kittens who know nothing about how awful life can be, and welcome you with purrs and snuggles. I know it's hard to see that stuff when the weight of the world seems to be on your shoulders, but it's always there. You just have to open your eyes to see it."

She was right. Of course she was.

Finley closed her eyes and did her best to keep her tears at bay. But it was no use.

"One more thing, then I'm done and you're going to get up and shower—because, girlfriend, your hair desperately needs washing—and make me a cinnamon roll. You're really lucky, Finley. That Hillary woman is gone. Dead. I know you'd never be so crass as to be relieved someone died, so I'll be relieved for you. And I'm sure the people of Fallport are just as affected by what happened. They'll be more aware from here on out, at least for a while. They'll be a little more watchful of their friends and neighbors, and if something seems off, I'm guessing they'll do what they can to find out why. What happened to you was awful...but it's over. *Done.* And I'm so jealous, it's hard to explain. The person who caused you so much pain and trauma is no longer a threat to you or the ones you love."

Finley opened her eyes and stared at Khloe. Her mind spinning with her words...

"The person who caused *you* pain and trauma is still a threat, isn't he...or she?"

Just like that, a shutter slammed down over the emotion Finley saw in Khloe's eyes. "It doesn't matter."

It *did* matter. She had a feeling it mattered a great deal.

But when her friend stood, Finley realized the moment of sharing had passed. Khloe had said what she wanted to say.

"Get up," she said crisply. "Shower. Wash your hair. I'll be in the kitchen, waiting for my cinnamon roll. If you aren't out there in ten minutes, I'm coming in here after you. And trust me, you won't like it if I have to come back."

Finley smiled for the first time in what seemed like forever. "Okay."

Relief filled Khloe's eyes. "Okay," she said a little gentler. Then she turned and walked out of the room.

She didn't make Khloe's ten-minute window, but twenty minutes later, Finley was in Brock's kitchen gathering the ingredients to make cinnamon rolls. It was a surprise to see how full the fridge was. She'd had no idea so many people had brought food by.

"Brock's been handing out free food all over Fallport," Khloe informed her. She was sitting on the counter, watching her as she moved around the kitchen. "The first place he brought food to was the Fallport Fire Department. He brought some to Davis. Then he went to the Mangree Motel, and Edna said she'd distribute it to the long-term tenants."

Finley wanted to cry again. She hadn't even asked what

Brock had been doing while she'd been lost in her head. Not only had he done whatever he could for her, he'd been taking care of those in Fallport who needed it.

She'd been extremely selfish for the last week. Yes, she needed some time to deal with what happened, but she'd taken it too far. Brock had gone above and beyond, and she hadn't shown him the least bit of appreciation.

Worse, she knew he'd been feeling just as guilty as she was...and she'd done nothing to soothe him.

She began to prepare the dough without a word. And bless Khloe, she didn't try to fill the silence with meaningless chitchat. It wasn't until she'd gotten a tray of cinnamon rolls in the oven that Finley turned to her friend. "I want to re-open The Sweet Tooth, but I'm scared," she admitted.

Khloe hopped down off the counter and leaned against it. "I can understand that. But it seems to me, this is a perfect time to make some changes."

"I've already made so many," Finley protested.

"So, make more," Khloe said with a shrug. "What are you scared about, specifically?"

"Making deliveries."

"Then don't."

"It's not that easy," Finley protested.

"Why not? It's your business, you set the rules. You can make a no-exception policy that all catering orders have to be picked up by close of business each day. Or, because I know what a soft heart you have, you could hire someone to deliver for you."

"I wouldn't want to put anyone else in the same position I was," Finley said with a shake of her head.

"Look, you own The Sweet Tooth. You make the decisions when it comes to what you bake each day, what time you open, what time you close, the services you offer, and how you spend your money. Do what you want and what makes you comfortable. The people of Fallport will adjust."

Finley stared at Khloe. She was right. More than that, it sounded as if the things she was saying came from experience. Finley was going to ask if she'd followed her own advice, but decided this wasn't the time or place. "You're right," she said instead.

"I know."

The two women smiled at each other.

"Fallport needs you," Khloe said after a minute. "It needs your goodness. Your decadent treats. Your caring. You'll bounce back. I know you will."

"I used to think you were a hard-ass," Finley teased. "But here you are, being all sappy."

"I *am* a hard-ass," Khloe said. "I'm standoffish and a total bitch. Just ask anyone."

"Maybe I'll ask Raiden," Finley couldn't help but say.

And just like that, Khloe shut down again. "How much longer until my cinnamon roll is done?"

Finley looked at her watch. "Not long now." She was more curious than ever about what was going on between Khloe and Raid, but she didn't want to upset Khloe. Not after she'd cared enough to come over and pound some sense into her.

The door opened, and a sweaty and half-naked Brock walked into the house. "Something smells delicious," he said with a smile.

And just like that, Finley's libido kicked into gear.

"No," Khloe said firmly.

Finley turned to her. "Huh?"

"I came for a cinnamon roll, and I'm not leaving until I get it. You and your boyfriend can have sex after I leave."

Finley laughed. Khloe was definitely a pushy little thing.

Brock approached and gently ran his fingers down her cheek. "You're back," he said quietly.

She nodded shyly. "I'm sorry I've been so self-absorbed."

He shook his head. "Nothing to be sorry about, Fin."

"Cinnamon roll," Khloe reminded them.

"It's so good to see you smiling and hear your laughter," Brock told Finley. He leaned down and kissed her. It wasn't a long kiss, but it wasn't a peck either. When he lifted his head, he said, "I'm going to go shower."

"Yes. Shoo," Khloe said.

Finley laughed again, glad to see that Brock wasn't offended in the least.

When he was out of earshot, Khloe fanned herself with her hand. "Whew! That man is *hot*!"

Finley giggled. "He is. And he's all mine."

"Of course," Khloe said. "He doesn't have eyes for anyone but you."

By the time Brock was done showering, Finley had three cinnamon rolls dished up and waiting on the table. They were still piping hot and the icing she'd drizzled over them immediately melted into a puddle of sugary goo.

Khloe didn't stick around after she finished hers. She stood and said, "I've got to go. *Some* of us have jobs."

Finley stood and hugged her. Khloe was a little stiff, but she did return the embrace. Then it was Brock's turn. He tugged the small woman into his arms and bent his head. He said something into her ear that Finley couldn't hear, but she saw Khloe blush and nod. Then he pulled back and stared at Khloe for a long moment, before leaning down and kissing the top of her head.

Khloe headed for the door, waving as she went. "I'll see myself out. If I run into Davis, I'll tell him to meet you at the bakery tomorrow morning," she said.

"Not until six. I'm changing the hours of the shop. We now open at eight."

Khloe turned back around and sent Finley a huge smile. "Good for you. Don't forget to call Liam and tell him."

"I won't. Khloe?"

"Yeah?"

"Thank you. Anytime you need to kick my ass in the future, you're welcome to."

"I'm gonna take you up on that," she said, then she opened the door and was gone.

Before she could move, Brock was in front of her, framing her face with his hands. He leaned in and inhaled deeply. "Cinnamon," he muttered. Then he said, "You okay?"

"I am now. I'm sorry I've been so horrible."

"You haven't been horrible. I get it, you've been trying to process what happened."

Finley nodded. "Are *you* okay?"

"Me?"

"Yeah. You've been taking care of me for a week. And apparently running all over Fallport delivering the extra food people have brought over. Have you been going to work at all?"

"No. Jesus is taking care of the shop."

Finley frowned. "I'm sorry."

"I'm not. There's nowhere I'd rather be than by your side. I just wish I could've done something to make you feel better."

"You did. You were there for me." When the frown didn't leave his face, Finley grabbed his wrists. "You *did*," she insisted. "If you'd have pushed me, I think I would've shut down more. I needed your concern. And love."

"Well, those you have. In spades." Then Brock got down on his knees in front of her and lifted her shirt. He kissed her belly reverently. "Have I thanked you for taking care of our Little Bean?" he asked.

Finley's throat threatened to close. But he didn't give her a chance to reply.

"I want this baby so much, but I want you even more." He looked up at her, love shining in his eyes. "Marry me, Finley. As soon as we can make it happen. No ceremony. No huge party...although we can have one later if you want. I need to make you mine. Make this baby ours."

"I *am* yours," she countered. "As is our baby." When he didn't say anything, just continued to stare up at her, she asked, "Are you sure? As I've demonstrated over the last week, I can be moody. And selfish."

"You aren't selfish. Not in any way, shape, or form. And I don't mind your moodiness. Please marry me, Finley. I've waited for you my entire life."

She nodded.

"Yes?" he asked.

"Yes," she confirmed.

Finley thought he'd smile, stand up, kiss her, then maybe even carry her back to bed and make long, slow, sweet love to her. It had been a week since they'd been intimate. And the wounds on her arms and hips were healing nicely. She barely even felt them anymore.

But instead, when he stood, Brock immediately turned away from her and picked up his phone from where he'd put it on the counter after he'd come in from mowing the grass.

"Brock?" she asked in confusion.

"Yeah?" he asked, distracted by whatever he was searching for on the phone.

"Um...I was hoping maybe we could celebrate or something. You know, now that I'm kind of back to my normal self."

"Oh, we're gonna celebrate," Brock reassured her without looking up. "I spent the last week hoping you'd get out of bed and I'm about to take you back there without a second thought. And I'm gonna be there with you, to show you exactly how much I love you and our Little Bean. You might want to call Liam now because you won't get another chance anytime soon."

Finley smiled. She liked the thought of that. All of it. "So what are *you* doing then?"

Brock looked up. "I'm searching for info on marriage licenses in Virginia and how long we'll have to wait."

Tingles shot through Finley. Brock wasn't kidding. He really did want to marry her as soon as possible. She watched as he read something on the phone. Love for this man almost overwhelmed her. He'd proven over the last week just how much he cared for her. She couldn't imagine anyone else putting up with her like he did. Yes, she'd been through something traumatic, but so had he. He'd told her more than once how terrified he'd been when he realized she was missing and something was wrong.

Brock's head came up, and he looked at her funny. "What?"

"There's no waiting period," he said.

"For what?"

"For getting married. We can get a marriage license from any circuit court in the state and there's no waiting period for the actual ceremony. Is that what you want to wear to marry me?" he asked.

Finley looked down at herself and laughed. "Um, fat pants and one of your T-shirts? No."

"Then you better go change, baby."

"Wait—you want to go *right now*?"

"Yes." Brock put the phone down on the counter and stalked toward her. He grabbed her around the waist and pulled her close. "I want you to be Mrs. Finley Mabrey more than I can say."

Finley went up on her tiptoes and kissed him. Hard. Brock returned the kiss almost desperately. The next thing she knew, she was lying on her back on the couch and Brock was pulling her pants down her legs. "I thought we were getting married." She giggled.

"I need you," he growled.

Mentally shrugging, Finley sighed, "I need you too. *Now*. Inside me, Brock."

But instead, he lowered his mouth between her legs and proceeded to drive her out of her mind.

Later—much later—they were lying in bed, completely boneless. Brock had been careful with her mostly healed wounds, but he hadn't held back in any other way. He'd been insatiable, just as she had.

"Tomorrow we'll get married," he mumbled into her chest. He hadn't shaved that morning and his five o'clock shadow was scratchy against the sensitive skin of her chest.

"I need to get back to work," she told him gently. "As do you. Jesus is great, but it's not fair to let him do all the work at your shop."

Brock growled against her and he propped himself on his elbows. His biceps, which she loved so much, rippled as he moved. Finley couldn't keep her hands off him. She caressed up and down his huge arms as she smiled.

"Fine. Friday afternoon. We're getting married."

"Okay."

His muscles relaxed, and for the first time, Finley realized just how tense he'd been.

"I love you, Finley."

"I love you too."

"I'm proud of you. Awed by you. Admire you."

"I feel the same about you," she said gently.

"I knew you'd be worth the wait," he told her with a small smile. "You were so shy and awkward around me, and it only made me want you more."

"You're weird," Finley informed him.

He grinned down at her before lowering his head. Five minutes ago, Finley would've told him she was too tired to do anything other than sleep. But one touch of his lips on hers, and she was primed and ready to go again. She'd never get enough of this man. She'd been his from the second she'd seen him, but never thought she'd have a chance in hell to be right where she was, right now.

And soon she'd be his wife. And she was having his baby.

Khloe was right...life was hard sometimes, but the good times more than made up for the bad.

EPILOGUE

The wind whipped through the trees as Talon hiked through the forest. He wasn't on the trail, as that wouldn't be where he'd find what he was looking for.

He had no idea why he was so obsessed with the mysterious woman who had saved Brock and Finley. He'd heard the story more than once about how she'd appeared as if out of nowhere, like an apparition. She threw dirt in the face of the asshole who'd threatened Finley, giving Brock time to get them both out of harm's way.

But Brock's observations, more than anything else, stuck with Tal.

Her torn and dirty dress. Her tangled red hair. Her bare feet.

It was that last detail that haunted him.

Pulling the collar of his shirt up, Tal shivered. If he was cold, what was *she* feeling?

He had no idea if the woman was the missing Heather Brown or not. It didn't really matter either way. But he couldn't help but wonder, if so, what had her last two decades been like? She'd been kidnapped when she was eight. Did she remember her previous life? Why hadn't she come forward by now?

He had more questions than answers, and something wouldn't let him give up trying to find her.

She was out here somewhere, and Tal wanted desperately to help her. Something about her situation called to him. He'd found an old picture of Heather Brown around the time she'd been taken, and the mischief shining in her blue-green eyes made him extremely sad. The age-progressed images published since then had intrigued him just as much. She was a beautiful woman...or would've been, if she was still alive.

Tal stopped and stood stock still, listening. For what, he didn't know. Any kind of sound that was out of place. But all he heard was the wind and a few birds.

Knowing what he was doing might be for nothing, he shrugged off his backpack. He'd chosen this part of the woods for a reason...because it was where she was last seen. Near where Finley and Brock had been attacked and the woman had appeared out of nowhere to help.

He reached into his pack and extracted the slightly smaller bag he'd packed earlier. Two pairs of wool socks, a flint, some freeze-dried meals, an old sweatshirt of his, a chocolate bar, some leggings, and a note explaining who he was...and that he wanted to help if she'd let him.

This was as good a place as any to leave the supplies.

Suddenly, Tal couldn't shake the feeling he was being watched.

He hoped and prayed it was by her. It might be wishful

thinking, but...Tal had been a member of the Special Boat Service in the UK. They were special forces, much like the Navy SEALs in the US. He was extremely adept at getting in and out of places without being seen, and sensing when the enemy was near.

The mysterious woman wasn't a danger to him. He knew that as well as he knew his name.

The Appalachians were vast, and there was a larger-than-average chance the woman would never find these supplies. That animals would find the bag and tear it to shreds to get to the food. But if the way his neck was tingling was any indication, she was near. And since he didn't want to spook her, Talon forced himself to back away from the supplies he'd left against the tree, shrug his backpack on once more, and head toward the trail.

It took everything within him not to look back. He wanted this woman's trust. Needed it. And if he had to treat her as a feral animal until he gained that trust, he'd do so. It felt wrong to leave her out here in the cold. But she'd obviously been taking care of herself for a long time now, and he had to believe she'd continue...but maybe the things he left for her would make her life a little easier.

* * *

Sunset Meadowblossom stayed crouched behind the tree long after the man had left. He made her extremely nervous. She'd seen him before. Him and other men. They came into the woods when people got lost. She'd followed all of them more than once, curiously observing. But ever since she'd risked helping that woman with the knife held to her throat, this particular man had been back far too often for Sunset's peace of mind.

She didn't know what he wanted, but she was fairly sure he was looking for *her*. It unsettled her. She didn't like men. All they did was hurt. For as long as she could remember, men had caused her pain.

Though...she couldn't help but remember the man who'd been with that woman. She'd followed from a distance after they'd escaped the bad man with the knife, watching closely. He didn't hit her. Didn't do anything to cause her pain in any way.

When they'd crawled under the big rock, Sunset desperately wanted to do something to protect the woman. To keep the man from climbing on top of her and hurting her.

But to her surprise, the man didn't do what she'd expected. He'd put himself between the woman and the forest and simply held her.

Sunset had watched the pair until her feet went numb and she was soaked to the bone by the lightly falling rain.

She was used to the cold. And the heat. Women weren't worthy of any kindness in The Community. They were fed last, worked from sunup to sundown, and only allowed to speak when spoken to. They did all the cooking and cleaning, and never, *ever* disrespected the men.

Well...most of the women didn't, anyway.

Of course, since she'd been left behind, she was now free to eat any parts of the animals she trapped. She didn't have to give the best meat to the men of the group. She wasn't beaten, wasn't talked down to...didn't have to lie under Arrow and pretend she liked everything he did to her body.

Shaking herself from the bad memories, Sunset continued to follow the man who'd left the bag in the forest until he'd reached the trail and started back toward the parking area. She never went anywhere near where people congregated. Outsiders were dangerous. She'd heard stories all her life about the awful things they'd do if they ever found her. How they'd throw her in jail for breaking the law.

What law, she didn't know, but if Arrow Goodson said it was true, it was true. No one ever questioned him.

There were times since The Community disbanded when Sunset had seriously contemplated approaching one of the many people she'd seen in her woods. But the echoes of warnings from her fellow members always stopped her.

Gripped by a shiver that had nothing to do with the cold, Sunset considered her Community family. Arrow had died and his son had taken over as leader. Cypress Goodson was ten times more strict than his father had been. And meaner.

Thinking about Cypress made Meadow feel physically sick. He was horrible. All the women had been forced to follow his word without hesitation. Sunset had always had the protection of Arrow, but when he'd died, that protection died with him.

Cypress hadn't hesitated to take what he wanted. What only his father had previously owned.

Her.

Pushing those thoughts away yet again, more forcefully this time, Sunset crept back through the woods and toward the bag the man had left. She knew she shouldn't go near it. That it was probably a trap. But she couldn't resist. Curiosity was a trait Arrow had done his best to beat out of her, with minimal success.

When she got close, Sunset burst out of her hiding spot and ran as fast as a gazelle toward the bag. She didn't slow down as she snatched it up and disappeared back into her forest home. On her feet were shoes made from the hides of rabbits, so she left no footprints behind.

Sunset ran for miles back to the cave she'd made her home for the winter. She'd move once the weather got warmer, but for now, this was the safest place she'd been able to find. Crawling into the cave, she stirred the coals from the fire she'd built earlier. As soon as she placed a small log on the smoldering coals, it burst into flames, giving her enough light to see what was in the bag and to warm her chilled skin.

Crossing her legs, Sunset tucked her dirty dress around her thighs. She'd never worn anything but the dresses The Community required women to don.

She pulled out the items in the bag one by one.

The socks felt a little scratchy, but when she untied the rabbit skins and put them on her feet, Sunset sighed in giddy delight. They were so warm!

She stared at the leggings for a long time, uncertain. She'd never been allowed to cover her legs, none of the women had. But Arrow wasn't here now...

Lifting her chin defiantly, she slowly pulled the soft-as-butter leggings over her cold limbs and smiled with happiness to find they fit, and were just as warm as the socks.

Next up was the sweatshirt. Not even hesitating now, Sunset pulled it over her head. It was way too big, practically swallowing her frame, but it smelled so good. Clean.

She couldn't remember the last time she'd smelled anything as good as this. She lowered her head and brought the material up to her face and inhaled deeply.

Smiling excitedly now, she dug into the bag once more. She couldn't figure out what the sealed packages were, and decided to put them aside to examine in the morning when she had more light. She could read. Not well, and she made sure never to let Arrow or Cypress know how much she understood, but she could usually figure out the meaning of most words.

The chocolate bar caught her eye, and a vague memory of her before life pushed at her brain, but Sunset blocked it. She didn't want to remember that time, when she was a child. Knowing it would hurt so bad to let the memories in, she might never recover.

Instead, she peeled back the wrapper and smelled the candy. Then she took a huge bite.

The flavor burst on her tongue, and she closed her eyes at the absolute decadence of the treat.

She'd had chocolate before. Just once. After Arrow passed away, Cypress had brought a box to The Community from town and rewarded the women with small pieces when they pleased him. One night, after Cypress had forced her to join him in his tent, after he'd taken her in that forbidden place while she'd been on her hands and knees, he was satisfied enough to let her have a piece of chocolate. The treat hadn't taken away her pain, but she'd enjoyed it anyway.

The terrible memory threatened to overwhelm Sunset, but she refused to let it. Cypress wasn't here now. Neither was Arrow. As the new leader, Cypress had decided he was sick of the cold and moved everyone to Florida. Sunset never wanted to leave the mountains, and especially not with Cypress.

He'd wanted her to be his primary wife, and after witnessing the way he treated his other wives, how he'd already treated *her*, Sunset wanted nothing to do with him.

She'd hidden in the forest when the time came to leave. It was a little scary to be without The Community's minor protection, but she was managing just fine.

A white piece of paper was the last thing in the bag, and Sunset pulled it out. It was a note. The writing was messy but still readable.

Hello. My name is Talon. My friends call me Tal. You can trust me. You don't have to be afraid to talk to me. I swear I'll never hurt you. If you see me in the woods, please don't be afraid to say hello. I thought you might like these things. If you need anything specific, just let me know. Leave me a note where you found this bag. I'll find it and bring you whatever you want.

Your friend, Tal

Some of the words in the note, Sunset didn't know, but she understood most of it.

Talon. The claw from a bird of prey. It was a strong name. But she'd known many men with strong names who were not good.

She licked her lips, tasting the chocolate there. Talon hadn't asked her for anything. Hadn't demanded she do anything. He'd only asked her to trust him.

She didn't trust anyone. Especially men.

Sunset couldn't deny the gifts he'd left for her were wonderful, however. She could definitely use the flint, and she'd never felt as warm as she did right that moment, wearing the socks, leggings, and sweatshirt. Still, it wouldn't be smart to write him back, and she should stay far away from the man who was too curious about her for her own good.

But as she lay down for the night, the note from Talon clutched in her hand, Sunset couldn't help but think if there was an outsider she *could* trust...it might be him. She'd never seen him yell at his friends. He'd never struck any of the lost souls he found in the woods, even when the people were terribly rude to him. And even though she could tell he was frustrated he hadn't been able to find her, he still left gifts.

She wasn't ready to show herself to an outsider...but maybe if she thanked him, he'd leave her more presents. Sunset didn't have any utensils to write with, hadn't needed them or been allowed to have them back when The Community was active, but she could find a stick and use some mud to acknowledge his offerings.

Deep down, she knew no gifts came without strings, but with the taste of the chocolate still in her mouth, she couldn't help but wonder what else the man might leave for her. He both scared and intrigued her.

Sunset made the decision right then and there to thank him...what would happen after that, she'd just have to wait and see.

* * *

Who is this mystery woman? Is her name really Sunset?

Tal not only has to find her, but he has to also somehow get her to trust him...which could be the harder of the two tasks. Find out how he does both in *Searching for Heather*

Want to talk to other Susan Stoker fans? Join my reader group, Susan Stoker's Stalkers, on Facebook!

Also by Susan Stoker

Eagle Point Search & Rescue

Searching for Lilly
Searching for Elsie
Searching for Bristol
Searching for Caryn
Searching for Finley
Searching for Heather (Jan 2024)
Searching for Khloe (May 2024)

The Refuge Series

Deserving Alaska
Deserving Henley
Deserving Reese
Deserving Cora (Nov)
Deserving Lara (Feb 2024)
Deserving Maisy (Oct 2024)
Deserving Ryleigh (TBA)

Game of Chance Series

The Protector
The Royal
The Hero (Mar 2024)
The Lumberjack (Aug 2024)

SEAL Team Hawaii Series

Finding Elodie
Finding Lexie
Finding Kenna
Finding Monica

Shielding Aspen
Shielding Jayme (novella)
Shielding Riley
Shielding Devyn
Shielding Ember
Shielding Sierra

SEAL of Protection Series

Protecting Caroline
Protecting Alabama
Protecting Fiona
Marrying Caroline (novella)
Protecting Summer
Protecting Cheyenne
Protecting Jessyka
Protecting Julie (novella)
Protecting Melody
Protecting the Future
Protecting Kiera (novella)
Protecting Alabama's Kids (novella)
Protecting Dakota

Badge of Honor: Texas Heroes Series

Justice for Mackenzie
Justice for Mickie
Justice for Corrie
Justice for Laine (novella)
Shelter for Elizabeth
Justice for Boone
Shelter for Adeline
Shelter for Sophie
Justice for Erin

Justice for Milena
Shelter for Blythe
Justice for Hope
Shelter for Quinn
Shelter for Koren
Shelter for Penelope

Ace Security Series

Claiming Grace
Claiming Alexis
Claiming Bailey
Claiming Felicity
Claiming Sarah

Mountain Mercenaries Series

Defending Allye
Defending Chloe
Defending Morgan
Defending Harlow
Defending Everly
Defending Zara
Defending Raven

Silverstone Series

Trusting Skylar
Trusting Taylor
Trusting Molly
Trusting Cassidy

Stand Alone

Falling for the Delta
The Guardian Mist

Nature's Rift
A Princess for Cale
A Moment in Time- A Collection of Short Stories
Another Moment in Time- A Collection of Short Stories
A Third Moment in Time- A Collection of Short Stories
Lambert's Lady

Special Operations Fan Fiction

http://www.AcesPress.com

Beyond Reality Series

Outback Hearts
Flaming Hearts
Frozen Hearts

Writing as Annie George:

Stepbrother Virgin (erotic novella)

ABOUT THE AUTHOR

New York Times, *USA Today* and *Wall Street Journal* Bestselling Author Susan Stoker has a heart as big as the state of Tennessee where she lives, but this all American girl has also spent the last fourteen years living in Missouri, California, Colorado, Indiana, and Texas. She's married to a retired Army man who now gets to follow *her* around the country.

She debuted her first series in 2014 and quickly followed that up with the SEAL of Protection Series, which solidified her love of writing and creating stories readers can get lost in.

If you enjoyed this book, or any book, please consider leaving a review. It's appreciated by authors more than you'll know.

www.stokeraces.com
www.AcesPress.com
susan@stokeraces.com

facebook.com/authorsusanstoker

twitter.com/Susan_Stoker

instagram.com/authorsusanstoker

goodreads.com/SusanStoker

bookbub.com/authors/susan-stoker

amazon.com/author/susanstoker

Printed in the USA
CPSIA information can be obtained
at www.ICGtesting.com
BVHW012002310823
669004BV00004B/15